CHAPTER ONE

Hollowgrove Plantation had been a South Georgia landmark for almost 200 years. Its 9400 acres spread along the banks of the Blood River like a lady's shawl, draping and folding in and out of various districts and municipalities, covering marshes, open fields, rich bottom lands, and deep forests. Once, the still black waters of the river had brought dry goods and slaves to the plantation and taken away bales of cotton and sugarcane. Now those same waters brought to Hollowgrove the new cash crop of the South: tourists.

The Hollowgrove Hunting Club was one of the most prestigious in the country. Luminaries, politicians, and the obscenely wealthy paid upwards of $50,000 a year for the privilege of shooting quail in its vast baited fields. The elegant Victorian mansion hosted only the most exclusive weddings, fundraisers, and celebrity events. More than one movie had been filmed there. Hollowgrove employed 75 people full-time, most of them on its 3000-acre farm and vineyard, all of whom lived on site.

The Whitleys, who had built Hollowgrove in 1833, still owned and operated the plantation, and those who were left made their home there. There had been talk of opening up the mansion as a B and B, but it was generally understood that would not happen as long as the elder Whitley, Jarrod the Third, continued to reside there. It was for that reason that the family had finally agreed to build a 30,000-square-foot luxury lodge on the back 12 acres of the estate to accommodate guests of the hunting club. The lodge, which had been almost two years in construction, was scheduled to open with quail and dove season this November —assuming it was completed in time.

Edison Quigley, general contractor, thought that was looking less likely with each passing moment.

Behind him, the rumble of the excavation equipment had stopped. The two operators huddled close to the largest earth mover, talking excitedly in Spanish. Ed could see a cloud of dust coming down the dirt road toward him. That would be Don Estes, the plantation manager, whose job was to investigate whenever the sounds of construction stopped. Sometimes Ed let the equipment run, burning fuel, just to avoid a confrontation with Estes. But there was no avoiding it now.

Ed stood on the edge of the trench that would one day be a swimming pool and spa and gazed down at the jumble of bones scattered across the sandy soil. He thought about jumping in there to have a closer look, but there really was no point. The small skull was clearly visible, as were two long bones that looked like leg or arm bones, and half a dozen smaller, less readily identifiable bones. There was no doubt about it. Those bones did not belong to a dog, a deer, a bear, or a raccoon. They were unmistakably human.

That meant police. That meant questions, an investigation, a work stoppage. That meant people in uniforms crawling all over the place, looking into things. And if there was one thing Ed had learned about Jarrod Whitley over the years, it was that he did not like people looking into things.

Ed glanced up as the pick-up truck screeched to a halt a few dozen feet away and the plantation manager got out. He slammed the truck door and strode toward Ed. Ed took off his hat, wiped a hand through his sweaty hair, and went to meet him.

"The boss," Ed told Don Estes gravely when he reached him, "is going to be pissed."

CHAPTER TWO

Buck Lawson awoke in a pool of sweat to the not-so-gentle poke of his wife's sharp-nailed forefinger in his bicep. "Wake up," she commanded. "It's almost 7:00."

Buck groaned and flung his arm over his eyes. "It can't be," he muttered. "I haven't been to sleep yet."

"Oh, please. You snored like an ox all night."

"That's because it was too hot to breathe."

"Get up," she repeated, tugging at his pillow, "and help me strip the bed. These sheets are a sweaty mess."

"You're telling me." Buck slid his arm from his slick face and opened his eyes reluctantly. He had lived here eight weeks now—a lifetime in terms of drama and trauma—but there was still a moment of disorientation every morning when he first woke up. Where was he? What was he doing here? Whose bed was this? The high mahogany ceiling with its elaborate crown molding, the tall windows looking out over an unfamiliar landscape of cultivated gardens, Spanish moss-draped trees, a still, dark river... this was not his country. This was not his place. None of it was familiar to him, and every morning, upon opening his eyes, he was reminded all over again how far from home he was.

The air was thick and fetid smelling, thanks to the open windows and the unfortunate sulfur smell that issued from the Blood River only a few hundred feet away. The fan overhead whirred at full speed, stirring the soupy mess into a hot goop. In the mountains, the air was crisp and green, and the water smelled as fresh as ice.

Nonetheless, Buck smiled as Jolene's face materialized, her dark skin glistening against the white bath towel that enveloped her from breast to knee, her hair caught up in a terrycloth turban. He reached for his wife. "You're a vision," he murmured. "Come back to bed."

She slapped his arm away. "You are delirious," she replied. "I just got out of the shower and don't have time to take another one. Get up. I'm not telling you again."

"I guess this means the honeymoon is over."

"You got it, Ace."

Buck rolled out of bed and stumbled to the bathroom. He splashed cold water on his face and impulsively ran his head under the faucet, shaking the excess water from his hair. He braced his hands on the sink and looked blearily into the mirror.

He was a good-looking man eighteen months shy of his fortieth birthday with a thick head of sandy hair, kind hazel eyes, and a slow, soft smile that females of all ages seemed to find irresistible. He was Buck Lawson, Chief of Police of Mercy, Georgia, population 12,800, a town he did not know and to which he did not belong. And as was so often the case these days, when he looked into the mirror, a stranger looked back.

A cruel scar bisected his torso, a tribute to the surgeons who saved his life a year ago by removing his spleen and part of his lung. On his back, just below his shoulder and visible only with a mirror, was the ugly puckered scar where the bullet had entered. On his left thigh were similar scars: the dented purplish entry wound that throbbed when he was tired and with every change of weather, and the neat long surgical scar that was the reason he could walk today. Sometimes, when he looked at himself in the mirror, he felt the same kind of momentary disassociation he felt when he looked out the window in this strange new place. Who was this guy? What was he doing here?

Buck Lawson had been born and raised in the mountains of western North Carolina, as had generations of Lawsons before him. He'd been in law enforcement for all his adult life, first as a road deputy, then as county sheriff, then as chief investigator. People who knew him thought Buck was as solid as the granite mountaintops from which he hailed and just as immoveable. He had thought so, too. Until he wasn't.

He turned abruptly away from the mirror, pulling on a tee shirt and yesterday's pair of rumpled jeans. He smothered a groan as he checked the time and temperature on his phone. 6:45 AM, and already 82 degrees.

"You know that expression 'hotter than the Fourth of July'?" he said as he came back into the bedroom. "I know where it was invented, now. Mercy, Georgia."

"Your problem is your body hasn't adjusted to the heat yet." Jolene tossed him the bundle of sheets from the stripped bed. "I saw it all the time with white guys in Afghanistan. Me, not so much."

"Because of your superior genetics."

She gave him an arch look. "Correct."

He took the sheets to the laundry chute in the hallway and returned with a fresh set from the linen closet. "I'm just worried about your mom and Willis trapped here all day in this oven."

"Don't be. Mama's volunteering at the library and Willis has a play date with the Baker kids. They'll be in the pool all day."

"Maybe I'll go with him."

"You are such a wuss." She unfolded the fitted sheet he handed her. "People have lived without air conditioning for thousands of years." This from the woman who was half an hour away from getting into her air-conditioned car and driving to her air-conditioned job, where she would spend several hours in an air-conditioned classroom, have lunch in an air-conditioned cafeteria, and drive home again in the same air-conditioned car.

The stately antebellum brick home in which they lived had been built, it was true, in an era when the stifling heat and humidity of south Georgia was a fact of life from which there was no escape; one simply made the best of it. The historic Aikens House was situated on a knoll overlooking the Blood River to take advantage of the cool breezes coming off the water; its high ceilings, tall windows, and wide verandahs were built to mitigate the heat. Live oaks and magnolias shaded the rolling lawn.

The old house would not have been Buck's first choice of a place to live, but it had come with the job when he took over as police chief. The street was quiet, the houses were far apart, and riverfront property—even if the town was Mercy and the river was the Blood River—was not easy to find. It was close enough to town to walk to the police station, though Buck did that as seldom as possible. Furthermore, it came to him practically rent-free by virtue of some kind of tax deal the Aikens family had made with the city. Most importantly Jolene, for some reason, liked the place.

She was right, of course: multiple generations of Aikenses had survived the summers just fine in this house. But by the time Buck had moved in, the big old house had been updated to accommodate twenty-first-century living, and that included state-of-the-art air conditioning...which had chosen the hottest week of the year to break down.

Buck stretched his corner of the sheet over the mattress. "I wish somebody would tell me how they did it," he grumbled, "because this mountain boy can't take much more of this."

"Mostly," replied his wife, "I think they spent the summers in the mountains. Of course," she added with a mischievous glance at him, "you could always ask your good friend Billy when you see him next."

Buck returned a sour look as he moved to the next corner of the bed.

Billy Aikens, the former owner of the house in which they lived— and the former holder of the office of chief of police, which Buck now held — had been dead for over two months. Buck had only met the man a couple of times, but they had become close friends via telephone and video chat during the time Buck had been preparing to take over the job. He still had vivid dreams about Billy in which they continued those conversations, Billy giving him advice and telling stories, Buck asking questions and enjoying the older man's company. Jolene liked to tease him about it, calling Billy Buck's own personal ghost. Buck suspected the dreams had more to do with the fact that the man whose job he now held and in whose house he now lived—whose life, in fact, Buck had virtually taken over—had been murdered in the performance of his duties only days before Buck arrived in Mercy.

Buck muttered, "Maybe I will." He snapped open the flat sheet, expecting her to catch one corner of it, but she was staring out the window. "I swear, Jo, if they don't get the AC fixed today, we're moving to a hotel. Three days of this is more than anybody should have to take."

Jolene did not even turn around. She just continued to stare in a kind of frozen way at something on the ground below. She said, unblinking, "Is that him?"

"Who?"

She didn't move. "Billy."

"What?" Buck let the sheet drop and came to stand beside her, frowning. "Where?"

"There on the porch," she replied in a hushed tone, "talking to Mama."

Billy Aikens had been, by anyone's account, an impressive figure of a man. Broad-shouldered, good-looking, with a thick white mane of hair and a neatly trimmed beard to match. There were pictures of him all over town: on the memorial wall of City Hall, in the police station's parade of chiefs' display, in the American Legion rec hall, and in the high school gymnasium that had been named for him. Buck had a photo of Billy in his study downstairs, and Jolene's mother found an oil portrait of Billy in the attic that she hung at the top of the stairs, much to Buck's amusement and Jolene's disapproval. There was no mistaking what Billy Aikens looked like.

The man who sat in the rocking chair on the corner of the front porch that was visible from the master bedroom looked enough like Billy to be his twin. The shock of it made Buck's heart lurch in his throat, and for just a second he was as dumbfounded as was his wife. But just for a second.

He turned quickly for the door. Jolene followed, pausing only to slide open her lingerie drawer, where they kept the gun safe. Buck tossed her a glance that was as puzzled as it was amused. "I don't think you're going to need your Glock to talk to a ghost."

"No," she retorted, her hands scrambling through the drawer, "but I might need my underwear."

Buck didn't wait for her. He descended the stairs in his bare feet, his hair still dripping from its impromptu dousing. He paused when he reached the screen door that led to the front porch, though, listening to the sound of soft laughter coming from outside. He opened the door cautiously, muffling its squeak with his other hand.

His mother-in-law, Eloise, was sitting in the rocking chair across from the visitor, her sunhat and gardening gloves resting on the white wicker table between them. She looked up when the door opened and exclaimed delightedly, "Buck! There you are. You won't believe who I found outside the gate this morning."

Even before he rose, Buck could tell that the man was not Billy. His hair was more platinum blond than silver, his beard shorter, and his physique a little softer. He was at least twenty-five years younger than Billy had been when he died. Still, the resemblance was uncanny, and Buck was surprised by the twinge of disappointment he felt when the other man extended his hand and said pleasantly, "Bill Aikens, Junior. Folks call me Junior. It's a pleasure to meet you, Chief Lawson."

Buck shook his hand. "You're Billy's son." That much was obvious.

"Yes, sir, that's right. I don't mean to intrude this early in the morning, but I was walking by and saw Miss Eloise pruning the roses out front. She was kind enough to ask me up on the porch."

"We've been having the nicest chat," Eloise said. "I've been trying to talk him into coming in for a bite of breakfast, but so far, no luck. See what you can do, Buck, while I go start the coffee."

She gathered up her things and went inside. Buck and Junior looked at each other awkwardly for a moment when she was gone, then spoke at the same time.

"I didn't mean," said Junior.

"I sure didn't expect," said Buck.

Buck smiled and gestured for the other man to resume his seat. "You look a lot like your dad," he said.

Junior seemed a little embarrassed by that. "I've been told. I really don't mean to stay, Chief."

"Call me Buck," Buck said.

"All right, Buck it is." He smiled. "Like I said I was just out for a morning walk and thought I'd pass by the place. Except for the funeral, I haven't been back here in years. Thought it might be nice to have one last look."

Buck nodded toward the door. "Well, you have to come in, then. Have some breakfast, spend as much time as you like looking around. Miss Eloise is an amazing cook," he added, "and my wife will want to meet you. She thought you were a ghost," he confided.

Junior grinned, although it seemed an automatic thing that didn't quite reach his eyes. "Maybe another time," he said. "I'm staying at the Magnolia House B&B across the square and I figure if I'm paying for breakfast I ought to enjoy it."

Buck chuckled. "I guess that's right. You're living in..." he struggled to remember what he had heard. "St. Louis now, is it? How long are you in town for?"

"That's right, St. Louis. But I'll be around 'til after the Fourth, probably. I left the wife and kids at our beach house in Destin and figured this was as good a time as any to drive over and go through the things we left in storage when Daddy died. I like the beach as much as the next fellow, but it's the last place I want to be on the Fourth of

July. Wall-to-wall bodies, all of them drunk and sunburned."

Buck smiled and nodded his understanding just as the screen door creaked open. Jolene came out, dressed for work in dark pants and a crisp white shirt, and extended her hand to Junior. "Mr. Aikens," she said. "I'm Buck's wife, Jolene Smith. And just for the record..." She shot a quick dark look at Buck. "I did *not* think you were a ghost. My mother sent me out to make sure you came to breakfast. She's making waffles."

"It's a pleasure to meet you, ma'am." Junior shook her hand and added, "But please tell your mother not to go to the trouble. I can't stay."

Jolene assured him, "Mama is cooking for a six-year-old. It's never any trouble. But if you won't stay for breakfast, we insist you come for dinner. Is tomorrow night good for you?"

Buck stared at her. He had married a soldier with two tours of duty under her belt; a no-nonsense cop with the looks of Nefertiti and the personality of Genghis Khan whom he had personally seen subdue a suspect twice her size without breaking a sweat. Whenever she pulled the perfect-wife-and-hostess bit on him he couldn't help feeling he was being set up as the butt of a bad joke.

Junior seemed as caught off guard as Buck was, and before he could stammer out a reply Buck stepped in to put him at ease. "Tell you what, Junior," he said. "Why don't we grab a burger at the Copper Kettle this afternoon and hammer out the details? I'll have my assistant set it up. She keeps my schedule and is the very devil to live with if I screw it up without consulting her."

Junior relaxed. "Lydia, right? She handled the funeral arrangements. She seems very... efficient."

Buck grinned. "She is that. I'm guessing she has your cell number?"

But the sound of thundering paws on the stairs inside the house interrupted Junior's reply. Willis, dressed only in his underpants, pushed open the screen door and a big curly-haired dog galloped through, hotly pursued by the little boy. "Thor!" he called. "Thor, you come back here!"

The dog ran up to the stranger and began sniffing his feet and ankles. Buck grabbed the dog's collar and pulled him away. Willis skidded to a stop, staring at the newcomer.

"Holy crackers," he said softly, his eyes big. "Are you a ghost?"

The two men chuckled, but Jolene snatched her little boy up and turned him back inside the house. "What a question! And what are you doing running around half-naked in front of company? Get back upstairs and get some clothes on before you show your face at the breakfast table."

"But it's hot!" he protested.

"And take that dog with you." Jolene clapped her hands sharply and opened the screen door. The dog scrambled through after Willis as soon as Buck released his collar.

"We have a painting of your daddy hanging inside," Jolene explained to Junior apologetically, "and you do look a bit like him. You know little boys and their imaginations. Maybe you'd like to have the painting?" she suggested hopefully. "We found it in the attic along with a bunch of other boxes and such that I guess no one had a chance to go through. You're welcome to do that anytime, though."

"No ma'am," he said firmly. "Whatever was left behind stays with the house. There's nothing in this place that I want."

The way he said that, with a slight edge of harshness to his tone, caused Jo and Buck to exchange a quick look. Junior seemed to notice and cleared his throat uncomfortably.

"Well," he said, "I'll let you all get on with your day. It was nice meeting you both." He shook each of their hands again and turned toward the steps.

"Don't forget dinner," Jolene reminded him.

Buck added, "Lydia will be in touch."

He smiled and nodded, but they could not help noticing he didn't reply.

"Well," said Jo as they watched him move down the sidewalk back toward town. "That was interesting."

"Seems like a nice enough fellow," Buck observed, "but he sure didn't inherit his daddy's personality."

"Seems to me he was in an awful hurry to get away from here," Jo added.

Buck said, "He told me that except for the funeral he hadn't been back here in years. Maybe something happened between him and Billy."

"Or maybe he just didn't like seeing his ancestral home occupied by Black folks."

Buck gave a noncommittal lift of his shoulder. "Possible, I guess." He slanted her a glance. "You invited him to dinner."

"Of course, I did," she replied innocently. "It would have been rude not to."

"And you're *never* rude."

She gave him a warning look.

His wife was one of the toughest cops Buck had ever worked with, and he had never known her to waste effort on trying to be pleasant. Three days a week she taught sensitivity and de-escalation techniques to rookies and veteran law-enforcement alike at the POST center two hours away, which in itself generated a certain amount of incredulity in those who knew her. Nonetheless, since taking the job Jolene had mellowed considerably, or at least she had appeared to. Sometimes Buck suspected her of practicing on her family the techniques she was preparing to demonstrate to her students.

Into her silence, he pointed out, "We don't even have a dining room table."

"We'll eat in the kitchen."

"Or air conditioning."

"So?"

"So, it just seems to me you're going to an

awful lot of trouble to be the gracious hostess to somebody you don't even know."

She retorted, "All right, hot shot, tell me you're not just as anxious as I am for a chance to interview one of the last living descendants of the legendary Aikenses."

He grinned at her. "'Living' being the key word."

She scowled at him, and he kissed her lightly before she could reply. "Going to take a shower," he said and turned back into the house.

"I did *not* think he was a ghost!" she called after him.

Buck was careful not to let her hear him chuckling as he went back up the stairs.

CHAPTER THREE

Patrice Miller—everyone called her Trish—knew she was good at her job. She had graduated in the 96th percentile of her class, excelled at every continuing education course since then, and had left her previous employer with a stellar recommendation. Nonetheless, this would be her first in-person meeting with her new boss, and she was nervous. The guy was a legend, after all. She was, by comparison, a nobody.

Trish rehearsed the upcoming interview in her mind as she drove. She lived twenty minutes outside of town with her parents—a situation that was entirely temporary, she assured everyone who asked—and the rural road on which she drove was practically deserted. She stretched out her fingers on the steering wheel, forcing tight muscles to relax, and focused on the interview ahead of her.

Impressive resumé, he would no doubt say, because it was. *What made you decide to leave Orlando for a little town like Mercy?*

"I was born here, sir," she said out loud to the empty car. That was an easy one. "It's my hometown. I always hoped to come back here if I could."

What did you like least about your last job? They always threw in something tricky like that.

She said, forcing easy confidence into her voice, "I didn't think my skills were being put to their best use in my previous assignment. I hoped for something more challenging."

No, no. She couldn't say that. That was stupid. She left a town the size of Orlando hoping to find challenge in Mercy, Georgia, population 12,800? He would laugh. He would think she was an idiot.

She cleared her throat and tried again. "I felt I was being under-utilized. People tend to underestimate me because of my age." And her petite size, and her blonde hair, and her tendency not to speak unless spoken to, none of which she could say out loud without sounding pathetic and self-pitying.

Why do you want to work for me? He was sure to ask that one.

She cleared her throat. "I've heard excellent things about the changes you've made here since you took over. I want to be part of a team that's moving toward the future. Also, I saw you on television and I really liked the things you said."

No, absolutely not. That made her sound like a groupie. She couldn't say anything about television, or about how seeing that one interview with him had made her decide to quit her job and move back home. Come to think of it, she probably *was* a groupie.

"I want to be part of a strong, progressive team," she said firmly. "I think I have a lot to offer."

There. That was better. She blew her bangs out of her eyes and decided to abandon the rehearsal, at least for now. She was already starting to break out in a sweat, just thinking about it. Instead, she pushed the button on the steering wheel that resumed the inspirational podcast she had been listening to on her phone.

"You are powerfully and wonderfully made," said the speaker. "Repeat after me."

"I am powerfully and wonderfully made," Trish said, squaring her shoulders.

"You are a child of the Creator of the Universe. You have everything you need to achieve your destiny."

"I have everything I need to achieve my destiny."

"God does not make mistakes."

"God does not make mistakes," she repeated, firmly.

"You are well able to master whatever comes before you this day."

Trish slowed to make a turn that led through a tunnel of trees draped with Spanish moss. It was the prettiest part of the drive. Lacy shadows played across the windshield as she asserted, "I am well able..."

She slammed on the brakes as a shape lunged across the road toward her car. "Fuck!" she screamed, twisting the steering wheel, standing hard on the brakes. But it was too late. "Fuck!"

She felt a thump on the hood of her car, saw the terrified face, and then the body rolled away, leaving nothing but a bloody handprint on the windshield.

CHAPTER FOUR

The Mercy police station was two blocks away from the police chief's house, a stately brick building with a long and colorful history, just like most buildings in Mercy. Usually, Buck walked to work, mostly at the insistence of his wife, who was determined the exercise was good for his health. Today he felt absolutely no shame in firing up his pickup truck and driving the two-and-a-half minutes to the employee parking lot behind the police station.

Lydia was waiting for him in the blissfully cool corridor of the administrative offices, as she was every morning, his coffee cup in one hand and a clipboard in the other. "Good morning, Chief," she said, handing the coffee to him. She turned to accompany him to his office, her heels clicking on the linoleum floor. "It was a quiet night. Two traffic accidents, no injuries, a noise complaint, one drunk and disorderly, and one false alarm on a security system. The reports have been uploaded to your computer."

"Good deal." Buck kept pace with her, sipping his coffee. "Any word on my air conditioning?"

"Still waiting on the part, sir."

"Call again."

"Yes, sir. I was about to do that."

When Buck had first heard of the inimitable Lydia, who ran the police station with an iron fist, he had pictured a gargoyle in her sixties with pursed lips, granny glasses, and a ship's-prow bosom. Lydia turned out to be an exceptionally attractive woman in her mid- thirties with an hourglass figure and an impeccable sense of style whose crisp, professional manner had intimidated him—as well as every other officer in the building—from the first moment they met. Buck was convinced that the police department would function just fine without a chief, a second-in-command, or detectives. But without Lydia, it would fall apart.

He said, "Did you know Billy's son, Junior, is in town?"

"No, sir, I didn't." She didn't sound surprised, but very little ever surprised Lydia.

"I told him we'd have lunch today. Can you give him a call and set it up?"

"I'd be happy to, sir, but today isn't possible. The mayor called first thing and wants you to meet her for lunch at Hollowgrove Plantation."

Buck frowned. He had spent every free moment since his arrival in Mercy studying maps, memorizing street names and intersections, and riding his territory. Of course, given the state-of-the-art sat-nav system in his cruiser, he knew the effort wasn't strictly necessary, but he did it anyway. He wasn't yet familiar with the location of every road, landmark, or business in the county, but he did know that Hollowgrove was at least twelve miles outside of town—and therefore out of his jurisdiction.

"What on earth for?" he demanded. "That'll take up half the day. Can't you reschedule?"

It was a moot question, and the look Lydia gave him over the rims of her dark-framed glasses said as much. One did not reschedule Mayor Corinne Watts. "I've adjusted your day accordingly," she said, "and..." She gave him another quick up-and-down look. "I'll have your summer uniform coat and tie pressed within the hour."

Buck groaned. "Coat *and* tie? It's a hundred degrees out there." Buck's standard summer uniform was dark trousers, a white short-sleeved shirt with insignia and badge, and no tie. Billy, he was given to understand, had always worn a tie.

"Eighty-six degrees," Lydia corrected, "Relative humidity seventy-eight percent. And it's a private club. Coat and tie for gentlemen."

For a small town, Mercy had more private clubs and restaurants with formal dress codes than any place Buck had ever been. He supposed that had something to do with the Old South sensibility that still lingered in small pockets around the region. He was not a fan.

"Oh, all right," he grumbled. He held out his hand for his updated schedule—or, as he liked to call it, The Bible, since its writings were as sacred to Lydia as any holy text ever produced. "Can you call Junior and apologize? I doubt he'll care about missing lunch with me, but Jo did want to have him to dinner. See if you can set something up this week."

"Certainly, sir." Lydia handed over the schedule. "You're interviewing a new hire at 9:00, you have a video conference with the state police at 10:00, and you should leave for lunch by 11:45. Mason Williams, this year's parade coordinator, is scheduled for 3:30, followed by the Director of Riverside Events at 4:00. Don't forget tomorrow's Events Committee meeting at 2:00. Sully wanted a moment with you this morning, so I penciled him in at 9:30. Also," she added, "we have another request from a true-crime podcaster for an interview. I sent her the standard reply: The Mercy Police Department is not giving interviews to the media regarding the Torrance case, and any information disseminated to the public about that case will be considered unauthorized and therefore unreliable."

He nodded absently. Even two months after the event, Buck's office received at least one of these requests per day, and not just from amateur reporters seeking to make their careers on a blog or a podcast. *20/20* was particularly persistent, as was some publisher in New York who offered a very compelling book deal, complete with ghost writer. He turned them all down, partly in deference to his agreement with the mayor, but mostly because he was smart enough to know that walking in the spotlight tended to lead to unexpected falls.

He said, "I figured everybody would've moved on by now. Isn't that the whole beauty of the twenty-four-hour news cycle?"

"Yes, sir." Lydia hesitated. "The problem is that the media doesn't like silence. And when they can't get the truth from the primary source..."

"They make it up," Buck supplied.

She smiled faintly. "They tend to go to other sources, which may or may not be as reliable. Just something to think about, sir."

Buck had, in fact, thought about that. And he hadn't much liked his own conclusions.

Lydia handed him a folder, all business again. "Here are the latest applications for fireworks show permits for your signature. The First Baptist Church on Friday, The Boy Scouts camp on Saturday, several restaurants along the river to coordinate with the main fireworks show on the Fourth."

"Good God," Buck muttered, flipping through the folder. "It would be easier to give out permits to people *not* planning a show."

"It's all routine, Chief," she assured him. "I finished transcribing the first fifty pages of your revisions to the Policy and Procedures Manual. They're on your desk, waiting for your approval."

"Excellent. Be sure to put in an overtime request for that."

"Also on your desk. And I need a decision on the Fourth of July barbecue if I'm going to get it in the department newsletter this afternoon. Some of the officers have been asking."

He didn't look up. "What barbecue?"

"Billy always hosted a department barbecue the first weekend after the Fourth," Lydia explained, "as a way to thank the officers for putting in overtime during the holiday. Family-friendly, of course, beer and wine only. The wives usually bring a covered dish, and we supply the hamburgers and hotdogs from the discretionary fund."

"Sounds simple enough," he murmured.

"Billy usually got a tray of pulled pork from Joe's Place," she went on, "and one year he deep-fried catfish in the turkey fryer, but that didn't turn out so well. It usually starts around 4:00 and ends at dark with a fireworks show."

He said, "And this is at my house?"

"Yes, sir. You can expect about a hundred people, counting the children."

He stopped walking. "At my house?"

"Not everyone stays all day," she assured him.

"But we just moved in. We don't even have a dining room table."

"Most barbecues take place outside, sir."

Buck frowned uncertainly and started walking again. "I don't know, Lydia. This sounds like something I should talk over with the family."

"It is a tradition, sir," she reminded him. "And all of the systems are in place as soon as I send out the newsletter. Tables, chairs, covered dishes... everyone signs up for something. And," she added, her voice gentling just enough to make him look at her curiously, "if I might say so, I think it would be a huge boost to department morale this year in particular, given everything we've been through."

There was no arguing with that. If there was one thing this department needed at present it was a boost to morale. He clearly didn't have a choice. "All right," he said, somewhat reluctantly. "The Saturday after the Fourth. What is that, July 9? I'll square it with Jo and Miss Eloise."

"It will be an excellent opportunity for them to get to know the community," Lydia pointed out. "And yourself as well, sir."

"I guess," he agreed with a sigh.

"I'll get the newsletter out this afternoon," she said. "I'm sure everyone will be pleased that the barbecue will go on as always." They had reached his office. "Also, a Mr. and Mrs. Gilford are waiting in your office. I tried to get them to speak with one of our officers, but they insisted on seeing the chief of police. They seemed quite upset."

He glanced toward his closed office door curiously. "Any idea what it's about?"

"I'm sorry, sir, no. Shall I interrupt you after

five minutes?"

"No, that's okay. I'll handle it. And Lydia..." He glanced back, his hand on the doorknob of his office. "Air conditioning first."

The newly decorated office of the Chief of Police was as stately and impressive as the women in charge—Lydia, Jolene, and a perky young designer named Deanna—thought the title deserved. The carpet was plush, the furniture burled walnut, the draperies tied back with gold braid. The wall behind his desk was painted deep teal and featured a framed print of an oil painting of the marsh at sunset. The desk was flanked by an American flag and a Georgia flag, and on the opposite wall was a collection of framed photographs of all the former Mercy chiefs of police, from the town's inception until now. Buck's photograph was the last.

The blue velvet sofa that stretched along one wall was the most hideous piece of furniture Buck had ever seen, and he suspected his wife of ordering it as a joke. He grimaced whenever he passed it and tried to avoid looking at it when he could. That was not possible today, however, because a young couple sat stiffly on the sofa, their hands tightly linked. Both were well-dressed in the manner of young professionals; he in a blazer and khakis, she in heels and a skirt. The woman's blond hair was cut in a wispy bob that fell just above her ears, and she clutched a damp tissue in one hand. Her eyes and her nose were red with crying, and most of her lipstick was gone. Circles of smeared mascara darkened her eyes.

Buck said, "I'm Buck Lawson, chief of police."

The man got to his feet. "Jeff Gilford, and this is my wife, Beth."

Buck shook his hand and went to his desk, placing the papers and coffee cup on top. "What can I do for you folks today?"

The woman said tightly. "Our baby. Our baby has been..." Her voice broke and she brought the tissue to her eyes, pressing hard. "Our baby has been stolen!"

Buck, in the process of sitting down, moved his finger to the intercom button instead. "Lydia," he said, "get Frankie in here. Sully, too."

The woman had her face buried in the tissue now, her shoulders shaking with silent sobs. Buck looked at the husband. "When did this happen? Where did you last see your child?"

The man's arm was around his wife's shoulders, and he looked at Buck helplessly. "We didn't see her. We never saw her, that's the problem. She was born last night, and we were supposed to pick her up this morning. But when we got here..."

"When we got here," the wife exploded angrily, swiping the tissue across her eyes, "they wouldn't let us in! They told us there was no baby!"

Buck looked around for the tissue box, which he was certain he had seen somewhere. He found it on the credenza opposite the sofa and brought the box to the young wife. She snatched a handful of tissues from the box and buried her face in them.

Buck sat on the corner of the desk, closer to the couple. "I'm afraid I don't understand. This was an adoption?"

"We paid almost a hundred thousand dollars for a blonde-haired baby girl!" the woman cried. "A hundred thousand! We've been waiting almost a year! They lied, everything they said was a lie, and we've been waiting so long! We even…" now she started crying again, "hired a muralist to paint sheep and clouds on the nursery wall, and we put together the crib and the changing table and the stroller with the removable car seat…"

There was a soft tap on his door, and Frankie came in, followed closely by Sully. Buck said, "Mr. and Mrs. Gilford, my lead detective Frankie Moreno and my second in command, Don Sullivan."

He gestured to his two officers to be seated and they took the matching wing chairs –silk upholstered, thanks to the perky Deanna, but at least in an acceptable print—and turned them to face the couple on the sofa.

After a somewhat rough start that had resulted in the firing of almost a third of his police force, Buck was starting to gain confidence in most of the officers under his command. These two, however, were among the ones in whom he had the most faith. Sully was tall, lanky, and bald, but his laconic demeanor disguised the fact that he was as solid a cop as Buck had ever met. Frankie was a short, plain-faced woman with an unattractive haircut and absolutely no sense of style—something that was particularly baffling when one took into account that she was married to the impeccable Lydia, who by all appearances, had never had a bad hair day in her life. When Buck first met Frankie, he'd thought she was an incompetent slacker and hadn't expected her to last more than a week under his command. Giving her a chance to prove herself had been among the best decisions of his life. She was now one of the most reliable officers on his force, not to mention the sharpest.

Buck resumed his perch on the edge of the desk and turned to Jeff Gilford, who appeared to be the more coherent of the two. "Why don't you start at the beginning?" he said.

Gilford looked at his wife, patted her hand, and turned back to Buck. "We've had fertility issues," he said. "We went through five rounds of in vitro but..." he shook his head. "We decided to adopt three years ago, but the process for an infant is so long, so complicated...every time we'd get close something would go wrong. We just didn't know how many more disappointments we could take."

Buck glanced at the wife, who had started crying again. She fumbled another tissue out of the box and pressed it to her eyes.

"This lawyer I met at a corporate retreat said

he'd done some work with Hope House here in Mercy," the husband went on.

Buck looked at Sully, who explained, "It's a kind of home for unwed mothers out in The Ranches." He referred to a sprawling, upscale, and mostly undeveloped neighborhood near the edge of town. "They take in girls for the length of their pregnancy and help them place the baby afterward. Privately funded."

"Funded by *us*," put in Beth Gilford bitterly, wiping her nose with the tissue.

Her husband cast a pained, uneasy look toward her and then turned back to Buck. "Naturally, we came down here to check the place out and it seemed fine. More than fine. Luxurious, even. The pitch was that the experience the babies had in-utero influenced their personalities, so everything was very spa-like. Peaceful."

Buck said, "Where are you all from?"

"Atlanta," replied Gilford.

"There must be plenty of adoption agencies in Atlanta," observed Sully.

Gilford nodded. "But like I said, the wait can be years. And this place... they promised us a baby within months."

Frankie said, "Did you meet the mother?"

"We only saw pictures," the man replied. "There were several potential mothers. We never knew their names, for what we were told were privacy reasons. Our agreement was that we would have first choice of whichever child was born first that met our specifications. Here." He reached into his jacket pocket and brought out an envelope. "We have the documents and everything. A legal intent to adopt, and a receipt for all the funds we paid."

Buck took the envelope and passed it to Frankie. "We'll make a copy of this and return it to you."

"But we didn't get the baby," Beth said harshly. "We did everything they said and... *we didn't get the baby.*"

Jeff Gilford wrapped his hand around his wife's and squeezed hard.

Buck said, "Why don't you tell us what happened when you arrived here to claim your adopted child?"

"They called yesterday to tell us one of our prospective mothers was in active labor and expected to deliver within twelve hours. Naturally, we wanted to come right away but they said it would be best to call in the morning for an update. When we called early this morning—just after midnight, in fact— they said a baby girl had been born with blonde hair and blue eyes and she would be ready for us to take home as soon as she was checked out medically. But when we got here this morning a little after six, they wouldn't even let us through the gate. They said the facility was closed to visitors. When we told them we weren't visitors, that we'd come to get our baby, they kept us waiting for over an hour. Finally, someone came to the intercom and said they had no record of our application. So, I demanded to speak with Mrs. Summerfield, the head of the place, and when she finally came on the intercom, she said there had been some kind of mistake and there had been no births there in the past week. We spent the next hour trying to get inside, trying to talk to somebody and find out what had really happened, but we got nowhere. Finally, the only thing left to do was go to the police."

"They gave our baby to someone else," Beth Gilford said tightly. "They took our money and stole our baby and now they're too afraid to face us. I want them arrested! I want them arrested *now*."

Lydia opened the door that separated their two offices and came silently across the room to hand Buck a note, then left as unobtrusively as she had come. Buck glanced at it. *Code 466 at Hwy 27, mile marker 13. Supervisor requested.* Buck passed the note to Sully, who glanced at it, took out his phone, and excused himself from the room.

"Mr. and Mrs. Gilford," Buck said, "I know how upsetting this is, and we'll definitely look into it. It's likely this is a matter you'll have to work out in civil court, but I'll send a couple of detectives out there to see if we can get to the bottom of what happened. Right now, you should go with Detective Moreno. She'll get the details from you and open an investigation."

Buck saw the three of them to the door just as

Sully returned, tucking his phone into his pocket. "Don't make me ask what a 466 is," Buck said. Mercy, like many small towns, used its own set of police codes in addition to the more widely used 10-codes. Buck had not yet begun to memorize them all.

"Officer-involved traffic accident," Sully replied. "Vehicle versus pedestrian. No word on the condition of the victim yet."

Buck swore softly and grabbed the keys to his official vehicle from his desk drawer. This was definitely a situation that called for the presence of the chief of police at the scene. "Who's the officer?"

Before Sully could answer they were passing Lydia's door. Buck poked his head inside and said, "Lydia, my nine o'clock..."

"Cancelled, sir," she replied, glancing up from the telephone. "And your car will be waiting at the back entrance."

"That was easy," Buck muttered as he strode with Sully toward the back door. "Usually getting her to cancel an appointment is like calling off a state dinner."

"That's because she knows who the officer involved in the accident is," Sully replied.

The door buzzed as Buck pushed it open, and he glanced at Sully curiously. "Who?"

"Your nine o'clock," replied Sully.

CHAPTER FIVE

An ambulance and two patrol cars were at the scene of the accident when Buck and Sully arrived. Another two units pulled up behind them, having been summoned by Sully for traffic control—although on this rural, tree-lined road there was little traffic to control. Blue lights strobed through the faint, hot morning mist that rose off the pavement, and a film of tiny insects moved through the humid air as Buck got out of the car. He stood still for a moment, looking around.

A late-model CRV was stopped crossways in the road, headlights pointed east on a road that ran north and south. Skid marks traced the last thirty feet of its journey. Leon Baker, one of his top officers, was taking a statement from the young woman who was apparently the driver of the vehicle. Behind them, EMTs worked to transfer another woman—light-haired, dirty, and spattered with blood—to a backboard. They had already fitted her with a cervical collar and hooked her up to an IV and oxygen mask. So, she was still alive, thank God. Before they covered her with the blanket, Buck noticed the victim's feet were bare. He also noticed that the driver could barely tear her distraught gaze away from the proceedings long enough to answer Baker's questions.

The driver was a young, petite woman in the short-sleeved navy uniform of a Mercy police officer. Her blonde hair was pulled back in a tight bun, as per regulation, and her fresh face, now drawn into pale, anxious lines, was clear of makeup. She seemed dwarfed by the utility belt she wore, like a child dressed up for Halloween.

"So, we're hiring teenagers now?" Buck murmured as Sully came to stand beside him. "I didn't know things were that bad."

"She's the one with the A-plus rating," Sully reminded him. "Graduated top of her class. Three years with the Orlando PD."

"Right," said Buck, not remembering.

The Mercy Police Department was down almost one-third of its complement, and they were filling the slots as fast—and as efficiently —as they could. It wasn't as though people were lining up to become police officers these days, despite the attractive salary and benefits package Buck was able to offer. Over half of the applicants he had looked at had been immediately rejected for malfeasance of office in their last job; another percentage had failed Buck's rather strenuous training requirements. Sully had done the final interview of those who made the cut, and while Buck approved the hiring of the ones Sully recommended, he usually didn't meet them in person until they came in for their welcome interview on the first day. Patrice Miller—whose name he had learned on the way over—was a surprise.

Baker glanced over at them, said something to Miller, and started their way. Sully said, "I'll check on the victim." as Baker reached them. Buck nodded.

Baker said, "The driver is Patrice Miller, twenty-four years old, 1359 Reynolds Way, a rookie with the Mercy Police Department." He slanted Buck a look that was almost wry. "Which I guess you know."

Leon Baker—the same Baker who owned the pool in which Buck's stepson planned to spend the day—was a tall, stern-faced Black man who had been with the Mercy Police Department for four years and was in that elite group of officers that Buck knew, without a doubt, he could trust. For that reason and others, Baker was being fast-tracked for promotion to detective. For the next six months, he would gradually be given more responsibility and his work would be closely scrutinized by both Buck and lead detective Frankie Moreno. So far, Buck was relieved to note, he had not disappointed.

Baker glanced down at his notes. "According to

her statement, Miss Miller—"

"An officer with the Mercy Police Department," Buck reminded him.

"Yes, sir, sorry. Officer Miller," Baker went on, "was traveling in the north-bound lane at approximately 7:45 AM this morning when she noted a figure run across the road from the west. Officer Miller estimates her speed at thirty-five miles per hour. She braked and turned the vehicle to the east but was unable to avoid striking the victim. The victim hit the passenger side of the vehicle, rolled onto the hood, and tumbled off it into the street. Officer Miller immediately exited her vehicle and checked the condition of the victim. She found her unconscious but breathing. Officer Miller called 911 and covered the victim with a blanket from her car. She continued to monitor her pulse and breathing until the EMTs arrived, approximately twelve minutes later, and took over."

Buck looked over to where Miller stood, her shoulders straight, her stance erect, her jaw set. He knew for a fact that there were officers on his force who would not have been able to hold themselves together half as well after something like this. Good for her.

Behind her to the west there was nothing but a field of tangled brambles and low-growing scrub grass, partially shielded from view by a stand of live oaks heavy with Spanish moss. This time of morning the shadows were deceptive, with bright patches of sunlight painting the road in checkerboards of light and dark. It would be easy not to see a person running through those shadows.

"No ID on the victim," Baker went on. "She was unconscious when I reached the scene at 8:16. The EMTs were working on her and reported they were unable to determine the point of impact at that time. I noticed her hands appeared to be scratched and bloody, as were her feet, which were bare." He looked up at Buck, finishing his report. "She was wearing what looked like a cotton nightgown, and it was bloodstained."

Buck looked back to the stand of moss-covered trees and the field beyond. "What's back there?" he asked. "Houses, roads? Abandoned buildings?"

Baker said, "Nothing like that, as far as I know. This part of the county is mostly farmland. A lot of empty fields these days."

"So, a woman wearing nothing but her nightgown takes off without her phone or her purse and doesn't even stop to put on shoes," Buck speculated. "It sounds to me like she was scared of something. And if she wasn't running from her house, maybe she was running from somebody who took her from her house."

"Yes, sir, makes sense," Baker agreed. "You're thinking maybe somebody brought her out to this field somewhere and assaulted her? Or left her on the side of the road?"

Buck said, "I'll get Sully to assign a team of men

to check it out."

Buck walked over to the car. Behind him, officers were measuring and photographing the skid marks. Buck circled the car, noting the smear of blood on the front windshield, passenger side. The headlights were undamaged, the finish unmarred. There were no dents. There was, however, another smear of blood low on the passenger side fender, just in front of the door. There was also a faint blood streak on the passenger door handle. Buck pointed these out to Baker.

"Make sure we get pictures of this," he said, "and of the blood on the windshield, before the car is moved."

"Yes, sir." Baker made the note and nodded toward the smear on the window. "Looks a little like a handprint, doesn't it?"

Buck said thoughtfully, "How do you reckon that blood got on this side of the car when the car was turning in the opposite direction?"

"I don't see any sign of impact, either," Baker observed.

Buck walked to the beginning of the skid marks and back again. He circled the car one more time. The ambulance was pulling away when he finished. He glanced at Patrice Miller, then looked back at Baker. "Okay," he said, "run Officer Miller down to the hospital for a blood alcohol and drug screen. Find out what you can about the condition of the victim, interview her if she's conscious. I want to know what the hell she was doing out here in her nightgown, and then I want to know everything she remembers about the encounter with Officer Miller's car. We need a complete forensics on the vehicle and the scene. Document everything and double-check it. The department's reputation is at stake, not to mention a young officer's career. I'm putting you in charge of this case, Baker, let's see what you've got."

If Baker was surprised, or pleased, his saturnine features never would have allowed the emotion to show. He replied simply, "Yes, sir."

"You'll report to Frankie, and I know you're smart enough to ask her for help if you need it."

"Yes, sir," agreed Baker, not quite smiling. "I am."

"All right then." Buck nodded reluctantly toward the young woman standing across the road. "Let's take care of the rookie."

Sully joined them as they crossed the road. "Contusion on the back of the head," he reported, "consistent with where she probably hit the pavement. Possible concussion. The blood pattern on her clothing and skin suggests sexual assault, but that's for the hospital to determine. Her hands and feet are cut up, maybe from running through briars. That's all we know now."

Buck said, "I need four or five men searching the field and the roadway. See if you can figure out how she got here."

Sully said, "Yes, sir."

They had reached the young officer, who squared her shoulders even further, as though bracing for a blow, and turned to greet them. Buck extended his hand.

"Buck Lawson," he said, "chief of police."

"Yes, sir." She gave his hand a strong, firm pump. "Trish Miller."

"Trish," he repeated. "Okay." He added, "I believe you know Officer Baker, Captain Sullivan."

She nodded to each man in turn, her jaw stiff.

Buck gave her what he hoped was a reassuring, if somewhat dry, smile. "Hell of a way to start your first day at a new job, Officer Miller."

"Yes, sir."

"You told Officer Baker the victim came across the road from the west," Buck said. "Could you determine whether she came from the woods there in front of that field, or from the road?"

She was careful with her answer. "No, sir, I can't say with certainty. I didn't see her until she was almost in front of my car. I was..." She cleared her throat a little and a very faint tinge of peachy color floated across her freckled cheeks. "I may have been a little distracted. I was listening to a podcast. Also," she hurried on, "as you know, eyewitness testimony after a trauma is not always reliable. Sir."

She had a cottony-soft southern accent that made her sound even younger than she looked, and her voice was not pitched to project authority. Neither one of these things should have affected her ability to be a good police officer, but Buck was not as confident as he would have liked to be. Then she spoke again.

"Chief Lawson," she said, unable to hide the anxiety in her tone now, "do you mind if I ask... the victim. Is she—will she be all right?"

Buck glanced at Sully, who answered, "It's too early to tell. They think maybe a concussion but couldn't find any other external injuries."

The young woman's pale brows knit together thoughtfully. "There was a lot of blood on her nightgown, but most of it was dried. I didn't see any cuts or gashes, except on her feet and hands."

Buck told Baker, "Make sure we take her clothing into evidence."

"Her manicure was expensive," Miller added, "and so was her pedicure. Rainbow ombre with daisies painted on the nails, not something you can do at home. And her hair was a mess, but the cut was good. The kind of cut that takes regular maintenance. The highlights were professional. I just think—I mean, I know we don't have an ID yet, but I think she has money. Someone is probably looking for her."

Buck glanced at Baker, who was writing this all down and looking mildly annoyed that he had not made the same observations. "Get a photo and circulate it," Buck said.

Buck turned back to Miller. "Have you had anything to drink this morning, Officer Miller?"

She looked momentarily taken aback. "Besides

coffee? No."

"Are you on any medications or taking any recreational drugs?"

She seemed mildly insulted. "No, sir."

Buck said, "Officer Baker is going to take you to the ER for a blood draw to confirm that, with your permission."

"Of course, sir." Her reply was crisp and certain.

"We'll be impounding your vehicle," Buck said. "Do you have a way to get to work tomorrow?"

She stared at him. "I'm sorry, sir?"

Buck explained, "I expect the examination of your vehicle to be completed by the end of the day, but you'll need a ride to work so you can pick it up at end of shift tomorrow."

She stammered, "But… does this mean I'm not fired? Or suspended? Or pending investigation…"

Buck said, "This is what our investigation shows so far. You did not strike the victim with your car. She approached you from the west as you were turning east. She tried to open the passenger door. Failing that, the trajectory of the vehicle forced her onto the hood of the car, passenger side, where she left a handprint on the windshield. She fell to the pavement when you came to a stop, sustaining a head injury."

At her uncertain look. Buck assured her, "I spent a lot of years as a road deputy and I know how to read an accident scene. We need to document the evidence of this incident, which is why we're impounding the car. But I see absolutely no wrongdoing on your part. You will report for duty at oh-seven-hundred tomorrow morning to Officer Baker, who will be your field training officer for the next six weeks. Any questions?"

There were two. The first came from a very startled-looking Trish Miller. "Are you sure?" This was followed quickly by a reddening of her cheeks and, "I mean, Yes, sir. Thank you, sir!"

The second was from Baker, who looked almost as surprised as the girl, and it came almost before she had finished speaking. "Chief, do you think..." He glanced at Miller and half turned from her, indicating Buck should do the same. He lowered his voice. "You're assigning the subject of an investigation to work with the officer who's investigating her?"

"No," Buck replied evenly, "I'm assigning a promising young recruit to the best officer I have for six weeks of intensive on-the-job training." He added easily, "You'll finish up the incident report clearing her by the end of the day. Tomorrow, she starts fresh. We're six men short on A-shift alone, and the Fourth of July is coming. We don't have time to waste."

"Yes, sir."

"And can you do me a favor?" Buck added. "Have Carol give Eloise a call about this barbecue I'm supposed to be giving next weekend. I have a feeling it's a lot more complicated than Lydia makes it sound."

"Sure thing. I'll text her now. I think she said Eloise was going to drop Willis by around noon. Y'all want to come over for cards tonight after supper?"

Buck had made it a point to get to know each of the people who worked for him personally, along with their spouses, in the short time he had been here. Naturally, he would become closer with some than with others. Sully was a good man to have a beer with on weekends and knew all the best fishing holes. A couple of the guys had kids on the same peewee soccer team that Jo had signed Willis up for, and they all usually went out for pizza together after practice. Baker's wife Carol had taken Eloise and Jolene under her wing from the moment they met, introducing them around, inviting them to lunch and club meetings, which soon expanded to socializing between the families. There was no rule against fraternizing with the boss at the Mercy Police Department, and if there had been, Buck would have changed it. The people under Buck's command knew where friendship ended, and the professional relationship began.

"Can't," Buck said. "Jo's working and Eloise has a meeting at church, so it's just me and Willis."

"Pizza night?"

"That's the plan."

Buck turned back to Trish Miller. "After you finish up at the hospital, take the rest of the day off," he told her. "We'll keep you updated on the victim. And Miller." He offered his hand to her again. "Welcome to the Mercy P.D."

She still looked a little stunned, but she shook his hand firmly and replied, "Yes, sir."

Buck and Sully walked back toward their vehicles. Buck said, "Let's try to keep this in the department for now. We haven't even gotten over the last scandal yet."

"You got it, boss."

Buck nodded toward the field, "So what's back there?"

Sully gave a more careful answer than Baker had done. "Depends on how far you want to go. Take this road we're on, turn left, go a couple of miles, and you're going to come up on a couple of housing developments. Turn right, go the same distance, you're in the swamp."

Buck grunted thoughtfully. "Neither one of them seems like a place a woman with ombre nails could've run from barefoot."

Sully shot him a puzzled look. "What's ombre?"

Buck said, "Have your men look for barbed wire, briars, maybe a creek with sharp rocks—anything that could have caused those cuts on her feet and hands."

"Yes, sir, boss."

"Did you know Junior Aikens was in town?" Buck said.

Sully gave a surprised grunt. "Wonder what for."

"He said it was to sort out some stuff he put in

storage. He looks a lot like his daddy, doesn't he?"

"Yeah, he does," Sully agreed. "Gave more than one person at the funeral a start, that's for sure."

"I can just bet. Do you know him well?"

"Can't say that I do. He's older than me, so we never hung out as kids. By the time I went to work for Billy, Junior was long gone. I don't believe he's been back more than a couple of times since. Once for his mama's funeral, then for his daddy's."

"Huh," Buck said, a little surprised. "Well, every family's different, I guess."

They had reached their cars. Buck said, "Lydia said you wanted to see me this morning. Anything important?"

"Just thought you'd like to go over the street closings and manpower deployment for the parade. It's pretty routine. And I have the duty roster for crowd control during the fireworks show. County deputies usually pitch in so it's not too much of a problem."

"Yeah, e-mail me all that. I've got to get back for a conference call and you've got your hands full here."

"On its way." Sully took out his phone and typed a few lines. "I heard you talking to Baker. So, the barbecue is back on. Glad to hear it. The men will be, too. You know," he added, returning his phone to his pocket, "we'd planned a big retirement party for Billy this year. It would've been the weekend after the Fourth."

"Damn," Buck said softly. He had forgotten.

Billy had planned to retire right after the Fourth of July, at which time Buck would have officially taken over as chief of police. Instead, Billy had been killed, and Buck had been fumbling his way through this job since May. "No wonder Lydia thought it was so important to go ahead with the barbecue."

"I think it'll keep folks' minds off things," Sully agreed. "Maybe lift their spirits a little."

Or, Buck thought but didn't say, it would only remind them that he was not Billy and never would be.

"Lydia said something about fireworks," Buck remembered. "Where do we get them?"

Sully grinned. "From the evidence locker. The men have been storing confiscated goods all year from people buying, selling, or displaying fireworks illegally."

Buck thought he probably should look into that, but he had learned to pick his battles when it came to the borderline policies of the City of Mercy.

"And the booze?" He thought he already knew the answer to that.

"Well," admitted Sully, "there's a limit to the amount of alcohol you can bring into the state without paying taxes on it. There's a Costco right on the Florida line where folks like to stock up on wine and beer because it's cheaper. Lots of them don't know about the limit."

Buck gave him a sideways look. "So you give

them a warning and confiscate the alcohol."

Sully shrugged one shoulder. "We've been known to pick up a case or two, especially around the time of the Georgia-Florida game."

Buck fixed him with a level look. "A case or two."

Sully grinned again and clapped him on the shoulder. "Don't you worry about a thing, Chief. It's going to be a hell of a party."

Once again, Buck chose to pick his battles. He opened his car door and replied, unsmiling, "See you, Sully."

CHAPTER SIX

According to the historic marker at the entrance to Sulfur Springs Park, the springs had been a point of contention between various indigenous tribes for centuries before the white man arrived. Valued for their healing properties and imbued with magical powers said to bring everything from strength in battle to immortality, legend had it that certain tribes would sacrifice the children of their enemies and throw their bodies into the springs to increase the efficacy of the waters. When Junior Aikens was a boy, the rumor was that if you stood at the edge of the springs and listened real hard, you could still hear the tormented cries of those sacrificed Indian kids from the black depths of the bubbling pool.

These days, the main spring—thirty feet wide, twenty feet deep—was surrounded by a plexiglass wall for the safety of visitors. There were plenty of other spring-fed pools into which tourists could dip their toes along the five miles of hiking trails, however, none of them were over three feet deep. People brought Mason jars and thermoses to collect water from the springs, and that was okay. The supply was endless. Children splashed in the waters and old people swirled their arthritic hands and feet in them, claiming a remarkable relief from symptoms afterward. That was okay, too. The miraculous sulfur springs of Mercy, Georgia, aimed to please.

"You've got to wonder," said a voice behind Junior, "whether the spirits of those Indian kids still haunt the place. Maybe that's why this town is so screwed up."

Junior turned from the green metal historic plaque to look at the man who'd come up behind him. He was Junior's age, with patchy red-brown hair and a weathered face, one corner of his lips now turned down in a faint dry smile. His belly was starting to paunch beneath the gray uniform shirt he wore, but otherwise he looked fit. Junior stared at him for several beats, then abruptly drew him into a fierce hug. "Zach Whitley, you son of a gun," he exclaimed. "Damn, it's good to see you."

Zach grinned and clapped him on the back. "You too, bro. You, too."

They broke apart, more awkward in their parting than they had been in the hug, and looked at each other for another moment, smiling. Then Junior said, "Thanks for meeting me."

Zach shrugged a dismissive shoulder. "The good thing about being the boss is you can come in to work late." He inclined his head toward a path that branched off toward one of the many bunting-draped concession stands that dotted the park. "You wanna grab one of those milkshakes the tourists call coffee and find a seat out of the sun?"

It was 10:00 in the morning and the park was already starting to fill up with visitors: sweaty parents in shorts and sunhats holding onto the hands of excited children, mothers pushing strollers, dog walkers, joggers dodging slow-moving tourists reading brochures. They lined up to buy tickets for pontoon boat rides down the Blood River or to rent kayaks and canoes; they bought snacks and ice-cream cones and over-priced sodas from food wagons all decked out in red, white, and blue for the upcoming holiday. The smell of suntan oil and insect repellent almost overshadowed the stench of the springs.

Zach and Junior got their coffees and found a seat on a curved iron bench that surrounded a giant live oak, its dappled shade providing a measure of refuge from the bustling crowd. A bed of red, white, and blue petunias separated them from the intersection of walking paths beyond. A sign post directed visitors to the park's various attractions: museum and welcome center to the left, river boats and carousel to the right, botanical gardens and hiking trails straight ahead. They sat for a moment sipping their coffee and watching the crowd, then Junior said, "How's

Leah, the kids?"

Zach replied, "Doing great, just great. Leah wants to have you out to Hollowgrove for supper before you leave."

Junior smiled briefly but did not reply. They both knew that wasn't going to happen.

Zach picked up the small talk. "How about your crew? Growing like weeds, I reckon."

"You got that right. Dillon's just about as big as I am. Says he wants to play football next year, but his mama has a problem with that."

Zach nodded and sipped his coffee. "Listen, Junior. I wanted to say I'm sorry about missing the funeral. We've been having trouble with our supplier in Texas, and I had to make a run down there to pick up some parts. I thought I'd be back in time, but..." He trailed off, watching a little girl with a balloon skip down the trail beside her dad, begging him for something or another while he tried to persuade her to wait. A temper tantrum was imminent.

Junior said, "Ah, that's okay. I doubt he missed you." He, too, was watching the father and child. "To tell the truth, I would've skipped it myself, if I could have."

Zach nodded his understanding and took another sip from his cup. He took a breath, as though bracing himself, and said, "Junior, look..."

Junior spoke over him. "So how did you ever end up back at Hollowgrove, anyhow? I'd've thought that was the last place you'd want to be."

Zach looked relieved to be distracted from what he was about to say. He replied, "Free rent. The business needed room for a warehouse, an office, and the old man offered it. He also carved out eight acres for Leah and me to build a place on. It's at the back of the property, away from everybody else but near the main road. We've got a nice house, good place for the kids, and plenty of privacy. Not to mention it's a five- minute drive to work." He smiled tightly and added, "I figure Dad felt guilty after Mom died and all. It was the least he could do."

Junior nodded noncommittally. "So business is going well?"

"Twenty-three trucks," replied Zach, making an obvious effort not to sound proud, "serving three counties and supplying parts to just about everybody in the lower half of this state. It's worked out okay."

Junior agreed, "It'd be hard not to make a killing in air conditioning in this part of the country."

"What about you?" Zach returned. "The insurance game isn't treating you too bad, I hear."

Junior sipped from his cup. "I do okay."

They were silent for a moment, sipping coffee, watching the tourists. Then Zach said, "I guess we both did okay. All things considered."

Junior agreed flatly, "Yeah."

A Pekinese on a retractable leash plowed through the flower bed and lunged at them, barking furiously. His harried owner, a red-faced woman in her sixties, jerked him back. "Sorry!" she called. Junior smiled and raised his cup to her.

Junior watched them leave, the woman tugging the barking Pekinese down the path behind her. He said, "I met the new police chief this morning. He seems like a stand-up guy."

Zach gave a mirthless grunt of laughter. "Too bad for him. He'll have a hard time fitting into this place."

Junior thought about that for a minute. "Maybe."

Zach said, without looking at him, "I never meant for you to come all the way down here, you know. I just thought... you ought to know."

"No problem." Junior sipped his coffee. "We were coming this way anyhow." He breathed in, breathed out. When he spoke, his voice was even. "What did you do with it? The hat."

"Burned it, like you said." Zach's voice, in contrast to Junior's, was choppy and full of breath, as tight as the fingers that gripped his paper coffee cup. "I mean, Jesus, it had his initials on it, Junior, embroidered right there on the bill for anybody to see! If Don had gotten ahold of it, or Daddy, they would've recognized it. They would have known. It was just plain luck I happened to be there when they dug it up, and the crew supervisor didn't know what they'd found."

Junior swallowed hard, and the coffee on the back of his tongue tasted as bitter as bile. "It was only a matter of time," he said.

"It wasn't just the hat," Zach continued tightly. "It was what they were going to find next. There was no way to stop it."

Junior nodded slowly, his gaze fixed on the colorful mix of foot traffic across the way. "This new guy, the chief... do you think he'll open an investigation?"

"How the hell should I know?" returned Zach gruffly. He took a gulp of coffee, and added in a marginally calmer tone, "Maybe not. It was a lot of years ago."

"Maybe I'll talk to him," Junior said, "see what his thinking is. He said something about having lunch today." He turned to look at Zach, his expression grave. "Or we could both talk to him. Tell him what happened. Like you said, it was a lot of years ago."

Zach's eyes went hard. "There's no statute of limitations on what we did, Junior," he said flatly. He shifted his gaze away. "Anyhow, nothing to find if they do investigate. Nothing that concerns us, anyhow." He looked again at Junior. "Right?"

Junior smiled thinly in agreement.

Zach finished his coffee and stood. "Well, I've got to get to work. Busy time of year." He offered his hand and Junior stood to shake it. "Good to see you, buddy," he said. "I mean that."

"Yeah, you too," Junior replied. "I'll be in touch."

Zach turned to leave, and Junior added, "Hey,

Zach."

Zach looked back.

"The police chief's AC is on the fritz," Junior said. "You might want to move him to the top of your list."

Zach gave a dry half smile. "I'll take care of it myself," he told him.

Junior sat back down to finish his coffee, watching the tourists and trying not to think about the past.

CHAPTER SEVEN

The Hope House Center for Women was discretely located at the end of an unmarked drive on a dead-end road. The building itself was a long low brick structure centered on a beautifully landscaped lot with walking paths and flowering hedges. Detective Frankie Moreno observed that it looked more like a private sanitarium than a maternity center, not that she would necessarily know what either one looked like.

She had made an appointment with Eliza Summerfield, the facility administrator, and was buzzed right through the gate. Given the reception the Gilfords had reportedly received only that morning, Frankie was somewhat surprised by how easy it all had been. She waited only a few moments in the plush reception area, with his pale pink and beige silk upholstery and delicate Queen Anne furniture, before the secretary returned to escort her to the administrator's office.

Eliza Summerfield in no way resembled the cold-hearted harridan Beth and Jeff Gilford had described. She was in her sixties and seemed comfortable with the fact, not trying to hide the thirty or so extra pounds or the silver in her short, practically styled hair. She wore a navy suit with a pretty floral print blouse, and she stood when Frankie entered, reaching across the desk to shake her hand.

"Detective Moreno," she said. Her voice managed to be both warm and distressed at the same time. "Please have a seat. I am so sorry you had to come all the way out here. As I told you on the phone, this is the most upsetting—and embarrassing—incident in the history of Hope House. Can I get you a coffee? Water?"

Frankie took the chair she had indicated, a pretty but exceptionally uncomfortable club chair upholstered in pale green velvet, and assured the other woman she required neither water nor coffee. She took out her notebook, but before she could ask the first question, the older woman sank back into her desk chair and began, "This is all a terrible misunderstanding. I've been trying to reach the Gilfords all morning, as you can imagine. When I finally got through, Mr. Gilford told me in no uncertain terms that all further communications should be through his lawyer." She spread her hands helplessly. "So, you see, I am really at an impasse. My own lawyer has advised me that any communication I have with the Gilfords from this point on would not only be inappropriate, but disadvantageous to Hope House. I just don't know what else to do. I'm sure this could all be cleared up in one conversation if we could just sit down and talk."

Frankie nodded her understanding. "Yes ma'am. In my line of work, I've found that's almost always the case. But the Gilfords have filed a complaint, and I have to compile a report. So why don't you tell me what happened?"

Mrs. Summerfield sighed. "We are a licensed adoption agency, as I told you on the phone, and a fully staffed maternity center. Many of the young ladies who come to us do so through a surrogacy situation, and in those cases, the only role we play is in providing the best possible prenatal environment and a nurturing, personalized birth experience for the whole family—biological and adoptive parents alike. When a woman comes to us wanting to place her unborn child, we take her into our facility and encourage her to choose the adoptive parents from our qualified applicants as early in the pregnancy as possible. As soon as a match is made, both parties sign a contract agreeing to the adoption. However, in Georgia, the mother has ten days to change her mind." She smiled wearily. "I'm afraid that's what happened in the Gilfords' case. The mother simply changed her mind after the baby was born."

Frankie nodded, consulting her notebook. "Mr. Gilford told me that he received a call informing him that the baby they had agreed to adopt had been born, but that when they arrived here, they were refused entry at the gate, and were told their baby wasn't here."

"That, I'm afraid, is where the confusion begins," she admitted regretfully. "They arrived at 6:00 a.m. The staff doesn't get here until 8:00. No one was available to answer their questions and that is a matter of gross incompetence on our part which has been dealt with, I assure you."

Frankie said, "Mr. Gilford also said that when he eventually talked to you it was only through the intercom and that you told him there hadn't been any births in the past week."

She looked mildly puzzled. "Well, I'm sure he misunderstood. When he demanded to be let inside to claim his baby, I told him there was no baby to claim. But before I could explain further, he began shouting accusations and threats and broke the connection. It was very upsetting."

"Why didn't you simply invite them in and explain the mother had changed her mind?" Frankie said. "I'm sure you can understand their frustration."

"Of course. And that's exactly what I would have done if I had been given a chance."

Frankie said, "According to the Gilfords' statement, they paid over one hundred thousand dollars to Hope House for this adoption."

"I'd have to check our records to confirm that. Our agreement is that the adoptive parents pay for all the birth mother's expenses, including her stay here at Hope House."

"What happens to their money, now that the mother has changed her mind?"

"It's all covered in the agreement," Mrs. Summerfield said. "A certain amount will be forfeited and the rest returned to them, or they can choose to stay on the list for the next available infant."

"They believe you gave their baby to someone else," Frankie said, "or that perhaps there never was a baby at all."

Mrs. Summerfield simply smiled. "That's nonsense, of course."

A few months ago, Frankie would have closed her notebook, thanked the woman for her time, and gone back to the station to write her report. She had investigated. She had found no evidence of fraud or criminal activity. This was very likely exactly what it appeared to be—an unfortunate misunderstanding. Otherwise, it was a matter for the civil court.

But perfunctory investigations and easy conclusions didn't pass muster with the new police chief, not for a minute. These days the Mercy Police Department acted on solid investigative procedure, clear evidence, and completely unimpeachable reporting. A lot of the guys on the force groused about that, but Frankie admired the standards set by the new chief and was determined to live up to them.

So, she said, "Thank you for your cooperation, Mrs. Summerfield. I just need to talk to the mother and verify the infant's safety. Also, I'll need a copy of the surrender papers the mother signed for our file."

Mrs. Summerfield's smile did not waver. "I'm terribly sorry, Detective, but none of that will be possible. I can get you a copy of our boilerplate agreement, of course, but the names of our guests are held in the strictest confidence. As for the mother and her baby, well..." She turned both hands, palms up, on the table. "I'm afraid they're gone."

And *this* was why the chief insisted upon thorough investigative procedure.

Frankie said, "What do you mean, gone?"

"I mean," replied the other woman, "that as of 7:00 a.m. nurses' rounds this morning, neither the mother nor the child was in residence. We don't hold them captive, you know. Our ladies are free to leave whenever they wish."

Frankie said, "I'll need her name and her check-in file."

Mrs. Summerfield smiled. "As I think I've previously made clear, that's not possible. Protecting the privacy of our clients is our first priority."

"Then may I talk to the nurses, the other residents, anyone who may have come in contact with her?"

Eliza Summerfield shook her head. "I'm so

sorry, no. No one who isn't staff or resident is allowed beyond this wing."

Frankie said, "Do you have a forwarding address or contact information on the mother?"

Mrs. Summerfield looked genuinely regretful. "Detective Moreno, as I indicated, our privacy regulations..."

Frankie waved a dismissing hand. "What about the father? Other next of kin?"

The other woman shook her head sadly. "I really am sorry."

Frankie looked at her for a long moment. In another lifetime she might have threatened her with subpoenas and warrants, but one thing Buck Lawson had taught her was never to give away your hand...assuming, of course, that you had a hand worth playing. And Frankie thought she did.

She closed the notebook, smiled, and stood up. "Thank you, Mrs. Summerfield. I think this is all I need. I'll talk to the Gilfords, but of course, it's up to them to determine how far they want to pursue this. If you decide there's anything else you can share..." Frankie placed her business card on the desk.

"I really am afraid there's not." The other woman stood as well, ignoring the card.

Frankie inclined her head. "Then thank you again and have a good day."

The secretary saw her to the door, and Frankie could feel eyes watching her as she made her way to her car. She wished she could have a look around the grounds and was trying to figure out whether it might be possible to breach the six-foot tall stockade fence when the call came in from Baker.

That changed everything.

CHAPTER EIGHT

It was protocol for the escorting officer to wait at the hospital for the lab results when requesting a blood alcohol, and usually it was easy duty—a chance to get a coffee or a bite to eat, chat up the nurses or make personal phone calls. Most of the time the only complaint was that the hospital was too efficient, and the officer—along with his prisoner, in most cases—was back on the road too soon. But this was not a typical case, and Leon Baker was having a hard time keeping his frustration from showing as he checked his watch once again.

The Corley County Hospital had twenty-two inpatient rooms, two operating rooms, and three emergency bays. A single traffic accident could exceed their capacity, and Baker knew the reason he had been waiting over an hour for a report that should have taken twenty minutes was because of the emergency the EMTs had brought in that morning. *His* emergency. His case. Because he had been waiting over an hour for an update on her, as well.

Baker's charge, the young blonde rookie, sat serenely in a plastic visitor's chair across from him, her features composed, her hands folded quietly in her lap, the band-aid on the inside of her elbow the only indication that her presence here might not be as official as her uniform indicated. He had told her to help herself to coffee or snacks from the vending machine, but she had politely refused. He wondered if she could really be as untroubled by the events of the morning as she appeared and decided in the negative. She might look as Zen as a yogi, but her nostrils were flared, and her breath was quicker than it should have been. That reassured Baker, in some way. He didn't think he could trust somebody who was as controlled as she was pretending to be.

"Officer."

Baker got up quickly and walked to the nurse's station, where a young woman held out a paper to him. "Just came in," she said.

He could feel Officer Miller's anxious gaze on him from across the room as he scanned the report. He said, "Okay, thanks. Could you try calling one more time about the condition of that Jane Doe they brought in? I need to speak to her as soon as possible."

The nurse picked up the phone. "Hold on."

Baker jerked his head toward Miller, and she got up, coming to him quickly. "You're clear," he told her, folding the paper into his pocket. "I'm waiting for a report on the victim, and then I'll get you home."

She showed no visible reaction to the news —except, perhaps, a slight relaxation of her shoulders. "Yes, sir." She added uncertainly, "Um, sir? Does this mean I'm working the case with you? Or am I still a principal?"

"It means," he replied, trying to keep the impatience out of his voice, "you're an off-duty officer waiting for a ride. I'll be with you in a minute."

He turned back to the nurse as she hung up the phone. "Dr. Wiggins is on her way down," she said.

"All right," he muttered. "Now we're getting somewhere." He took out his phone and walked toward the elevator, checking his texts. He wasn't aware that Trish Miller was following in step until he put his phone away and found her standing at his shoulder.

Leon Baker had been told—most recently by his boss—that he needed to work on his people skills. He didn't disagree. He just didn't see the value of amiability when he could do his job perfectly well without it. Nonetheless, making detective was important to him and he appreciated the opportunity the chief had given him. He therefore resolved to try harder to present a more genial face to the public and his colleagues. His wife thought he was making progress. He wasn't so sure.

He said, striving for an even tone, "Look, Officer Miller, why don't you..."

The elevator dinged, and the doors opened on a woman wearing a white lab coat over her scrubs. "Dr. Wiggins?" he said. "I'm Officer Baker, and this is Officer Miller. I understand you're in charge of the Jane Doe who was brought in earlier."

The doctor led the way back to the nurse's station, consulting her clipboard. "She was transferred to my service from the emergency room, yes, but I was unable to perform anything beyond an initial exam. According to the EMTs, she was struck by a car, but we only found superficial injuries. Some dehydration and excessive bleeding, which is why I recommended she be admitted for observation. At this point, we're more concerned about her newborn, which is why I wanted to talk to you in person."

Baker stared at her. "She had a baby?"

Trish demanded urgently, "How long ago did she give birth?"

"Less than twenty-four hours," replied the doctor.

Baker said, "We need to talk to her. Is she conscious?"

"She was," admitted the doctor. "But talking to her might be a problem since she left the hospital before being transferred to her room."

"Alone?" said Trish.

"No," Dr. Wiggins answered. "My understanding is that someone came for her.

An aunt, a mother? You'd have to speak with the emergency room staff for the details. The attending physician was..." She flipped a page in her chart. "Dr. Timori." She looked from one to the other of them. "She was very uncommunicative; I can tell you that. Quite distressed, as I suppose is to be expected, but when I saw her, she was unable —or unwilling—to give as much as her name."

Baker took out his phone and punched Frankie's number.

"So, she didn't say anything to you," Trish insisted, "anything at all that might help us uncover her identity, or even where she gave birth?"

The doctor shook her head helplessly. "Nothing."

Frankie said, "Could we see the security footage? Maybe we can find out who she left with."

The doctor shook her head again. "HIPAA regulations. You'll need a warrant."

Baker said into his phone, "Sergeant. I'm at the hospital with the Jane Doe who was involved in the 466 this morning. The doctor says she gave birth less than twenty-four hours ago. We might be looking at an abandoned newborn."

There was a brief silence, then Frankie said, "I think I might have a lead on that. Meanwhile, we'll get out an all-points. Any progress on her ID?"

"No, ma'am. She left the hospital without talking to anyone."

"Security footage?"

Baker glanced at Trish, then at the doctor. "We'll need a warrant."

"All right. Get her photo on the network and we'll start circulating it. Somebody's got to recognize her. This town is not that big."

Baker cleared his throat uncomfortably. "Actually, ma'am, I was waiting until she recovered consciousness to get the picture."

Frankie said, "You don't have a photograph of the victim? Standard procedure, Officer Baker."

"Yes, ma'am, I..."

Miller tapped him on the shoulder, and he turned to her in annoyance. She was holding up her phone with a photograph of Jane Doe, taken at the scene of the accident, filling the screen.

"Standard police procedure," she explained, a little apologetically.

Baker turned his attention back to his conversation, scowling. "Cancel that, Sergeant. We have the photo. Uploading it now."

"Excellent," Frankie replied. "You know what to do. Talk to the last people who saw her. Canvas the neighborhoods around where she was found. Coordinate your progress with Captain Sully. I," she added with a grim note of determination in her voice, "have to get a court order. Keep me informed, Baker."

"Yes ma'am."

He disconnected the call and turned back to Miller. She met his gaze with the kind of hopeful expectation he hadn't seen in anyone's eyes since his kids' Labrador was a puppy. "I could help interview the ER staff," she volunteered.

Baker scowled. "I'm supposed to take you home."

"I don't mind," she answered quickly. Then she added, "I'd really like to help, sir. I feel, you know, responsible."

Baker debated another moment, then took out his phone. "I'll clear it with the captain. Let's go."

CHAPTER NINE

Baker talked to Dr. Timori, who once again reminded him of the HIPAA regulations which prevented him from talking about Jane Doe's medical condition. Baker assured him they were far less interested in the woman's medical information than the fate of an endangered newborn. While they were thus engaged, Trish glanced around the white-tiled room, meeting the glances of curious nurses and smiling at the ones who did more than glance. The nurses were the ones who actually dealt with the patients, after all, and they almost always knew more than the doctors did. Trish walked over to one of them and showed her the picture of Jane Doe on her phone.

"Were you here when the EMTs brought this woman in?"

"I was," she admitted cautiously, "but..."

"I just want to know if she said anything about her baby," Trish assured her quickly. When the woman hesitated, she added, "I'm the one who, ah..." She didn't want to say, "hit her with my car," since the chief himself had assured her that was not what happened. So, she said instead, "I was first on the scene. I got the impression she wanted to ask me for help, but she lost consciousness before she could. Is there anything you can tell me? Anything at all?"

The other woman's expression softened a bit. "She was very upset. She wouldn't give us her name, or any of the information we needed for her paperwork. All she kept saying was, 'I'm sorry.'" The nurse glanced around and lowered her voice. "I got the feeling she was afraid of something, or someone. Probably the police. I hate to say it, but I've been a nurse for thirty-five years and I've seen this kind of thing before. I think she might have left that baby to die somewhere, or it was already dead."

Trish winced inside but refused to let it show on her face. She said, "Did you see her leave the hospital?"

The nurse shook her head. "I asked her if I could call anyone for her, and she asked to use my phone. It was the only time she was really coherent. I gave her my phone and I overheard her telling someone she was here in the emergency room and wanted to go home, but that was really all she said. They took her up for a CT scan after that, and I didn't see her again."

Trish said, "Could you show me the number she dialed?"

The nurse took her phone out of the other pocket and scrolled down to the number, showing it to Trish. Trish reached for the phone. "Do you mind?"

Baker came up just as Trish pushed the "dial" button. "Jane Doe called someone before she left the hospital," she explained and put the phone on speaker.

After three rings, a rather tense female voice answered, "Hope House."

Trish glanced at Baker, and he returned a small nod.

Trish said, "This is Officer Miller with the Mercy Police Department. Could I speak with the, um, administrator, please?"

There was a pause, then, "One moment."

Trish said to Baker, "Hope House?"

Baker replied, "It's one of those... what do you call them? Where women go to have their babies."

The nurse supplied, "Maternity homes."

The receptionist came back on the line. Her voice was crisp. "I'm sorry, Mrs. Summerfield is not available at the moment. I'll be happy to take a message."

Trish left her own mobile number and returned the nurse's phone to her. "Thank you for your help," she said.

Baker took out one of his cards and gave it to her. Trish's own cards wouldn't be issued until after her probationary period.

"If you think of anything else," Baker told the

nurse, "please give me a call."

Baker and Trish walked out together.

"So," Trish said, "we know where she came from, but not who she is."

"Or," Baker reminded her grimly, "what she did with her baby."

CHAPTER TEN

Marianne didn't know what to do. It was not supposed to have happened like this. She had thought it out so carefully, planned every detail, talked it through for months. She had never believed it was going to be easy, but she was in the right, and no one would dare try to stop her. Stop them. Or at least that was what she had thought.

She had driven fifty miles in a state of panic and shock before it finally hit her: she was a kidnapper. An Amber Alert had probably already been issued. There would be a BOLO on her car. There had been witnesses. People knew who she was. And Giselle...Giselle knew where she was headed. Someone would have contacted her parents by now. There would probably be federal agents waiting for her. She had to get off the highway.

She took the next exit and drove toward the big Wal-Mart sign. By this time, the sun was up and there were even a few cars in the big parking lot. Better, there were a couple of RVs and an eighteen-wheeler parked at the end of the lot. She pulled her Escort into one of the parking spaces between the truck and an RV, so that she was mostly shielded from view. She turned off the engine and sank back against the seat, breathing shakily.

How could it all have gone so wrong?

Marianne unfastened her seatbelt and twisted to look into the back seat, half-kneeling on the console to see into the infant seat that was securely fastened there. The tiny, red-faced infant was fast asleep, her little fist pressed against her cheek, her delicate nostrils flaring with each breath. She had hardly made a sound since their desperate journey had begun, which was a blessing. Newborns spent most of their first twenty-four hours sleeping, but that wouldn't last forever. Marianne had grabbed a handful of diapers and a bottle of infant sucrose water from the nursery, but she was going to need more supplies. The diaper bag, so carefully packed with everything they would need for the trip, the folding portable crib she had spent almost a week's salary on, the extra boxes of diapers, the receiving blankets... they were all back at her apartment.

Marianne wriggled herself over the console and into the backseat, trying not to disturb the sleeping infant as she sank into the seat beside her. "Oh, Daisy," she whispered, "I am so sorry."

She reached out a tentative finger and stroked the baby's cheek lightly. The tiny eyelids fluttered, but she didn't wake. "I never meant for this to happen. Never."

They had been calling her Daisy since Marianne had seen the ultrasound that revealed the baby was a girl. The policy was, of course, not to reveal the gender to the mother, but Marianne knew it was essential that the mother start to bond with her infant as soon as possible. So, they decided on a name, and it was Daisy. Marianne hadn't counted on the fact that the only one who was bonding with the child was her.

She would need formula. Maybe not now, but soon. She hadn't planned on that.

Marianne reached forward to the front seat and dragged her purse to her, pulling out her wallet. Seven dollars and twenty-two cents. She had credit cards and an ATM debit card, but in every cop show she'd ever seen the fugitive had been captured by tracing his card activity. Maybe that was fiction, but at this point could she really afford to take a chance?

Kidnapping. Dear God. That was a federal offense.

Her phone lay inert in the pocket of her purse that was designed to hold it. She stared at it for a long time. She knew she had to do it. She had to call her parents. She had tried to keep them out of this, lying about her job and her whereabouts for half a year because she didn't want to get their hopes up, didn't want to rekindle the pain of the past that they had almost, almost been able to put behind them. Hoping that when she returned triumphant with Giselle and the baby all would be forgiven. But she wasn't returning triumphant. She had screwed everything up and she wouldn't be able to go home at all without help.

Slowly, she pulled the phone out of her purse, drew a deep, steadying breath, and pushed the wake button. Nothing happened. She tried again, and again. The phone was dead, and her charger was back in her apartment, on the nightstand by her bed where she had left it.

Marianne leaned her head back against the seat and closed her eyes briefly, drawing slow breaths in, pushing slow breaths out. She hadn't eaten since lunch yesterday. She needed coffee. She needed solid food. She needed a phone charger, formula...She needed to *think*.

She glanced at the big box store across the parking lot from her. It would have all those things. It would also have security cameras, and a woman in hospital scrubs carrying a newborn wouldn't exactly be inconspicuous. And seven dollars and twenty-two cents would barely buy her a cup of coffee.

She wouldn't be able to stay here much longer. In another hour, the temperature would be too high to sit in the car, even in the shade. Besides, she was pretty sure there were security cameras in the parking lot, too, and if she stayed here too long someone was liable to get suspicious.

She had fifteen hundred dollars in cash tucked into the toe of a running shoe back at her apartment. Her emergency money. She supposed part of her had always known there was a good chance this plan would go south.

She really didn't have a choice. She had to turn herself in. And what would happen then? Even if she told them what was really going on at that place—what she *suspected* was going on—they would take baby Daisy from her, and most likely send her back to the very same situation from which Marianne had rescued her. No. What she had to do, the only thing she *could* do was get Daisy to safety. After that, whatever happened to her would happen. She could deal with it.

Her mother would take care of Daisy. She might not approve of how she had come into this world, but she would not let an innocent child suffer for the sins of the mother. Marianne's father knew lawyers. He would make sure no one took Daisy from them.

She had half a tank of gas, which just might be enough to get her to her destination. At this point, all she could do was try.

Marianne dropped a kiss lightly atop the baby's head. "It's going to be okay, sweetheart," she whispered. "I promise. We can do this."

Then she climbed back over the console, got behind the wheel, and started home.

CHAPTER ELEVEN

Buck got an update from Sully before he left the office.

"Even though we know she made a phone call to Hope House," he explained, "and the likelihood is that she was a resident there, the Gilfords couldn't positively identify the woman in the photo as one of the mothers they'd seen. She was unconscious, her face was swollen, her hair not the same, and it's been months since they'd seen her. They said it could be, but they weren't positive. Based on this, Judge Warren asked for more time to consider the search warrant."

Buck punched the intercom. "Lydia, get Judge Warren on the phone." He added to Sully, "If she called Hope House, it was probably someone from there who came to get her from the hospital. She could be there now, and she's the only one who can tell us where her baby is."

"We have eight teams searching the woods, the riverbank, and the marsh within a two-mile square of the place Jane Doe encountered Officer Miller's vehicle," Sully went on. "Also, every available officer is searching dumpsters, public restrooms, and trashcans in our jurisdiction. Corley County is lending an assist. Four teams, led by Officer Baker, are canvasing houses and businesses within the perimeter we've set up. Also, Officer Miller requested to join the search. Her labs came back clean and the accident site has been cleared so I okayed it."

"I like a woman who hits the ground running," Buck murmured.

The intercom buzzed. "I'm sorry, Chief, Judge Warren is in court until 5:00. I left a message."

Buck bit back an oath and said instead, "Thanks, Lydia."

"Chief," Sully said solemnly, "in my opinion, we're not going to find that baby. Best case scenario, the Gilfords were right and it's already been given to somebody else. Worst case, it's in the river somewhere. I'm sorry to be blunt."

"Damn it," Buck said softly. Every bone in his body ached to be out in the field, directing the search, even though he knew Sully was right. These things rarely turned out well. He said, "What's the deal on this Hope House place? Are they legit or what?"

Sully said, "According to Frankie, their papers

are all in order. No complaints with this department or any state agency that we can find. If they're up to anything off the books, they've been really good at it so far."

The intercom buzzed again. "Chief, the time..."

"Got it, Lydia," Buck replied, and disconnected. He looked at Sully for a moment, ruminating. "Thoughts?"

"This is not a high school kid giving birth in a bathroom and trying to flush the results," he replied, "or an illegal burying her newborn in the woods because she can't afford to lose her job as a maid." Sully's tone was flat, but his eyes were in turmoil. Buck's stomach turned even as he spoke. "But we've got to treat it like it was. My opinion, given the circumstances, something bigger is going on. I say let Frankie do her job."

"Yeah," Buck agreed, heavily. "Right."

He called Jo on his way out of town, knowing it was her lunch break.

"Hey babe," she said around a mouthful of something. "What's up?"

"We're giving a barbecue for a hundred people next weekend."

"Yay," she replied. "Where's your grill?"

He smothered a groan. He hadn't seen the grill since they'd moved in. No doubt it was at the bottom of a stack of unopened boxes in the tool shed. "It's going to take more than one grill to feed a hundred people," he pointed out.

"You're going to be a busy boy."

"Also," he said, "we have a county-wide search for a missing newborn."

"Oh, hon." Her voice was immediately filled with compassion. "These things never turn out well."

"Not to mention," he went on grimly, "the mother of the missing newborn was the victim of a pedestrian-versus-vehicle collision involving one of my officers."

"Ah, crap," she said. "You're having a day."

"To say the least." His voice tightened with frustration. "Meanwhile, instead of being out there directing the investigation, I'm on my way to a priss-pretty luncheon with Miss Corinne to help her play politics. Why the hell did I even take this job if I'm not going to be allowed to *do* my job?"

"You took this job," she reminded him calmly, "because we have a little boy who's going to college in exactly twelve years, three months, and sixteen days. And because, two weeks after that, there's an open-air yurt in Bali with our names on it."

He smiled, more enchanted by the way she said, "we have a little boy" than by the reference to Bali. "Yeah, okay," he agreed. "I guess that's worth one more stupid wasted afternoon eating lunch. How's your day going?"

"I got clocked on the chin by a trainee during an exercise," she admitted. "Had to go to the dispensary for treatment, *and* file a six-page report."

The muffled exclamation he gave was part incredulity, part concern. "You okay?"

"Fine," she assured him dismissively. "But the poor kid practically pissed himself when he realized he'd hit me."

This time Buck couldn't quite stifle his laughter. "Baby, I can't even picture that."

"Yeah, well, laugh it up, big guy. All I need is a neck brace and a shyster lawyer to qualify for disability."

"So maybe that yurt in Bali is closer than we think."

"Now you're catching on. Gotta go, babe. Be nice to Miss Corinne. Go ahead and eat supper with Willis. I'll be home around 9:00 or 9:30."

"We're going to get pizza."

"No, you're not," she informed him. "Mama's making a taco casserole. All you have to do is serve it up."

"Even better."

"And Buck? Don't spend the whole time on the phone with the watch commander. I know you're worried about this case, but Willis has been looking forward to boys' night all week."

"So have I," Buck assured her. "Phone in the drawer. Promise."

"Love you," she said, and he replied, "More." That was the best part of his day.

CHAPTER TWELVE

The first time Buck visited Mercy, he had thought it looked like a movie set; a perfect replica of a small southern town captured in time circa 1860. Its slow-moving blackwater river, its weeping willows and waxy magnolias, its wide, shaded porches and white-columned mansions all combined to suggest a bygone era of quiet civility and easy refinement.

Buck knew, of course, that the antebellum epoch Mercy represented was neither civilized nor refined, but he had to admit that over the past few weeks he had been drawn into its charm. Old gentlemen in seersucker suits. His next-door neighbor, watering her roses every morning in a print housedress and portrait hat. The local paper highlighting Junior League dances and beauty pageants. None of it was politically correct or even sensible, and he, as police chief, knew better than most it was all a myth designed to shield those who longed for a gentler way of life from the harsh realities of the modern world. Still, it was a pleasant myth, and one he didn't mind indulging in from time to time.

Even so, he was in no way prepared for the outrageous example of Old South grandeur that was Hollowgrove Plantation.

His navigation system took him so deeply into barren countryside that he thought it might be malfunctioning. The roads down which he was directed were flat and featureless, the monotony broken only occasionally by an endless row of white pasture fencing or a field of soybeans stretching toward the horizon. He could smell the rich sulfur odor of the river even through his vehicle's closed air conditioning system, but he couldn't see it. According to the nav map, he had gone a little over fifteen miles when he was directed to turn right in one hundred yards. A discreet, custom-made white sign announced, "Hollowgrove Plantation."

After a mile, the paved road forked. To the right was a sign directing visitors to "Deliveries." To the left, the sign read, "Plantation; Restaurant; Office; Check-In."   Buck traveled down a marble-chip drive through a tunnel of interlocking oak trees that set the scene perfectly for the stately mansion that stood at the end of it. The marble drive widened to surround a tall, white-columned structure with twin curving staircases, a verdigris copper roof, and tall leaded windows that glinted in the sun. Two wings, east and west, appeared to be recent add-ons. Meticulously maintained flower beds were filled with bright pink, yellow and lavender flowers, and a neat boxwood hedge mimicked the curve of the twin staircases as it sloped away from the house. The lawn looked like a golf course, its green so bright it was hard to look at.

"Okay, Miss Corrine," Buck murmured, "I'm impressed."

The drive was bisected by a circular flower bed and a tall, three-tiered fountain. Buck drove behind the fountain and pulled to a stop in front of the steps. They were marble, he saw now, easily ten feet wide on each side. Unbelievable.

Directly ahead of him to the right of the house was an open car shed with three Mercedes inside, each with its own set of vanity plates: Whtly3, Whtly2, and the last one simply, MAYR. Roland, the mayor's son and driver, leaned against her vehicle, watching Buck drive up. A young Hispanic man in a red valet's vest trotted around the corner and reached Buck's car just as Buck was getting out.

"Good afternoon, Chief," he said. He was sweating in the white shirt and bow tie, his dark hair already damp. "I am happy to park your car for you." He held out his hand for the keys with a smile.

Buck pushed the button on the remote that locked the car and said, "This is an official police vehicle. Nobody touches it but me or..." He nodded toward Roland, who continued to watch laconically. "The head of the city motor pool over there. He looks kinda busy, so if it's all the same to you, I'll just leave it here." He dropped the keys into the pocket of his jacket, ready to get out of the sun.

The young valet must have been equally as anxious to seek shade, because, after only a momentary flutter of disappointment as he no doubt calculated his lost tip, he agreed cheerfully, "No problem, sir, I'm sure it will be fine here. Have a good lunch."

Buck took out his phone and checked his texts. A team had found an old barbed wire fence in the field about a quarter mile from the accident site, and blood on the grass nearby. The fence was less than a quarter-mile cross-country from Hope House. Nothing yet from Judge Warren.

What about another judge? Buck typed.

Looking into it, Sully replied.

Jane Doe?

Nothing.

Buck put away his phone, his lips tightening in frustration, and went up the steps. A pretty young woman in a black sheath and elegant pearl necklace waited for him at the top of the steps. Her caramel-colored hair fell in a perfectly styled oval just past her shoulder blades, and the neckline of her dress formed a heart shape over her breasts, showing just enough cleavage to be intriguing while still managing to appear demure. Her skin and her eyes suggested Hispanic descent.

She extended her hand to him with a warm smile. "Chief Lawson, welcome to Hollowgrove." Her handshake was delicate, her teeth brilliantly —and expensively—maintained. "My name is Marina, and I'll be your hostess this afternoon. Mayor Watts and Mr. Whitley are waiting for you in the private dining room."

She opened the carved oak door and Buck stepped into a tall-ceilinged room highlighted by a crystal chandelier in the center and a sweeping staircase to the right. The glossy plank floors were accented with richly faded Aubusson carpets and antique furniture—a fainting couch, wing chairs, and a settee—done in gold brocade. The windows were arched and decorated with burgundy velvet, and to the left was an enormous mahogany arch, also accented with floor-to-ceiling red velvet. It was clear that whoever had designed this place did not believe in the principle of understated wealth.

"Quite a place," Buck remarked as Marina led the way through the arch and into another room, equally as lavish and easily twice as big.

"This part of the house was built between 1842 and 1848," she replied, falling effortlessly into the role of tour guide that she had no doubt played many times before. She had the faintest trace of an exotic accent that Buck could not quite place. It gave her voice a faint musical lilt that was a pleasure to listen to. "The floors are cypress, harvested from the swamps of Louisiana and brought down the Blood River via the Mississippi. The mahogany paneling..." she gestured backward toward the arch through which they had just passed. "... which you'll see throughout the home, was imported from the West Indies, where the original Mr. Whitely owned a shipping company as well as another sugar plantation."

Buck inquired pleasantly, "Where are you from, Marina?"

She replied, "I've lived here all my life, sir." She paused just outside another door and drew his attention to the wall of photographs adjacent to it. "Some of our more notable guests," she pointed out.

The photographs, all 8x10s in gold frames, were of presidents and presidents' sons, movie stars, and royalty. A Saudi prince; a famous, now-deceased news anchor; a couple of well-known billionaires. The photographs went back over fifty years, and almost all of them were taken posing with Jarrod Whitley. Buck couldn't help being impressed, just as he was supposed to be.

"Are all of them members of the hunting club?" he asked.

"No, sir, not all."

She gestured him to the right, into an enormous round room surrounded by more of those arched, floor-to-ceiling windows. Classical paintings of hunting scenes featuring boys in red jackets and noble hunting dogs hung in gilt frames around the room. There was a huge banquet-style table in the center with tall carved chairs pulled up around it. The enormous vase of hydrangeas and gladiolus in the center of the polished table would not have looked out of place in a hotel lobby.

"The plaster work in this room was done by the same Italian artist who worked on the pope's summer palace in Gandolfo. It took him two years to complete." She gestured to the elaborately decorated ceiling and gave Buck a moment to appreciate it. Buck tilted his head back and pretended to admire the workmanship.

"In 1863," Marina went on, "A cannon ball was fired from the Blood River and struck the west wall of the dining room near the fireplace, where it remains embedded in the exterior to this day. If you stand just here, you can see how the wall bulges inward a bit from the damage."

"Interesting," Buck murmured, although, in truth, he wasn't as charmed by old houses as someone who didn't actually live in one might have been.

"During the season, and of course during special events, the dining room is open to guests," she said, her heels clicking on the wooden floors as she crossed the room. "But family meals are served here, in the private dining room."

She opened a door that was so well concealed by painted paneling that Buck had not even noticed, and gestured him inside, smiling. "Mr. Whitley," she said, "Chief Lawson."

This room was somewhat smaller and not nearly as ostentatious as the ones through which they had just passed, although no one would mistake it for ordinary. There was a fireplace with an elaborately carved marble mantle, a long buffet displaying heavy silver serving pieces, and a tall hutch with crystal and China artfully arranged behind its glass doors. A table for six was nestled inside the curve of an enormous bay window, dressed in an ivory tablecloth and matching damask napkins, with a bowl of ivory roses in the center. The man Marina had introduced as Mr. Whitley half rose when Buck entered, but it was Corinne Watts who greeted him.

"Buck, darling, there you are."

Corinne Watts was somewhere on the north side of sixty, as best anyone could guess. Her platinum hair was cut stylishly short and tucked behind the ears, her creamy skin and sharp-boned features maintained at great expense by the best plastic surgeons in the South. Today she wore a red silk suit with short, puffed sleeves and a black blouse with a black-and-white polka-dot tie. Buck had never known her to dress like anything less than a fashion model, which was part of her mystique. Everything about her radiated power. She hid her deadly nature behind a fine façade of old-world charm, but those who underestimated her did so at their own peril. Corinne Watts ruled the fiefdom of Mercy with a ruthlessness any mob boss would have envied, but Buck had to hand it to her: she might be a despot who operated barely inside the law, but she was a brilliant despot. And there wasn't a single person in town who didn't love her for it.

"I heard you had some trouble in town," she went on. Her gentle Southern accent sounded just like magnolias looked—lush, sweet, and almost unbearably overdone, much like Miss Corinne herself. "I'm so terribly glad you were able to make it." She extended her hand to him, fingers down, the way a lady should, and at the same time turned her cheek for a kiss.

Buck's relationship with the mayor straddled the fine line between wary respect and outright mistrust, as did hers with him. They had, over the past two months, negotiated a cautious truce based on mutual need. For now, he was content to play her game.

He came around the table and bowed slightly over her fingers, then obliged her with a kiss on the cheek. Somehow the gesture did not seem quite as ridiculous in this setting as it might have elsewhere.

"Buck, honey, this is Jarrod Whitley, the owner of Hollowgrove. Jarrod, this is our police chief, Buck Lawson. Isn't he just the yummiest thing?"

Both men politely disregarded the last

comment as they shook hands and sized each other up. Jarrod Whitley was easily in his eighties, a portly man with liver-spotted skin and thinning white hair that fell, in somewhat scraggly strands, to his collarbone. He had a keen look in his narrow hazel eyes and a grip that was surprisingly strong.

"Well now," he declared, shaking Buck's hand, "if it ain't the legend himself." His voice was as strong as his grip, and it practically boomed in the empty room. "Sweeping into town like some kind of cross between Clint Eastwood and Elliot Ness, cleaning out the crime nest, and then sinking back into obscurity, too damn modest to even take a bow for himself. Goddamn pleasure to meet you, Buck."

Buck cast a mildly amused look toward Miss Corinne. "Elliot Ness and Clint Eastwood, huh?"

The mayor took a sip of her drink, blue eyes twinkling over the rim. "That's what they say, sugar."

"Sit down, Buck, sit down," commanded his host. "About time we got acquainted." He sank back into his own chair and waved Marina over. "Get on over here and see what the man wants to drink, darlin'. Let's get this cart on the road."

Buck sat down and Marina placed a leather-bound menu before him, centering it precisely on his place setting. Buck couldn't help noticing her nails, painted with an intriguing design that went from dark red on the tips to the palest pink near the cuticles. Little flowers were painted on the index finger of each hand.

She said, "What can I bring you from the bar, Chief Lawson?"

"The chief doesn't drink on duty, honey," Corinne answered sweetly before he could. "But I'll take another one of these when you come back." She lifted a half-empty glass of what might have been a Manhattan.

"I'll have a sweet tea, thanks, Marina," Buck told her. She smiled and nodded and left as discretely as she had come.

"You don't know what you're missing, Buck," said Whitley, raising his own glass. "The bourbon is my own special label. Triple distilled. Best in the country. So." He leaned back in his chair, took a sip, and regarded Buck with that narrowed gaze. "I hear you married a colored girl."

Miss Corrine groaned softly. "Oh, for God's sake, Jarrod. Nobody says 'colored' anymore."

The muscles in the back of Buck's neck tightened, but he did his best to keep it from showing. He unfolded his napkin in his lap, maintaining an expression that was carefully neutral, carefully pleasant. "My wife is part Haitian, part Sioux Indian, and part Irish," he replied easily. "Myself, I'm mostly Scotch with a little bit of Cherokee thrown in. I hope that's okay with you. If not..." He smiled. "I really don't give a damn."

There was a brief, static silence, then Whitley burst forth with a cackling laugh that echoed around the room. He slapped the table, jostling the silverware and causing the water to slosh in the cut-crystal glasses. "By damn, you're okay, Buck Lawson."

"I'm so terribly glad we got that settled," Corrinne drawled, but the look she gave Jarrod Whitely could have cut glass. "Now, Jarrod, if you would kindly stop acting as though you were raised in your mama's horse barn, perhaps we can get on with a pleasant lunch. Do you like game meat, Buck? The pheasant in porcini wine sauce is locally sourced, and absolutely scrumptious."

"Our chef won six awards last year," Whitley informed him, completely unfazed by Corinne's comment about his manners. "And the pheasant is from our own farms, naturally."

"I thought pheasant was out of season," Buck observed, meeting the other man's gaze.

Whitley returned a smile that left his eyes flinty. "Not on private land, son. Not on private land. You hunt?"

"I do," Buck said.

"You'll have to come out and join one of our hunts this fall. Free membership for all city officials for one year."

"Maybe I will," said Buck. The truth was he didn't care if he never set foot on Hollowgrove Plantation after today, and he didn't know how much longer he could conceal the fact. Then something occurred to him. "Whitley," he said. "As in Whitley Heating and Air? Is that you?"

"No, that'd be my son Zach. He operates out of here, though. You'll probably notice his trucks going out."

"Buck, honey, you're not still having trouble with your air-conditioning, are you?" Miss Corinne said. She turned a meaningful look on Jarrod Whitely. "We can't have that, now can we, Jarrod?"

Marina appeared just then with Buck's iced tea and Miss Corinne's Manhattan, and when she had placed each drink, she stepped back and inquired in a soft voice, "Shall we serve, Mr. Whitley?"

He made a circular motion with his wrist that Buck supposed was meant to be affirmative. When Buck glanced down at the leather portfolio in front of him, he realized it was not a menu in the traditional sense, but a list of what they would be served. The first course was apparently some kind of quail egg on toast, with something involving arugula on the side. He thought longingly of the fried chicken sandwich that was his usual go-to for lunch while he worked at his desk over-hauling the policy manual. He would have given a good deal to be working at his desk at that moment.

He said abruptly, "Miss Corinne, Mr. Whitley. I appreciate the invitation to lunch and it's all very nice, but I'm guessing this is not a social get-together. The truth is I have an active case back in town and I don't have a lot of time. So, if it's all the same to you, could we get to the point?"

Whitley gave a quick decisive nod of his head. "I like a man who keeps on track. So, here's the situation, Buck. Hollowgrove has been a working plantation for almost 200 years. Nine thousand acres in farmland and livestock, a commercial kitchen, packing plant, distribution center, the whole works. Not to mention our hospitality and sporting industries that bring in over two million a year. All this is to say we're a business. A business that runs on a budget and a very tight schedule and we can't afford to be shut down over some crazy-ass pottery shards or bone fragments or what have you. Not for a month, not for a week, not for a day. So, what we need from you is to do whatever it is you have to do with whatever agency you need to do it with and let us get on with the business of making money, which is what *we* do. How does that sound?"

Marina set the quail egg and arugula dishes before them with not so much as a clink of China, and discretely moved away. Buck said, "That depends. What exactly are we talking about here?"

Whitley picked up the tiny fork that had come with the first course and speared the quail egg. Yellow yolk soaked the square of toast and dripped into the arugula. He shoved a bite into his mouth and spoke around it. "We're talking about a mess, is what. We're opening a twenty-five-room lodge *with* a heated pool in less than six months and my contractor says he's uncovered a grave, maybe a whole goddamn cemetery. The Mexicans are too damn superstitious to keep on digging, and my plantation manager tells me we can't get up and running again until the authorities clear the site."

Buck paused in the act of cutting his toast. "You found human remains on your property?"

"Bones," clarified Whitley. "Could be a hundred years old as far as I know, maybe more. Legend is there used to be an Indian burial ground somewhere around here. That's how the place got its name. Hallowed Grove." He stuffed the last of the arugula into his mouth and scraped yolk off the plate. "So, you can see my problem."

Buck put down his fork. "I'm afraid I don't."

"History, son, history!" returned the old man impatiently. "You get the damn university out here with their little paintbrushes and tweezers and we could be shut down for months."

Buck said, "I doubt what you have are ancient artifacts. I don't think human bones can survive intact that long in this climate, but that's for the medical examiner to determine. Your manager is right. You can't continue excavation until law enforcement has been notified and the remains have been removed for examination."

"Well, what the hell do you think you're here for?" demanded Whitley.

Buck kept the irritation out of his voice with an effort. "This isn't my jurisdiction. You need to call the sheriff's office."

Whitley sucked in a breath to reply but Miss Corinne spoke first. "Well, actually, sugar, it *is* your jurisdiction. Hollowgrove contracts with the City of Mercy for police protection, just like so many other of the larger hotels and businesses do."

The businesses she referred to were all within a mile or two of the city limits, and it made sense for them to prefer to work with Mercy. But Hollowgrove was much too far out to expect a timely response from the police department in case of an emergency. As far as Buck knew, they didn't even patrol out here.

"And of course," Miss Corinne went on, taking a final sip of her Manhattan, "we knew you'd want to take care of this personally, seeing as how discretion—and expeditiousness—are of the utmost." She glanced at her empty glass and then looked around the room. "Now, where do you suppose that sweet girl has gotten off to?"

On cue, Marina returned with their main courses, including a fresh drink for Miss Corinne. Buck's fingers itched to check his phone for updates on the case he had left behind, but at least he knew what he was doing here now. Money. Whatever Hollowgrove was paying the City of Mercy for police protection—and from the looks of the place, they could afford to pay plenty—Miss Corinne did not want to lose them as a client, so to speak. And from Buck, she expected nothing less than concierge service.

He gritted his teeth and picked his battles.

"I'll have a look at the site," he said, "and try to

get somebody from the M.E.'s office out here today. Beyond that, I can't make any promises."

Miss Corinne reached across the table and patted his hand, smiling benignly. "All we can ask for, sugar." And to Whitley, she said, "What did I tell you? He's just a sweetheart. Now, look at this lovely pheasant. Jarrod, you must tell Buck about the hunt dinners you host here during the season."

CHAPTER THIRTEEN

Marianne was two hours into her trip when the state patrol car pulled out behind her. She felt her heart thud against her ribcage and her bowels go weak. She checked her speed. 40 mph. She had no idea what the speed limit was. She was on a two-lane highway in the middle of nowhere. The last signs of civilization had been half an hour back. She was the only car in the west-bound lane and the trooper paced her. He was running her tag, of course he was. Any minute now the lights would start to flash, the sirens would wail.

In the backseat, the baby started to fuss.

It had been a slow and painful trip. Keeping with her resolve to avoid the expressway and major highways, Marianne had crept along the back roads, never going more than five miles an hour under the speed limit. She had gotten lost twice, and, without her phone, had to rely on blind luck to get back on track. She'd ended up going miles out of her way and using up more gas than she could afford. Finally, she had no choice but to stop and put five dollars' worth of gas in the tank. Another gallon and a half, but it just might be enough to get her home. Had someone spotted her at the gas station? Had they called in her description, and alerted the police?

The tiny, irritable mewling sounds from the baby grew more insistent. Marianne's throat was so dry she could barely whisper, "Shh, sweetheart, it's okay, it's okay..."

And then, suddenly, it was.

The patrol car abruptly sped up and passed her. No lights, no sirens. Before Marianne could release her tightly held breath, he was a quarter of a mile down the road, off on more important business than tailing her.

The baby was still whimpering when she pulled into the parking lot of a fast-food restaurant. She backed into a space beneath the speckled shade of a crepe myrtle and sat there for a moment, shaking, trying to calm herself with deep breaths. It was over. He hadn't pursued her. She was safe.

Marianne left the air conditioning running and fished a diaper and the sterile bottle of sugar water out of her purse. She got into the back seat and carefully lifted the delicate bundle of humanity out of its carrier. She couldn't help smiling at the screwed-up little face, the bleating cries.

"I know, baby, I know," she whispered. "You miss your mommy. I miss her too. This is not what you expected. Me either. She would have loved you if she could. But she was broken." Here Marianne's own voice broke, and she felt hot tears blur her vision. She blinked them away and concentrated on changing the tiny diaper, fastening the tabs, and re-wrapping the blanket. "That's not going to happen to you," she said, her voice firming. "I'm not going to let them break you."

Even as she said it, she thought about her father, who had taught her to fear God and everything else in life, and her mother, who was just afraid. How could she tell them what she'd done? How could she turn this tiny, innocent life over to their care?

And then it struck her: maybe she didn't have to.

She was so tired, she was so scared, she was so shocked at what had happened this morning, that her brain was working at bare minimum capacity. Even now, as she fumbled to remove the cap from the nursery bottle, as she brushed the nipple against Daisy's lips, urging her to take it, she could barely process her thoughts.

The state trooper hadn't stopped her. He had been behind her long enough to run her plates, and he had found nothing. The police weren't looking for her. And why should they be? No one had reported her.

Baby Daisy screwed up her face and let out a fresh cry, turning away from the bottle. Marianne bounced her gently in her arms, cooing nonsense words. She shook out a few drops of liquid from the bottle onto her finger and pressed it against the baby's lips. After a moment, Daisy began to suck her finger. Marianne smiled and substituted the bottle. Daisy sucked on it, her eyes closing in contentment. Marianne let that same contentment seep through her as she sank back against the seat, feeling her muscles unwind for the first time in days.

No one was looking for her. The people at that place couldn't afford to call the police. They couldn't allow anyone to look into their business, to ask questions, to uncover secrets. As for Giselle...she had made her choice, and Marianne had always known that the chances of her making the right one were not good.

"We're on our own," she whispered to Daisy, and the words sounded like the beginning of a whole new life. She couldn't help smiling with the power of them.

The baby had fallen asleep, pale blue lids fluttering, tiny nostrils flaring in and out with each breath. The nipple slipped from her mouth and Marianne took the bottle away. She carefully tucked Daisy back into her carrier and secured her safely, kissing her lightly on the forehead. "We're going to be okay," she whispered.

And this time she meant it.

CHAPTER FOURTEEN

L eon Baker had just about decided he was not cut out to be a training officer. The Mercy Police Department was structured so that, in order to qualify for promotion, an officer had to be on the force for three years, have a certain number of continuing education credits, and pass the Field Training Officer's exam. The exam was no problem, and since—up until recently—there hadn't been a lot of turnover in the department, Baker had never been called upon to put his skills to work. He was starting to wonder if Buck's decision to assign the rookie to him was designed to test more than his skills. His patience, for example.

It wasn't that there was anything wrong with the new girl. She did what she was told, and she did it courteously and professionally. She didn't engage in meaningless chatter or pester him with questions. She didn't play on her phone or try to tell him all about her personal life. She just sat there, looking tense and eager and excited, and it made him nervous as hell.

Baker liked riding alone. He didn't like trying to make conversation or worrying if he was being too gruff or too angry, or if he was showing enough consideration for his partner or pretending to be interested enough in her personal life. Most of all, he didn't like being responsible for somebody else. He just wanted to do his job, check out at end of shift, and go home to hang out with people he really liked being around. It didn't seem too much to ask.

They finished the search of their assigned territory around 1:30, and Baker pulled the patrol car into a strip mall with a sandwich shop, a beauty salon, a Laundromat, and an ice cream parlor. The sandwich shop at one end and the ice cream shop at the other each had a few tables and chairs set up out front. Baker said, "We get an hour dinner break. I usually spend it studying for the detective exam while I eat. After that, I need to get back to the office and work on the report about the incident this morning. I figure you could take the rest of the day off like the Chief said. Sub sandwich okay with you?"

"Oh," she said, sounding a little distracted. "Yes, fine. I was just hoping... sir, do you think it would be all right if I finished out my shift?"

Baker frowned. "How come? You got the day off

with pay, and you already worked half of it."

"It's just..." She chewed her lower lip. "My dad gets home at 4:00 and I don't know how to explain to him about the car, and all."

He stared at her. "How old are you again?"

Her cheeks flamed. "It's just that my folks never wanted me to be a police officer, and now I screwed up on my first day and I'm only living with them until I find a place of my own but still..." She drew an abrupt breath and stopped. "You're right." She darted him a quick glance, then stared straight ahead. "Not your problem. Sorry."

He looked at her for another moment, scowling, then put his hand on the door handle. "I'll get the sandwiches. You start showing Jane Doe's picture to these other shop owners here. We'll meet at the tables outside. What do you want?"

She looked confused. "What?"

"To eat," he replied impatiently, getting out. "What do you want to eat?"

"Oh." She fumbled to get money out of her back pocket as she got out of the car. With the heavy utility belt around her waist, it was no easy task. "Um, turkey sub is good." She finally managed to pull out a twenty and offered it to him. "And a water."

He waved the money away, figuring that would be his good deed for the day. "On me," he said, "this being your first day and all. And Miller."

He gave her a steady look that some might have interpreted as a glare and tapped his chest. "Body camera on whenever you get out of the car. Chief's rules."

"Oh." Her cheeks went red again as she quickly turned on her camera and stuffed the money back into her pocket. "Yes, sir. Thank you, sir."

Baker watched her move off toward the salon and then turned to go into the sandwich shop, shaking his head a little and wondering how he was going to get through the next six weeks.

Trish was wondering, as she pushed open the door of the salon, whether anyone in the history of the Mercy Police Department had ever made such a bad first impression, and whether there was any coming back from that. *I am strong, I am competent, I am fully equipped...* The mantra, however true it might be, did not sound nearly as convincing as it had before she had run a woman over with her car. Or almost ran her over, as Chief Lawson insisted. How *did* you come back from that?

The smell of bleach and perfumed hairspray hit her as Trish stepped inside the salon. A plump woman in a pink apron decorated with pictures of shears was cutting an older woman's wet hair at the station nearest the door, and she looked up when Trish came in. Another woman was under the dryer, reading a magazine, and a skinny young man with curly dark hair was sweeping the floor nearby.

The woman in the pink apron said, "Can I help you?"

Trish replied. "Are you the owner?"

"I am. What can I do for you, honey?"

Trish would have bet anything she owned that the lady would not have called Officer Baker "honey," and that didn't do anything for her self-esteem at the moment. She took out her phone and brought up the picture of Jane Doe. "We're trying to find out the identity of this woman," she said. "We're hoping you can help us."

The hairdresser paused in her clipping and winced as she looked at the picture on the phone. "My goodness, she doesn't look well, does she?"

"She was in an accident," Trish explained. "She hasn't been able to tell us her name and her baby is missing."

The hairdresser gasped. "Oh, my, that's terrible! But I'm afraid I can't help you. I'm sure I've never done her hair."

The woman in the chair craned to see the picture, and when Trish showed it to her, she shook her head sadly, making sympathetic noises. Trish was aware that the young man had stopped sweeping and was staring at her, but when she turned to look at him, he quickly went back to work. Trish thanked the two women and started to cross the room toward the woman under the dryer. On impulse, she turned back to show the picture to the young man, but when she held up the phone to him a look of sudden panic crossed his face. He threw the broom at her, striking her in the chest, but Trish batted it away as he bolted toward the back of the salon.

"Hey!" Trish cried. "Stop!" She put the phone away and raced after him, shouting, "Police! Stop!"

She ran after him into a small room filled with shelves and bottles, and at the rear of it, an open door. "I just want to talk to you!" she shouted.

She burst into an alleyway with a loading dock at one end and a cluster of dumpsters at the other. The boy was running toward the dumpsters. She ran after him, pressing the button on her collar radio at the same time. "Officer Baker," she gasped. "I've got a suspect fleeing east on foot in the alley behind the shops. Hispanic male, dark hair, red shirt, blue jeans. In pursuit."

He was only ten or fifteen feet ahead of her and she was fast, but he had a longer stride and was gaining ground quickly. It looked as though he planned to climb the fence that surrounded the dumpsters and use them to swing himself over the fence on the other side, landing in the parking lot. Trish did not want to climb the fence. She ran harder.

The back door to one of the shops burst open just as the kid came abreast of it. It struck him hard in the chest and he staggered back, almost falling, but regained his balance just as Baker lunged from behind the door and made a grab for him. All Baker caught was the fleeing man's shirt, but it was enough to send both of them to the ground, Baker landing hard on one knee as the kid pushed himself up with his hands and wriggled out of Baker's grasp. It was just the delay Trish needed. She launched herself at the suspect, slamming him back to the ground with her weight. She sat astride his skinny waist to keep him down and grabbed a handful of his hair. "What is your problem?" she shouted at him, adrenaline still pumping. "Are you crazy? I just wanted to talk to you!"

Baker appeared, limping a little, and snapped the cuffs on him. Trish rolled away and Baker hauled the boy to his feet. "What the hell?" he demanded.

"I don't know, sir," Trish replied, breathing hard. "He was sweeping the beauty salon when I went in to show Jane Doe's picture. When I started to come over to him, he threw the broom at me and ran."

Baker turned his glare on the boy, who looked sweaty and scared. "What did you run for?" he demanded. "You hiding something from the law?"

The boy shook his head, eyes growing bigger.

"He's hiding something," Baker grumbled. He turned back to the boy. "What's your name?"

The women from the beauty salon and a few other shops came cautiously into the alley, huddling near their doors. The boy's gaze traveled to them and then back to Baker. "Paulo," he answered, swallowing hard.

"Paulo what?"

"Paulo Ramirez."

Baker said, "You got anything in your pockets that's going to poke me or stab me when I search you?"

The boy shook his head.

"How old are you, Paulo?" Trish asked while Baker patted him down.

"Twenty-five," he answered.

"Sixteen," speculated Baker. He searched the kid's pockets and came up with a small bag of marijuana. He held it up for Trish to see. "Told you he was hiding something."

"Seriously, Paulo?" Trish gave the boy an admonishing look. "All I wanted you to do was look at a picture. Now you're going to jail."

"He's probably undocumented, too," observed Baker. He grabbed the suspect's arm and added, "You get the salon owner's statement while I secure the prisoner in the unit. Damn," he added, almost to himself, "there goes lunch."

Trish cleared her throat. "Um, sir?"

He glanced at her.

She plunged ahead. "According to Section Three, Paragraph 41-A of the Policy Manual, proper procedure is to call for another unit to take charge of the prisoner and complete the investigation while the arresting officer seeks medical treatment."

He scowled at her. "What are you talking

about? What medical treatment?"

Trish glanced at his leg. The pants were torn at the knee and stained with blood. "Yours, sir. You're bleeding."

He glanced down, noticing for the first time. "Son of a bitch tore my pants," he said, the scowl darkening. He pushed the suspect forward. "Now it's personal, punk. Let's go."

Trish, emboldened by the takedown and still flush with adrenaline, said, "Sir, excuse me, but section 18, paragraph 62 of the policy and procedure manual clearly states that all on-the-job injuries must be immediately reported on form 1128-dash-3, accompanied by a medical statement from the officer's personal physician or an emergency department attending physician as defined by county code 1432, section 8."

Baker stared at her. "What did you do, memorize the whole damn manual?"

"Yes, sir," she assured him earnestly. Then she flushed crimson. "Of course, you're the superior officer. If your judgment is to override procedure, that's your prerogative."

His jaw hardened. Trish could practically see him counting to ten. "My judgment," he said at last, tightly, "is to take this punk to jail and then to take you home. You've had enough training for one day. And just so you know," he added darkly, "the joke is on you. The boss is rewriting the whole damn book."

CHAPTER FIFTEEN

J arrod Whitley declined to accompany Buck to the excavation site after lunch but sent for his manager to bring the truck around. The pretty Marina wished them a good day at the door and Buck and Miss Corinne went down the steps together. The heat hit them like a steam bath, and Miss Corinne slipped on a pair of stylish white sunglasses, looking around for Roland.

"I do declare, that boy would just as soon see me have a heat stroke right here on the steps than be on time," she complained, fanning herself with her hand.

She spotted Roland, sipping from a soft drink can and scrolling through his phone in the shade of the car shed, and lifted her arm imperiously, as though hailing a cab. Roland didn't notice. Corinne scowled furiously, but it was pointless.

Had he not been her son, he wouldn't have lasted in that job half a day.

Buck took out his phone and texted Roland: *Heads up.* Roland glanced in their direction, took another drink from the can, and put away his phone. He ambled over to the mayor's car, clearly in no hurry.

In a moment, Corinne turned her attention away from her incalcitrant driver and smoothed out her features, turning back to Buck. "I'm real proud of you, sugar," she said, slipping her arm through Buck's. "Jarrod is an ornery old fart but more bluster than bite, you know. Smart as a whip, though. There's not a thing that goes on in his business he doesn't have his hand in. The trouble is, he's from a completely different time. You just have to be patient with him."

Buck squinted in the sun. "Why do I get the feeling he's a pretty big backer of your political career?"

She chuckled. "Did you notice all those photos on the wall outside the dining room? Jarrod has instructed his girls to make sure everyone who comes to Hollowgrove sees them. Do you know why?"

"Because he's a self-obsessed bastard who likes having his picture taken with celebrities?"

"Because every one of those men owes him a favor," she corrected. "It would be safe to say Jarrod Whitley is one of the most powerful men in the South. So, yes, we try to accommodate him when we can."

Buck said, "It's crazy for Mercy to be providing police protection way out here. You know that. He'd be a lot better off with the sheriff's office."

Miss Corinne said, "Jarrod lost his oldest son, Trey, about thirty years ago." She spoke matter-of-factly. "He was shot in the back of the head with his own hunting rifle one Thanksgiving. They found his body in the river but never did find out who did it. Eventually Sheriff Barker—that's who was in charge back then—called it a hunting accident and closed the case. Jarrod never forgave him for that and refused to trust anybody from the sheriff's office again. He hired his own private security force for insurance reasons—you know, with high-profile guests and all—and turned the rest over to the Mercy Police Department. For a hefty fee, I might add. So, you can see why it's very important to provide him with the stellar police service for which he's contracted. And you, my darling..." She squeezed his arm. "Are stellar."

Buck murmured dryly, "Right."

"I hear you're rewriting the policies and procedures manual," she remarked, watching as Roland brought her car around.

"In my spare time."

"Which I'm surprised you have any at all of, honey, given that your police force is down thirty percent and so, may I add..." She tilted her glasses down to the bridge of her nose at peered at him over the rims. "... are your revenues."

"Our job is to protect and serve," Buck replied, "not to balance the city's budget."

"Actually," she informed him sweetly, "your job is to find a way to do both. Ten seatbelt violations, twelve distracted driving violations, eight speeding citations, and three D.U.I.s per shift are the very minimum you need to survive. I do hope you put that in your policy manual because some of your people seem to have forgotten."

Buck said stiffly, "We don't have quotas."

She patted his arm affectionately. "Of course, we do, sweetheart. *Your* quota is exactly what it takes to keep the police department running throughout the fiscal year, not even including those expensive body cameras you bought. And if you had any idea how hard I worked to get the highway department to run both 215 and 127 through town so that you could meet that quota you'd be a lot less cavalier about it."

The mayor liked to play these little power games now and again, for no apparent reason other than that she could. The problem was that she did it so randomly that Buck had a hard time telling when she was serious.

"I thought we had an agreement." Buck kept his tone pleasant with an effort. "I don't tell you how to run the city, and you don't tell me how to run the police department."

Her smile was both condescending and genuinely amused. "No, sugar. What we agreed on is that you serve at the pleasure of the mayor of Mercy. Please try not to forget that."

They both turned to follow the sound of tires crunching on marble chips as Roland pulled the mayor's car around the circular drive and came to a stop behind the police chief's car. Corinne made no move toward the car, but neither did she look at Buck. "Buck," she said, facing straight ahead, "I'm going to tell you something. But if you repeat it, I will swear before God and all the saints that you're nothing but a bold-faced lying son of a bitch. Understand?"

Buck's attention was pricked, mostly because she so rarely used his name without following it with one of her trademark endearments. He said cautiously, "Okay."

"I'm starting to understand why Billy picked you for this job," she went on, "and, believe it or not, I think he made the right decision. You're just like him. I always did say Billy could charm the stripes off a pole cat, and Lord help us if you can't do the exact same thing. Folks like you. Hell, *I* like you, and not just because you're cute as the dickens and fun to look at." A dimple appeared briefly at the side of her mouth, then faded.

She tilted her sunglasses down and looked at him over the rims. Her eyes were as hard as fine diamonds, and as blue as cracked ice. "But here's what *you* need to understand," she said. "Billy stayed in office for thirty-five years because he knew how to work with the people in charge to achieve a common goal. That common goal was the good of the town he loved as much as I do. So, I need you to bring your police force up to full complement, and I need you to bring in the revenue that pays their salaries. Also..." She returned her sunglasses to their original position and went on mildly, "I need the draft of the new policy manual on my desk by the end of the day."

Buck took a moment to reply. Roland waited patiently in the air-conditioned car while the two of them stood broiling in the sun. Buck said carefully, "Let me be clear. I don't love this town. I barely even know it. But it pays my salary, and as long as it does, I'm going to do right by it, and by the people who live here."

She turned her gaze on him, impossible to read behind the sunglasses. "You know," she remarked casually, "you still have a couple of months to go on your probationary period. Up until then, I can fire you for looking at me crooked."

"Or," he pointed out, "I can quit because I don't like wearing a tie to lunch, at which point I would no longer feel obligated to keep any of Mercy's secrets." She looked at him sharply, and he went on, "But I don't see how that would do either one of us any good, do you?"

She did not reply.

"Now," he added, "I don't want you to worry your pretty little head about staffing the police force or meeting budgets. That's what you've got me for. As for the policy manual, you'll see it at the same time the rest of the council does, when I'm finished with it. Meantime, I don't see any reason we can't continue to work together just as well as we've been doing. For the good of the town, of course."

She continued to look at him, expressionless, for another long moment. Then she drawled, "I ought to smack you. 'Pretty little head,' my ass." A corner of her lips dimpled abruptly, and she leaned in to kiss his cheek. "Lucky for you, I *do* like you, you scoundrel."

She stood back down and demanded, "Now what in the *hell* is this I hear about one of your officers running down a pedestrian? For God's sake, Buck, that's the last thing we need. Fix it, will you?"

Buck smiled and opened the car door for her. "Fixing it," he assured her. "You have a good day, now, Mayor."

She paused before getting in and glanced up at him. "By the way, I hear Junior Aikens is in town. We're all going to have to get together for a drink before he leaves."

Buck said, "Is there anything that goes on around here you don't know about, Miss Corinne?"

She laughed lightly. "Don't be silly, sugar, of course not." She patted his arm. "Now, you do what you can for Jarrod, honey. And keep me up to date, will you?"

"I don't think that will be a problem, Miss Corinne."

Buck wiped the lipstick off his cheek as he watched her drive away, then checked his messages. Nothing from Frankie, which meant there was no break in the case, and no search warrant from Judge Warren. If the newborn had in fact been abandoned, its chances of survival were lessening by the minute. And there was absolutely nothing he could do about it.

Buck tossed his jacket and tie in the back of the cruiser and was rolling up his shirtsleeves when a black F-150 with "Hollowgrove Plantation" stenciled in gold on the panels pulled up behind him. A tall, cadaverously skinny man in a checked shirt, dusty jeans, and a Stetson got out. He strode forward and extended his hand to Buck in a firm, borderline-aggressive, handshake.

"Don Estes," he said, "plantation manager. The boss wanted me to take you out to the site."

The man smelled like cigarette smoke, diesel fuel, and sweat, not an altogether inappropriate thing for a fellow who worked on a farm. Buck said, "Buck Lawson, chief of police."

Estes replied gruffly, "I know who you are." He gestured to the truck. "Get in."

Buck murmured, "Okay, then." And climbed in the passenger side of the truck.

Estes lit a cigarette as soon as they were underway. He cracked the window on his side, but it let in more humid air than it let out smoke. He turned out of the drive onto a brief stretch of asphalt road marked by a sign that read "Exit to

Highway" then he took an abrupt left onto a dirt road. Fields of corn spread out on one side of the road, peanuts on the other. After they'd bounced along for a few acres, Estes said, "Road to the lodge is being paved. Gotta take the back way. We'll come out onto gravel up here a piece."

"Big place," remarked Buck. He held onto the overhead grab bar as they made another sharp turn beside a sign that read, "Equipment shed."

"One of the biggest working farms in the state." They passed through a long deep field of tall fescue, and Estes tapped cigarette ash out the window. "Quail and dove," he said, "deer and boar back in the woods."

They left the fields behind after a few miles and Buck turned his head to look at a long low concrete building set back from the road. "What's that?"

"Dormitories to the left, dog kennels to the right."

"Dormitories?"

"For the household staff."

"They live on-site?"

"Yep." He lifted his small finger to indicate another paved road branching off to the right. There was a gate and a sign that read "Private." "Family residences," he said. "Managing staff, security, they all have places further on."

"Including you?"

"Yep. Part of the benefits package."

Buck gave a small grunt of appreciation. "Not

bad. You work here long?"

"Thirty-eight years."

They rounded a corner and a gravel parking lot spread out to the left, surrounding a long metal warehouse building. There was an eighteen-wheeler pulled up beside it, along with several white box vans marked "Whitley Heating and Air." Buck thought in annoyance that it was no wonder it was taking so long to get his air conditioning repaired if the only service provider in the county was headquartered way out here. And then something occurred to him.

He glanced at Estes. "So how come Whitley is the only HVAC company in the area? Looks like there'd be plenty of room for more than one air-conditioning repairman in a climate like this."

Estes replied, "Whitleys don't like competition."

"Well, if they don't get somebody out to fix my unit pretty soon, they're going to have some," Buck remarked, "if I have to call somebody from the next county."

"Won't do you no good," said Estes. "They won't come over here."

Buck grunted thoughtfully. "So, the Whitleys have got the market locked down, huh? Just the air conditioning business, or everything else too?"

Estes smoked in silence, and for a moment Buck thought he wouldn't reply. Then he tossed his cigarette stub out the window and said, "I don't concern myself with the business part."

They came to a length of construction fencing, behind which were parked a couple of Bobcats and a flatbed truck filled with steel pipe and board siding. The gate was open and as Estes drove through Buck saw the construction site in the distance: a long two-story structure clothed in silver house wrap and scaffolding in the background, and in the foreground a shallow dusty pit around which several vehicles and four people stood. Two of the people, a man and a woman, appeared to be engaged in a heated conversation as Estes pulled up.

"I called security to stand guard," Estes said. "Gave everybody else the day off. Didn't want to take no chances of you all coming back and saying we disturbed anything." He jerked his head toward a man in a wide-brimmed straw hat and sweat-stained work shirt who was leaning against a pickup truck, watching them drive up. "That's Ed Quigley, the contractor. Thought you'd want him to stick around in case you had questions."

"Good thinking," agreed Buck, and opened the door.

The woman swung a hard glare on him as Buck got out of the truck, then turned back to the uniformed man to whom she had been speaking. "Just do what I told you and take care of it," she snapped. "You're supposed to be in charge of security, aren't you? And take that worthless brother of yours with you. It's about time he earned his way around here." Without waiting for a reply, she spun around and strode toward Buck, her expression fierce.

She was an athletic-looking woman in her mid-fifties with short, spikey black hair and a square face, strong hips, long stride. She wore tight jeans and a white tank top beneath an open denim shirt, and her face and throat gleamed with sweat. She thrust out her hand to Buck and said briefly, "Geraldine Whitley, Jarrod's daughter." She jerked a thumb over her shoulder to the bearded man in green uniform pants and a white polo shirt to whom she had been talking. "Over there, my brother Carter."

The man she indicated wore a Glock in a holster around his waist and didn't look up from his phone conversation. The word "security" was embroidered on his shirt pocket.

Buck shook her hand, but before he could speak, she went on, "You're the new police chief. Daddy said you're going to get this mess straightened out so we can get back to work."

He replied, "I'll do my best. The name's Buck Lawson, by the way."

She did not appear in the least interested. She gestured impatiently to the empty pit and said, "Just get this cleared up. I've got to get back." She turned away and barked, "Carter! Get this man whatever he needs and then get to work. You've already wasted half the day." To Buck, she said briefly, "Excuse me."

She strode over to an ATV and climbed aboard,

bringing it to life with a roar and spewing up dust as she chugged past them back down the road. Buck could not help noticing the hard, furious stare Geraldine Whitley gave Estes as she passed. Estes was leaning against the side of the truck, lighting another cigarette, and watched her go without a flicker of expression.

Buck walked over to the pit.

It was about thirty feet long and fifteen feet wide, deeper at the far end than the side on which Buck stood. The two security guards, one on each side of the pit, wore green short-sleeved uniforms, gun belts, and wide-brimmed hats. Each carried long rifles, which Buck thought was a bit of overkill on a private estate, but he knew these security types—the bigger the gun, the more important they felt. They had hard faces and narrow eyes, which made Buck think professional mercenaries. Most people would've been satisfied with retired police to fill a security team in a place like this.

Buck caught the eye of the man Estes had pointed out as the contractor and gestured him over. Buck introduced himself, and said, "You're Quigley, right? The contactor?"

"Yes, sir," the other man agreed. "I've done all the work on the lodge."

"What are we looking at?"

Quigley pushed back his hat, wiped his gleaming forehead with his sleeve, and gestured toward the excavation site. "Thirty-by-fifteen-foot lagoon-style pool, nine feet on the deep side, graduating to three on the shallow. Two waterfalls, a teak walkway from the lodge to the pool, a twenty-foot stone surround. Lots of landscaping in between. The pool contractors will be out next week to pour the concrete and set the stone, but Mr. Whitley likes to have all the scutwork done in-house. That'd be your heavy equipment operators, landscapers, like that. He keeps them on payroll. Still, I manage them like they were my crew. Something goes wrong, I take the hit."

Buck nodded, encouraging him to go on.

"We got the deep end dug last week," Quigley continued, "but had to stop on account of the rain. We got to the second pass on this end when the boys saw something in the ground. Thought it might be an irrigation pipe or something and called me over." His mouth formed a tight line as he directed his gaze toward the newly excavated ground. "I got down there with a shovel and moved some of the dirt. That's what I found."

Buck knelt beside the shallow end of the pit, his bad leg protesting. About three feet below, on a slight incline and dusted with red Georgia clay, was the dome of a small skull. Below that, fully uncovered, was a short bone, discolored with age but completely recognizable as a fibula. A few feet away was another small skull, and, protruding from the earth near it, another partial bone. Buck swore softly.

He heard Carter, the security guard, end his telephone call and sensed him come to stand beside him. Without looking up, Buck said, "You got a tape measure?"

The contractor turned to get one from his truck, but Carter, who apparently liked to be in charge, barked, "Estes! Tape measure!"

Buck took out his phone, snapping several photographs of the remains. When Estes returned with the tape measure, Buck lowered it into the pit next to the fibula, set the measurement, and snapped the picture. He took several other measurements and documented them. He stood, trying not to wince at the pain that shot through his leg, and dusted off his clothes.

"These are the bones of children," Buck said. "Two of them, at least."

"That's what I thought too," replied Quigley. "Probably some kind of old cemetery."

Buck asked, "What do you do with the fill dirt?"

Quigley gestured toward a dump truck that was parked a couple of hundred feet away. Already it was mostly filled with red Georgia clay. "We'll use it to build up the walking paths around the lodge."

"Don't do that just yet," Buck advised. "Did you notice anything else while you were digging?"

Quigley shrugged. "The usual. Old beer and soda cans, pieces of old fertilizer sacks and burlap." He thought about it for a moment. "Some rotten pieces of cloth, a baseball hat, and part of a tennis shoe. A Timex watch that was rusted through. You know, the things people lose or forget working outside."

Carter said impatiently, "I don't know what the fuss is about over a bunch of old Indian bones. Can't you just certify them or whatever it is you're here for, and let us get on with it?"

Buck glanced at him. "You law enforcement?" he asked bluntly.

The other man smiled thinly. "UGA business school."

"Guess they don't teach much about forensic science in business school," observed Buck. "In the first place, Indians didn't bury their dead three feet deep. Most times they didn't bury them at all. They especially didn't bury them with beer cans and Timex watches. And bones of any kind wouldn't still be intact after 200 years. Maybe in the desert, but not here."

The other man, instead of being embarrassed, stared him down.

Buck looked around. "What used to be here, before you started building?"

It was Don Estes who answered. "The ground lays fallow every other year. In between, since the eighties, it's seeded for dove. Before that, cotton."

Spoken like a man who knew his business. Buck gave him an appreciative nod and returned his tape measure.

Buck called the medical examiner's office, explained the situation, and asked them to send a team out. The assistant on the other end replied they could probably have somebody out in the morning. Buck told him that Mayor Corinne Watts considered this a priority. He was put on hold and thirty seconds later the assistant reported that a recovery team would be there within the hour. Buck smiled as he put away his phone. It worked every time.

"Y'all should be good to go by the end of the day," he told Carter. "The recovery team will have to finish the excavation, make sure they get all the bones, and take pictures. Keep your men in place until the team from the M.E.'s office gets here, just to make sure no one disturbs the remains. As soon as they finish, unless they notify me otherwise, you're clear to resume construction."

Carter nodded, his mouth tight. "Seems like a helluva lot of trouble over old bones."

Buck chose not to argue the point. "Your sister didn't seem that pleased to have the police involved."

Carter replied flatly, "We're used to taking care of things ourselves on Hollowgrove."

"Yeah, I figured," Buck replied amiably. "You guys are practically self-sustaining out here. Your own little city." He glanced over at the two men guarding the site. "How many on your security team?"

"Eight," replied Carter, "split between two shifts."

"They look like they've got military training."

"They get the job done."

Buck was more pointed. "What's the job?"

"Patrol the premises for trespassers," replied Carter as though by rote, "protect the women. Keep the farm workers under control and the knife fights to a minimum."

Buck wasn't sure whether he was joking. "Knife fights?"

"They're mostly Mexican and Central American," Carter explained. "Hot-blooded, you know. Cutting each other is as natural to them as breathing."

Buck said, "The farm hands live on site?"

He nodded briefly. "The old man decided it was more efficient that way. Now, if there's nothing else, I've got someplace to be."

"I was just wondering," Buck said easily, making no move to go, "being as how you all are used to taking care of things yourselves, and how this mess has already cost you a day's work, why you decided to call in outside help."

Instead of replying, Carter just jerked his head toward Don Estes. "*We* didn't," he replied pointedly.

Buck looked him over for a minute, thinking about this. "Well, it's a good thing your manager knows the law," he said.

Once again, Carter didn't even blink when Buck held his gaze.

Buck took out a card and handed it to him. "In case you have any questions," he said. "Do you have a card? I'll probably need to check in with you to file my report."

After what seemed like a long moment, Carter took out his wallet, found a card, and handed it to Buck. *Carter Whitley, Security Manager, Hollowgrove Plantation.*

"Mr. Whitley," Buck said politely, tucking the card into his pocket. "I'll be in touch."

As he was walking back to the truck where Estes was waiting for him, something occurred to Buck. He dialed Judge Warren's office and asked the clerk to get a message to Her Honor regarding the search warrant they had requested for Hope House. The message was simply, "Mayor Watts has requested this be a priority."

Ten minutes later, as they were bouncing down the dirt road toward the construction gate, he got a text from Frankie: *Warrant in hand. On our way. Thnx.*

Buck smiled and put his phone away. It worked every time.

CHAPTER SIXTEEN

When Marianne first moved to Mercy, she had told her parents she was joining a traveling nurses' team and wouldn't have a permanent address for a while. They didn't question, nor did they seem very interested. They had their church, their jobs, their community service, and—if one was being honest—their sanctimony to occupy them. She called them every other Sunday to report things were fine, and that seemed to satisfy them.

Marianne wasn't entirely sure why she'd lied. When she'd first gotten the report from the private detective she wasn't sure it was valid, of course. Then she wasn't sure her plan would work. Then she'd sworn secrecy to Giselle. But whatever the reason, it turned out the lie had worked in her favor. No one was looking for her. No one was worried about her. She had time to make a new plan.

She thought she'd head toward Savannah. She'd always loved the romance of the place and thought it would be fun to live there. Savannah had several big hospitals and she'd have no trouble getting a job. Some of them probably even had daycare, and if not, she could find an in-home caregiver for Daisy. Things might be tight financially for a while, but she would manage. Savannah was the kind of city that was big enough to get lost in, but small enough to feel like home. She thought she'd like it there.

Now that she was no longer worried about the police, Marianne took the time to stop for gas and used her credit card to fill the tank. She made a quick stop at a roadside Dollar Store for diapers, formula, and sterile water, keeping the tightly swaddled baby close to her chest the entire time. She ordered fast food from a drive-through and felt her head clear and her resolve strengthen with every bite. Savannah. It was a good plan.

She arrived at her apartment a little before noon. Most people were working that time of day, so there was no one around to notice as she carried the baby, still sleeping in her carrier, inside. Once there, she breathed a huge sigh of relief and let the tension slowly drain from her back and shoulders. With all the blinds still closed, the place was dark and cool, and the baby, who had started to fuss again, fell back asleep as soon as she was changed. Marianne would have liked to catch an hour or two of sleep herself, but she didn't dare. Just because no one had reported her to the police didn't mean no one was looking for her. She couldn't afford to stay here.

It didn't take long to pack up her apartment. The place had come furnished, so all she needed to take were her clothes, toiletries, and personal electronics. It all fit into two suitcases, which she stored in the cargo space of her vehicle along with the folding crib. She made up several bottles of formula and packed them in a cooler because she didn't know how long they would have to stay in a motel before she could find a place with a kitchen. She took time to shower and change and to make sure baby Daisy was clean and dry before shouldering the diaper bag and picking up the baby carrier once again.

She paused before opening the door, sweeping her gaze around the impersonal little apartment one last time. She had thought about this day so often. It was supposed to be the first day of the rest of their lives—hers and Giselle's and Daisy's. Instead, it was the beginning of Marianne's new life as a single mother.

That was okay. It wasn't what she'd planned, but it was good. Better, even.

Marianne took the sleeping Daisy back out into the humid air, refastened her safely in the car seat, and hurried to start the engine, turning the air conditioning on high. She glanced at the sleeping infant in the rear-view mirror before putting the car in gear. She smiled, just as though the baby could see her. "Okay, sweetie," she said, "here we go. Off on our big adventure."

Whatever doubts she might once have harbored were gone. Yes, she was nervous, even a little scared. She knew nothing about this would be easy. But she also knew, with every fiber of her being, that this was the right thing to do.

She pulled out of the parking lot for the last time and did not look back. She didn't see the black pick-up truck that had been parked a few spaces down pull out behind her. And she didn't realize the truck was following her until it was too late.

CHAPTER SEVENTEEN

As they drove back to his car, Buck asked Estes about the farm workers Carter had mentioned. "He said they live on site?" He made it into a question.

Estes was puffing on another cigarette. "We used to truck 'em in every day but that never worked out. We can afford to feed and house twice as many for what it was costing us in lost time and labor."

"Where do they live? In dormitories like the household staff?"

"Nah. They've got a trailer camp at the south end of the property, their own cook house, latrines, everything."

"Can we drive by the camp on our way out?"

"No time," replied Estes briefly, tossing his cigarette out of the window. "Boss said you had to be back in town by 3:00."

Buck just nodded and let it go. Instead, he said, "Seems like you lost a few points on the popularity scale for calling me out here."

The other man replied, "Didn't have a choice. If I hadn't reported it, Quigley would have."

Buck said, "I got the feeling, from the way Mr. Whitley was talking, that it's not that unusual to find artifacts like this on the property."

Estes gave a snort of laughter. "Artifacts. That's a good word for it."

Buck said plainly, "Do you have any idea how two kids might have come to be buried out there in the field? And spare me the Indian theory."

Estes drummed his fingers on the wheel. Buck was ready to repeat the question when Estes said, "Back in the day, farm workers used to bring their families with them. The women and kids would pick cotton, dig potatoes, whatever. They all lived in the camp, or in the slave cabins next to it. You gotta remember, this place was a lot more isolated back then, help was harder to get in an emergency. So, if a person got sick or snakebit or whatever, and he didn't pull through, they'd bury him here, usually in the old slave graveyard, but not always. It happened now and then over the years."

Buck said, "How long ago was this?"

He shrugged. "As far back as the forties, I hear. They stopped letting families live here about ten years after I came. Now it's men only."

"Do you remember anybody being buried here

during your time?"

"Can't say that I do," replied Estes. "But then, I don't know everything that goes on with these people."

Buck thought that was unlikely. "Where's the slave graveyard?"

Estes lit another cigarette and pointed with it out the window. "Back over near the swamp, behind the labor camp. Not much of it left now, but I reckon you could tear through some of the vines and find a rock marker or two. There was some folks out from the university doing just that ten or twelve years ago. Something about preserving Black history. Mr. Whitley told them to get the hell out, and even set up a guard around the place. Their lawyers fought him on it for almost a year."

Buck asked, "Who won?"

Estes shot him a dismissing look. "Whitley, of course."

And that, Buck surmised, was where Jarrod Whitley got his contempt for archaeologists.

Buck said, "The field where the bones are is a long way from the swamp."

Estes just shrugged. "I reckon."

It was clear Buck had learned all he was going to from Don Estes, and they completed the trip in silence. When they reached the house, he thanked Estes for his time and Estes, not getting out of the truck, reminded him, "Just drive straight ahead and you'll hit the blacktop that'll take you right back to the main road."

Buck waited until the other man was out of sight to get into his car and drive toward the exit. He did not, however, intend to go there.

The first road that led due south was the one marked with the sign "equipment shed." He followed it for a couple of miles, his tires spewing up a plume of red dust in their wake, until he came upon a chain link enclosure guarding a metal barn. There was a fuel station and a couple of tractors outside the building, along with a harrow, a rock rake, and a two-ton open-bed truck. But the dirt road continued past the equipment shed, and so did Buck.

The road ended at a wide turn-around half a mile later. A double gate and a long expanse of chain link surrounded a dozen rusty single-wide trailer homes, a row of porta-johns, and a long, low-roofed screened building which, judging by the trestle table that ran the length of it, appeared to be the chow hall. Behind that, some distance away, stood a smattering of weathered cedar shacks that Buck took to be the old slave cabins. The dirt yard was scattered with burn barrels that fogged the area with green-wood smoke—a practice, Buck knew, that was supposed to discourage mosquitos. A handful of brown-skinned men in sweat-stained khaki work clothes were gathered inside the chow hall, playing a card game and talking animatedly in Spanish. They fell silent when Buck pulled up, turning suspicious, covert glances in his direction.

The gate, he couldn't help noticing, was locked with a double padlock and chain. A security guard in aviator sunglasses stood in front of the gate, holding an AR-15 across his body. He wore a side arm and a radio on his belt.

Buck got out of the car. "How're you doing?" he greeted the guard as he approached.

The guard made no attempt to pretend to be accommodating. "This is a restricted area," he replied. His hands tightened on the rifle, which made Buck want to snatch the weapon out of his hands and smack him upside the head with it.

Instead, he jerked a thumb back toward his vehicle, which had "Chief of Police" stenciled in gold across both sides, and replied easily, "I'm authorized. Is this the camp where the farm workers live?"

The other man seemed to think about it for a moment before he replied grudgingly, "That's right."

Buck nodded toward the gate. "What's with the padlock?"

The guard set his jaw and did not reply. Buck waited a good thirty seconds.

"Dude," he said, with what he thought was admirable restraint, "it's hot and I'm running late and I was ready to put this hellhole in my rear-view mirror about an hour ago. Answer the goddamn question before I slap you in cuffs just to take the edge off my misery."

The man sucked in a breath through flared nostrils. He replied tightly, "Word came down we have a situation in the compound. No one is to leave or enter the worker's camp until I receive the all-clear."

Buck said, "What if I want to interview some of the workers?"

"Then you need to speak Spanish," replied the guard. Buck was sure he did not imagine the faint bite of smug sarcasm there. "And you need one of the Whitleys to escort you."

The impression Buck had first gotten of a prison yard was only reinforced. Only most prison yards he'd visited were cleaner. He looked around. "Where is the old slave graveyard from here?"

Now the guard looked absolutely blank. It was probably the first honest expression Buck had seen on the man's face since he'd driven up. "I don't know what you're talking about."

Buck stared him down for a long moment. Then he said, nodding toward the rifle, "What's the cannon for?"

The guard replied without expression, "Gators."

Buck regarded him for another beat, then nodded. "Carry on," he said, and he turned and went back to his car.

He followed the dirt road back the way he had come for another hundred yards or so and turned right onto a flat grassy track that he had noticed on the way in. It curved back toward the swamp, slightly away from the fenced compound he had just left but close enough that he could still catch glimpses of the old slave cabins through the brush. The path grew narrower as it progressed, with scrub pines and brambles that scraped the side of his car, and when he felt he couldn't go any further without getting bogged down, he stopped and got out.

Knotty tupelos and moss-draped oaks shaded the area, but the calf-high wild grass testified to the fact that it had once been cleared. As Buck stepped out of the car, cursing his dress shoes and watching for hidden dangers in the grass, a bird shrieked a warning. He turned his head and, sure enough, saw a four-foot-long black snake swipe its way along an overhanging branch, no doubt eyeing the bird's nest in the crotch of the tree. Buck kept his hand on his sidearm as he made his way carefully forward toward what, by his calculations, had to be the site of the old slave graveyard.

He picked up a fallen branch to beat aside the weeds and brambles, and after a moment came upon a bare rock planted in the dirt. He moved aside the vetch and vines and found another rock approximately six feet away. Grave markers, not inscribed, just there. He looked around. Flat earth, covered with ground vines and dotted with the occasional sapling or wild blackberry bush. Possibly there had been wooden grave markers at some point, but now they were long gone. He walked a few feet forward and uncovered another stone, and another. No names, no dates. Pets today receive more respect upon their passing than these people had two hundred years ago.

He moved toward the back of the cleared area and noticed the undergrowth was thinner, the weeds shallower. When he used his branch to lift aside a patch of viny ground cover, he saw fresh earth underneath. Estes had said the archeologists had been out here ten years ago. But whoever had disturbed this ground had done so a good deal more recently than that.

He heard the familiar rumble of an ATV coming down the dirt road, and he turned back toward his car. He reached it, sweat-drenched and batting away a cloud of insects, just as Geraldine Whitley arrived. He leaned against the car door and waited for her to dismount. Given the amount of time that had elapsed, Buck figured the guard must have radioed her the minute Buck's car had turned onto the dirt road.

Buck noticed a 20-gauge shotgun behind the seat of the vehicle as she got out. She strode toward him and demanded in a tone that was not the least bit welcoming, "Are you lost?"

"Just curious," Buck replied. He squinted against a salty drop of sweat that rolled into his eyes and nodded back toward the way he had come. "The old slave graveyard, right? A real piece of history."

Her eyes were like flint. "We don't give tours."

Buck said, "I'm told if I want to talk to any of your workers, I have to be accompanied by one of the Whitleys."

"What do you want to talk to them about?" Her tone was as hard as her gaze.

"Oh, this and that," he replied easily, enjoying the annoyance that built in her eyes. "Where they're from, how long they've been here, how they like working for you. That kind of thing."

"They like it here a hell of a lot better than where they came from," returned Geraldine shortly, "I can tell you that much. Free room, board, medical care, even the clothes on their backs. Nobody's complaining. I don't see what any of that has to do with your investigation."

"All fully documented, I'm sure."

"Of course," she returned coolly. "If you want to see our records, you'll have to come by the office. It's that small brick building next to the main house. Now, if you'll excuse me..." She started to turn back to her vehicle.

Buck said, "What about the household staff?"

She returned that cool contemptuous gaze to him and replied briefly, "What about them?"

"I understand they live on-site, too. How many are there?"

"Ten or twelve."

"That seems like a lot," observed Buck.

"It's a big house," she returned impatiently, "plus guest cabins."

"And they live in the dormitories down the

road?"

She made no attempt to disguise her impatience. "That's right."

"Why not just hire people from town?"

She replied, "Honestly, Chief, I can't see how the way we do business is any of your concern. Aren't you here to sign off on those bones they uncovered on the other side of the plantation? Have you done that yet?"

"Not yet," Buck replied mildly. He had to admire her gall, if nothing else. He added, "Who else lives here on the plantation, besides the farm workers and the household staff?"

She replied shortly, "Estes. Some of the security guards who don't have families. My brother Carter, myself, my stepbrother Zach, and his wife and two kids. My father lives in the main house. The rest of us have our own places."

He said, "Is there a family cemetery on the property?"

She frowned a little. "There is. It's old, hasn't been used this century, for sure. And it's at least a mile away from the lodge where they found the bones."

He nodded. "I might want to have a look at it, depending on what the medical examiner says."

"I'm not a tour guide. You'll have to set that up with Daddy." She walked back over to her ATV and added pointedly, "You can follow me out."

Buck got in his car, feeling the intensity of her stare until he started the engine. He thought he should probably give ICE a call in the morning. That would piss off Miss Corinne mightily, but that was just a bonus. There was something off about this whole place, and the sooner he could find some other agency to take it off his hands, the better.

Still, the dusty, dank miasma of the place followed him all the way back to town, and all he could think about for the rest of the day was going home and taking a shower.

CHAPTER EIGHTEEN

Baker couldn't suppress a small grunt of admiration when he pulled up in front of the white brick mansion Trish Miller called home. It was located inside a gated community with a golf course and a keypad entry, and from what Baker could tell, the Miller home overlooked the water feature. He'd also gotten a glimpse of a pretty fancy screened pool and outdoor kitchen in the backyard as he'd come around the corner.

"Nice place," he remarked.

"It's only temporary," she said quickly, flushing. "I mean, as soon as I start drawing a regular paycheck, I'll find a place of my own."

"Why?" Baker returned with a lift of his eyebrow. "Looks to me like you've got it made."

Instead of answering, Miller said earnestly, "I don't mind helping with the paperwork, honestly.

Or if Detective Moreno wants help conducting interviews…"

Baker looked at her steadily. "You know, as your FTO I have to do an assessment on you at the end of every shift. You want to know what my first-day assessment is going to be?"

She managed to look both miserable and eager. "Yes, sir. Of course. That would be good."

He replied, "My assessment is: good instincts, lacks confidence. You've got a good record, Miller, and you proved it today. But you're not going to go far in this department if you don't learn to stick up for yourself. If you've got something to say, don't be afraid to say it. You've got an idea, put it out there. You know, be assertive. And…" he nodded toward the house. "That doesn't only go for work."

She nodded, cheeks flaming, looking straight ahead. "Yes, sir. I know. It's just that…" she ventured a glance at him. "When you look like me, you don't naturally command a lot of respect. I always pulled the low-ranking assignments—public relations, communications, school resource officer. Not," she added hastily, "that those assignments aren't important, and I always took them seriously, but I guess I never had much of a chance to assert myself. And after a time, it got to be easier to just kind of stay quiet and do what I was told. Not draw attention to myself."

Baker was thoughtful for a moment. "Well, I

guess I know a thing or two about being judged on the way you look. But the thing I've learned is that once people make up their minds about you, nobody can change them but you."

She smiled in brief gratitude. "Yes, sir."

"Now," he said sternly, "Get on out of here so I can get back to work."

"Yes, sir." She quickly unfastened her seatbelt and opened the door. Then she hesitated and looked back. "Sir," she said, "that kid we arrested today. Paulo?"

He said, "Yeah?"

"It's probably nothing, but you told me to speak up and..." She took a breath. "I don't think he ran because he was carrying weed. I'm not even sure he realized he had it, or that it was illegal here. He looked surprised that that was why he was being arrested. But before that, he looked terrified. Not just of the police, but of something worse."

"Do you think he knows something about our Jane Doe?"

"He was close enough to see the photo when I showed it to the salon owner. And when I tried to show it to him, that's when he got that crazy-scared look in his eyes and ran. I think he recognized her."

Baker gave a thoughtful grunt. "Yeah, okay, Miller. Thanks."

She gave a quick shy shrug and opened the car door. "Like I said, it's probably nothing." She got out of the car.

"Hey, Miller."

She bent down to look at him.

"I'll pick you up here at 6:30 in the morning."

She said quickly, "Oh, sir, you don't have to do that. I can ..."

"6:30," he repeated sternly. He put the car in gear. "Don't be late."

Trish barely managed to close the door before he drove off.

CHAPTER NINETEEN

B uck made it back to the office in time for both of his meetings and spent another twenty minutes with Sully going over street closures and personnel deployment for the Fourth of July parade. One thing he was still having trouble adjusting to in this job was that every minute of every day was either full-out or full-stop, with rarely an in-between. One minute he was gazing at the bones of children in a mysterious grave; the next he was talking about safety vests and parade routes. And each of those things demanded his full attention.

"We generally have a couple of units at the front of the parade," Sully said, "with an honor guard of four men walking beside. You want to do that this year?"

Buck waved an agreeable hand. "Sure,

whatever."

"Billy used to lead the parade," Sully added, "walking out front and waving to the crowd while Roland drove the chief's car."

Buck couldn't help chuckling. "I'll bet he did. I'm surprised he didn't ride on the hood."

Sully grinned. "That would've been just like him, all right." But their mirth faded sooner than it should have as both of them remembered their fallen friend. Sully added in a moment, "I was wondering if you..."

He didn't have to finish the sentence before Buck shook his head. "I don't know, Sully. Folks might not feel right about me taking Billy's place at the head of the parade. It's only been a couple of months. Let me think about it."

"Sure thing." Sully started to gather up the street maps he'd spread over Buck's desk. "You ought to try to make it a point to take the family down to the park for the fireworks show, though. It's really something to see."

The park he was referring to was Sulfur Springs Park at the edge of town, Mercy's main tourist attraction. There would be live music, food, and fireworks throughout the evening, but the main show would take place on the river, right in front of the docks. People would be lined up five and six deep.

Buck said, "I'd kind of figured on staying close to town that night."

"Well," Sully admitted, "the view's not bad

from your place, either, being on the river like that."

The intercom buzzed and Lydia said, "Excuse me, sir. Jarrod Whitley is on line one. Also, you wanted to know when Detective Moreno checked in."

Buck reached for the phone. "Great. Is Frankie in her office?"

"Yes, sir. I'll tell her you're on your way. I'm leaving for the day. Is there anything else you need?"

Buck glanced at his watch, surprised to see it was almost 5:00. He'd promised to be home by 5:30 so that Eloise could make her meeting on time. "Thanks, Lydia, I've got it from here. Have a good night."

"You too, sir."

Buck held up a finger to Sully. "Hold on a minute." He punched the button for line one. "Buck Lawson."

"Now, you listen to me, boy," spat Jarrod Whitley angrily. "When I do business with a man, I expect him to keep his goddamn word, you hear me? You sit at my table, you shake my hand, you do what you say you're going to do. So, by God, do it!"

Buck moved the receiver a little away from his ear and lifted an eyebrow, glancing at Sully. "Is something wrong, Mr. Whitley?"

"You're goddamn right something is wrong!" Whitley exploded. "You told my manager we'd be back to work by the end of the day and here it is 5:00 and those pointy-headed shovel-slingers are still out there sifting through dirt and telling my people to back off. What in the *hell* are you trying to pull? Didn't I tell you this is exactly the kind of thing that was *not* going to happen? Didn't I?"

"Yes, sir, you made yourself very clear on that point," replied Buck calmly. "Sounds like I'd better send a couple of men out there to see what's going on."

"You just do that," snapped Whitley. "Because I'm telling you right now, we've already lost a whole damn day and I'm sending in the heavy equipment at 7:00 AM in the morning whether anybody's in that hole or not."

He punctuated the declaration by disconnecting the call, and Buck returned his own receiver to the cradle with a small shrug. Buck started gathering up his keys and phones in preparation for leaving for the day.

"There's something dicey going on out at Hollowgrove Plantation," he told Sully. "Probably labor law violations."

"Wouldn't surprise me a bit," Sully said as they walked toward the door. "Those folks run their own little empire out there, never have worried much about the law of the land."

"Well, they might have to pay a little more attention to it now," Buck said. "An excavation crew found the remains of two children buried on the property."

Sully stared at him. "Okay. That *does* surprise me."

Buck paused to lock his office door. "They keep trying to say it's part of an old cemetery, but the facts don't line up. I don't suppose you have any thoughts?"

"No, sir, boss, I don't. That would've been county territory up until ten years ago, anyhow. We wouldn't have much to do with the goings-on out there."

"Yeah, about that..." Buck dropped his keys in his pocket. "How many other friends of Miss Corinne is the Mercy Police Department providing services for that I don't know about?"

Sully grinned and shook his head. "I couldn't tell you. There's probably some even I don't know about."

"I guess you'd better send a car out there," Buck said, "with a couple of men to hold the perimeter until the M.E.'s team finishes its work. Jarrod Whitley is all red-in-the-face about it taking longer than it should and there's no telling what that crazy old coot is liable to do."

"Yes, sir, boss, you got it."

Baker met them in the hall. "I've got that report on the 466 you wanted," Baker said, handing him a folder. "The forensics bear out your initial conclusion—the victim ran into the side of Miller's car and the accident was unavoidable."

"Good work," Buck murmured, flipping through the report. "We're on our way to Frankie's office. Walk with us."

Sully asked, "How's Miller working out?"

"To tell you the truth," Baker replied, "I feel like I'm babysitting my thirteen-year-old niece. She's a good officer," he hastened to add, "but, damn, she's fresh."

Sully said, "How's your knee?"

Baker waved a dismissive hand. "It's nothing."

"Did you file an incident report?"

"On your desk."

Buck looked up from the report in his hand. "What happened?"

Baker looked embarrassed. "I fell chasing a suspect, scraped my knee. Miller did a pretty good job on the takedown, though, considering she can't weigh a hundred pounds soaking wet. The fellow—a Hispanic by the name of Paulo Ramirez —freaked when Miller tried to show him the photo of our Jane Doe and ran out the back door of the beauty shop where he was working. Turns out he was holding a baggie of weed. Probably undocumented, too." He hesitated. "Miller says she thinks something else was going on with him, too. She thinks he might have recognized the photograph and something about it scared him enough to send him running."

Buck grunted thoughtfully. "Is he in our jail?"

"Yeah, we'll hold him for twenty-four and if nobody comes to claim him, ship him out to county."

"Did you question him about the Jane Doe?"

"I did," Baker said, "but I didn't get anywhere. He wasn't exactly cooperative. I can take another run at him tomorrow if you want."

Buck said, "Can't hurt."

The door to Frankie's office was open and she was at the computer. Frankie turned her chair around when they came in, and Buck could tell by the look on her face that the news was mixed. She confirmed it with her next words.

"The good news is, the Gilfords went back to Atlanta. I told them we'd keep them informed, but they were already planning their lawsuit against Hope House. I can't say I blame them. More good news, we got a hit from the missing person's database on the fingerprints we took from the outside of Officer Miller's car." She consulted her computer. "Giselle Martindale, age 22. She disappeared from her parents' home in Mobile five years ago, probable runaway. No arrest record or employment record since then, no bank account, no housing record—at least not under that name. Both parents and a sister still living in Mobile."

Buck frowned a little, remembering what Trish Miller had said about the expensive hair and nails. Clearly, the woman had come upon better days since her time as a runaway.

"The bad news is the search of Hope House was a bust," Frankie went on flatly. "The place had been sanitized, the 'residents'..." She put this in air quotes. "...were on a regularly scheduled trip to the mall an hour away. The security cameras have been conveniently down for the past twenty-four hours and the guard who was on duty last night didn't answer my calls or his door. There were three staff members on duty, and all of them confirmed that the birth mother had simply changed her mind about the adoption. They all also insisted—along with Eliza Summerfield—that no one from Hope House had picked up Giselle Martindale from the hospital or brought her back to Hope House. The room that was identified as hers looked unoccupied, the bed stripped, drawers emptied."

Buck gave a grunt of surprise. "She called someone at Hope House this morning. Who did she talk to?"

"Mrs. Summerfield did admit to talking to her but said the conversation didn't go beyond Gisele confirming that she was all right and that she had decided to keep her baby." Frankie added matter-of-factly, "Summerfield was lying. But the warrant came through for the security footage from the hospital, and I got a pretty good look at Giselle leaving the hospital with another woman. It was no one I recognized from the interviews at Hope House, so maybe Summerfield was telling the truth about that part at least."

Buck looked at Baker. "The nurse at the hospital who loaned Giselle her phone. Was she sure she overhead Giselle asking someone to pick her up?"

"According to the nurse," Baker said, "she told whoever was on the other end that she was in the emergency room and that she wanted to come home. She was supposed to be admitted to the OB floor, but never got to her room."

Frankie went on, "There was a nice little nursery set-up at Hope House, but no sign of a baby. We weren't allowed to view any documents related to the identities of the so-called guests of Hope House, but I did get the financial records. Summerfield's lawyers followed us around like bird dogs, making sure we didn't ask the wrong question or open the wrong drawer."

"Which they were perfectly entitled to do," Buck reminded her. "It was a limited search warrant."

"I don't understand all the damn secrecy," Sully said. "Last I heard it wasn't illegal to have a baby."

"It was a real swanky place," Frankie went on. "The rooms the girls stay in were like luxury hotel suites. There's an indoor-outdoor pool, a yoga room, a mediation room, and a screening room that Steven Spielberg would envy. I'll tell you what, if I were doing the surrogacy thing, I'd make sure that a nice long stay at Hope House was part of the bargain."

"What about the medical care?" Buck asked.

"Oh, sure. There's a nurse practitioner on staff for regular prenatal care, an R.N. for every shift, and a doula or midwife attending every birth, with an OB standing by in case of emergency. I talked to the midwife who attended Giselle's delivery, but she didn't know anything about

Giselle leaving the facility. I haven't been able to reach the nurse yet."

"Have you been able to find anything irregular about the adoptions coming out of there?" Buck asked.

"Nothing in public records," Frankie said. "I'm going to start tracking down some of the individuals who've done business with Hope House, starting with that lawyer the Gilfords said referred them in the first place. And, oh." She took out her phone. "I got a screenshot of the hospital security tape showing the woman Giselle left with. I can run the whole thing for you if you like."

Buck leaned in to view Frankie's phone screen. So did the other two men. The shot was from a typical grainy, black-and-white camera roll, but at least it had been taken at a time of the morning when there was enough daylight to make out some detail. Two women were frozen in the frame beneath the hospital awning. One was wearing a hospital gown and robe and was almost certainly the same woman they had all seen being taken away in an ambulance earlier that day. The other woman was tall and slim, wearing jeans and a tee shirt, with short, spikey black hair. She gripped the girl's arm as though afraid she might get away.

"Son of a bitch," Buck said. He pointed to the dark-haired woman. "I know that woman. That's Geraldine Whitley."

Sully narrowed his eyes over the screenshot. "I've only seen her once or twice, but by God, I think you're right."

They straightened up, and Frankie turned the phone to study it herself. "How do you suppose a girl like Giselle got to know a woman like Geraldine Whitley?"

"And how," put in Sully, "did Whitley know she was in the hospital?"

"And," added Baker, "what did the girl do with her baby?"

Buck tapped the file folder Baker had given him against the back of his hand. "All good questions," he replied, looking at Frankie. "Do you suppose we might get some answers by tomorrow?"

"On my way to interview Ms. Whitley now," Frankie replied. She put away her phone and started closing computer files.

"Don't be put off by first impressions," Buck advised. "She's even meaner when you get to know her." He glanced at his watch. "Okay, I'm out of here. I'm playing Mr. Mom tonight and if I'm late they probably won't let me do it again."

The other three shared a grin. "Good night, Chief."

He thrust the file folder to Sully as he turned toward the door and almost told them to call him with any developments. Then he remembered his promise to Jolene and said only, "Y'all have a good one."

He left the building with ten minutes to spare.

CHAPTER TWENTY

A low bank of thunderheads was gathering along the river, teasing the promise of a cooling rain, when Buck turned into his drive. He left his truck in the garage and crossed the lawn through a blanket of steamy heat with the sun still three hours from setting. The sound of barking and galloping paws greeted him when he opened the back door, and also something else—an unexpected wave of cool air.

Buck knelt to pet the shaggy dog and had barely regained his feet when Willis plowed into him, crying, "Buck! You're home!"

Buck caught up the little boy in a hug, swinging him around once, and agreed, "I sure am!"

Willis was an exceptionally beautiful child. With his fawn-colored skin, striking green eyes, and the wreath of golden-brown ringlets framing his face, he turned heads wherever he went. Buck had seen pictures of Willis's father, an American soldier who had died in Afghanistan, and knew where he'd gotten his green eyes and light skin. Everything else was pure Jolene. Fortunately, his personality was as delightful as his looks, earnestly precocious and flawlessly mannered. Willis had never met an adult he didn't charm, and Buck was no exception.

Willis giggled with delight and Buck set him on his feet as his mother-in-law came into the kitchen, her purse over her arm.

"Why is it so cool in here?" he asked.

"The air conditioning man got here before lunch," Eloise replied. "He had the whole thing up and running in half an hour."

"Way to go, Lydia," Buck murmured.

There was a frosted cake on the counter, and Buck reached to take a swipe of the frosting with his finger. Eloise slapped his hand away.

"That's for my meeting," she said. She snapped a lid on the cake carrier and added, "I just put the casserole in to bake. The timer's set for one hour. You can make a salad, can't you, Buck?"

"Yes ma'am. I'm all over it." He dropped a hand onto Willis's shoulder. "Besides, I've got my number one helper here."

"We're all over it," Willis assured his grandmother sincerely.

Eloise smiled and bent to kiss Willis's cheek. "You be good," she told him. And to Buck, she added, "I'll be back before 9:00. If you need anything..."

"We won't," he assured her. "Have a good time. Do you need any help carrying the cake to the car?"

She made a dismissing gesture with her hand and picked up the cake carrier. "You've got fresh strawberries for dessert," she said. "Don't let Willis drown his in chocolate sauce the way he likes to do. That child isn't going to have a tooth left in his head if we're not careful."

Buck held the door for her. "We've got this, Miss Eloise."

"Yeah," Willis agreed, grinning, "We got this."

As soon as she was gone, Willis turned eagerly to Buck. "What do you want to do first, Buck?"

Buck pretended to think about it. "How about this for a plan? I go change out of this uniform, then we make the salad, then we set the table, then we eat. What do you think?"

Willis considered this. "Sounds a little boring, Buck."

Buck nodded thoughtfully. "You've got a point. How about this? I go change, we make the salad, take Thor out back for a game of ball, then we eat, then we all walk downtown for an ice cream cone."

Willis's eyes lit up. "Yeah!"

"Okay, sport, you got it. Give me five minutes."

Buck took the world's shortest shower and changed into shorts and a tee shirt. When he returned to the kitchen, Willis had lined up all the salad ingredients on the countertop, climbed atop a stepstool, and was reaching for a butcher knife from the knife block. Buck took one long stride forward and claimed the knife before Willis could. "I thought I'd get started chopping the tomatoes," Willis said innocently.

"Well, that's real thoughtful of you, bud." Buck's heartbeat gradually returned to normal. "But I'd just as soon skip the trip to the emergency room tonight if it's okay with you. How about you take over lettuce-tearing duty and I chop the tomatoes?"

Willis shrugged. "I don't like tomatoes, anyway." He thought for a moment. "To tell you the truth, I'm not that wild about salad."

Buck took out the cutting board. "You'll like it the way I make it. I put in peanuts."

Willis looked interested. "Peanuts?"

"It's a whole new world of flavor sensation," Buck promised him. "Wash your hands before you start on the lettuce."

Buck started chopping the vegetables while Willis washed his hands. "Did you have a good time at the Bakers' today?"

"Sure." Willis shook the excess water off his hands and onto Thor's coat, who didn't seem to notice. He hurried back to his stepstool and climbed up with the dog trailing his every step. "Ms. Carol made us peanut butter and jelly sandwiches for lunch, with corn chips *and* potato chips."

"Sounds better than what I had for lunch."

"Then we played Giganotosaurus on the Xbox while our food digested and then we jumped back in the pool and then Jamar taught me how to do a cannonball. It was awesome!"

"Sounds awesome," Buck agreed. He pointed with the knife tip to the lettuce. "Small pieces, like your mom showed you."

"Next time Jamar's coming to my house," Willis said. "Can we have a pool for our backyard?"

"I'm afraid not," Buck replied. "We're too close to the river, which means a shallow water table."

Willis looked at him thoughtfully. "I don't think I know what that is."

"If we tried to put in a pool, it would collapse into the river," Buck explained simply.

"Oh." He looked dejected for a brief moment, then brightened. "But the river is fun, too. Are you sure we can't swim in it, Buck?"

"I'm sure," Buck said firmly. "The river is for boating and fishing. Remember what I told you lives there?"

"Alligators!" replied Willis with enthusiasm.

"With teeth," Buck reminded him. It was important to make this distinction because of Hobo, the ancient, toothless, and practically tame alligator who wandered around town so harmlessly that he had been named the town's official mascot.

"And snakes," added Willis, wrinkling up his

nose.

"Also with teeth," Buck said. "Or fangs, as the case may be. How're you coming with that lettuce?"

"Almost done." He tore a few more strips of lettuce into the bowl and said, "You know what Jamar told me today?"

"What's that, buddy?"

"He said that a long time ago people that looked like you used to own people that looked like me. Do you suppose that's true, Buck? 'Cause Jamar makes a lot of stuff up."

Once again Buck felt the hot tingle across the back of his neck, and he worked hard to keep his expression easy. He tried to think of the right reply, but there really was only one.

He said, "Yes, sir, I'm afraid Jamar got it right this time." And even as he spoke, he was thinking, Damn it. *Damn it.* He didn't want to have this conversation now. He never wanted to have this conversation. "A long time ago there were some people who thought it was okay to own other people and keep them as slaves."

Willis looked up at him with big, curious eyes. "How come do you suppose they did that, Buck?"

Buck scraped the chopped vegetables into the bowl with the lettuce. "I don't know, Willis," he answered. He rested his palms on the countertop and looked at the little boy steadily. "But I can tell you this. It was wrong, and it will never happen again."

Willis looked puzzled, and Buck knew he was about to ask another question for which he had no good answer. But he was saved at that moment by none other than Thor, who barked and scrambled across the room, his claws clicking and sliding on the tile. A moment later something thudded hard against the side of the house. Buck heard a crash coming from the dining room.

Willis looked at Buck with wide eyes. "I think something fell down," he said.

Buck dried his hands on a dish towel and followed Thor into the dining room, Willis by his side. The room was empty except for some packing boxes and framed photographs—Buck and Jolene's wedding, Eloise's wedding, and Willis as a baby—they had hung on the wall. Eloise's walnut dining set, which included a full-length buffet and China hutch, was still in storage in Raleigh, awaiting a convenient time for the movers to bring it south. But she insisted there was nothing like family photographs on the wall to make a house feel like home, so as soon as the fresh paint was dry, she had turned the empty room into a family gallery.

There was a set of patio doors leading out to a small brick terrace, and Thor stood there, peering out eagerly and wagging his tail. On either side of those doors, a framed 14x18 photograph had hung—one of Buck's grandmother, one of Jolene's. The photograph of Jolene's grandmother had fallen to the floor, the glass spider webbed.

"Mama's not going to like that," Buck murmured. He crossed the room to pick it up and then he noticed something out of place on the patio just outside the door. It was a brick, probably from the stack outside the workshop that had been left over from some project or another. Buck was certain the brick had not been on the patio when he crossed the lawn from the garage less than an hour ago.

Buck ruffled Thor's ears absently and handed Willis the broken photograph. "Do me a favor, bud, and keep Thor inside, will you?"

"Sure thing, Buck." Willis wrapped his hand around Thor's collar. "You think there's a mean old gator or something out there? Maybe that's what knocked great-grandma's picture off the wall?"

"Probably not," Buck admitted, "but let me check it out anyway."

He stepped out onto the patio and picked up the brick, scanning the yard as he did so. There was a chip in the white trim around the doorframe and flakes of red brick on the patio where the brick had fallen, as though someone had aimed to hit the glass door and had missed. Perhaps he'd been scared away by Thor's barking before he got close enough to make a good shot. Buck was about to toss the brick away when he noticed something written on the underside. In bold black marker, it read, *Back Off*.

CHAPTER
TWENTY-ONE

F rowning, Buck stepped out into the yard, starting to retrace the path the vandal would have taken from the workshop. He had only gone half a dozen steps when Willis opened the door and called, "Buck! Company!"

Buck hesitated, looked at the brick in his hand, then at the hedge that separated the workshop from the house. He lifted his arm to Willis. "On my way," he called.

"I've got it!" Willis called back and scampered toward the front door with Thor at his heels.

Buck quickened his step. When he arrived in the foyer, the front door was open and Junior Aikens stood there, petting an enthusiastically wriggling Thor. Willis, holding the door, looked at Buck uncertainly. "Um, Buck," he said, "the ghost man is here."

Junior Aikens looked up from petting the dog. He had a small package in his hands and an apologetic look on his face. "I'm sorry to keep barging in on you like this. I realized I don't have your phone number, and I hated to call the station for something like this."

Buck placed the brick on the foyer table and said, "I'm glad you stopped by. Listen, you didn't see anybody just now, did you? In the yard or hanging around the house?"

Junior looked puzzled. "No, but I just drove up. Something wrong?"

Willis stood on tiptoe and whispered to Buck, "Aren't you going to ask the ghost to come in?"

Junior, overhearing, grinned, and Buck couldn't help doing the same. He put his hands on Willis's shoulders. "Willis, this is Junior Aikens, the son of the man who used to own this house. And your mama told you he isn't a ghost."

Willis stepped forward and extended his hand. "It's a pleasure to meet you, Mr. Aikens," he said politely. "My name is Willis, and this is my dog, Thor. I'm glad you're not a ghost," he added as Junior bent to shake his hand.

"It's a pleasure to meet both of you," Junior said, and the twinkle in his eye made him look more like Billy than ever.

"Come in," Buck insisted, moving forward to close the door. "I'm sorry about not following through on lunch. Lydia called you?"

"She did," Junior said. "But I don't mean to

bother you. I just stopped by to make sure you got your AC fixed. Which," he added as he stepped over the threshold, "it looks like you did." At Buck's puzzled look, he explained, "Your mother-in-law mentioned it to me this morning. I went to school with Zach Whitley back in the day—we practically grew up together in fact—so I made a call. He said he'd take care of it personally."

"Well, that was mighty good of you," Buck said, surprised. "We appreciate it."

"I also wanted to bring you this." He handed Buck the package. "I don't know how it ended up in Daddy's things. It belongs with the house."

Buck slid a carved brass plaque out of the paper bag in which it was wrapped. *The Aikens House, 1853. A Designated Historic Landmark Mercy, Georgia.*

"It used to hang by the front door," Junior explained. "I guess the screws rusted out or something and Daddy never bothered to put it back up."

"Thanks," Buck said. "I'll make sure it gets back where it belongs." Although he couldn't help wondering privately how many times he needed to be reminded that he was now in charge of preserving a history that was not his own. He gestured back toward the kitchen. "Come on in. Let me get you a beer."

He thought Junior would refuse, which was— if he was completely honest—why he had made the offer. The other man surprised him by saying,

"Thanks. That'd hit the spot on a day like this."

Willis tugged on the hem of Buck's shorts. "Buck, since the salad is all made, do you think it would be okay if I got a head start on playing in the backyard while you visit with your company?"

Junior's lips twitched with amusement and Buck said, "I think that's a fine idea. Maybe you and Thor could practice catching the ball until I get there."

Willis and Thor scampered down the hall toward the back door, and the two men followed at a more leisurely pace, passing rooms on the right and left that were still mostly unfurnished. Aikens Furniture had delivered the living room set only last week, but they were still waiting for rugs and occasional tables. Footsteps echoed on the ancient wood floors as Buck and Junior made their way to the kitchen.

"That is one cute kid," Junior said when Willis and Thor bolted out the back door.

"Yeah, he is," Buck agreed. "We're trying to keep it from going to his head, but I think he's on to us."

"I'm sorry to interrupt your evening," Junior said, glancing around the kitchen as Buck opened the refrigerator. "I can see you're getting ready to eat."

"You're welcome to join us." Buck put the salad in the refrigerator and took out two beers. He handed one to Junior. "It's just us boys tonight."

"Thanks," Junior said, "but I'm on my way to meet Cousin Corinne for dinner."

"Right." Buck twisted the cap off his beer. "I forgot the Aikenses are related to everybody in town." He gestured toward the back door. "Do you mind if we sit on the screen porch? I know it's a waste of good AC, but I don't like to leave Willis out there by himself this close to the river, especially with that fool dog likely to take off any minute."

"My mama was the same way," Junior agreed, following him out to the porch. "She was forever after my daddy to put up a fence, especially after Cousin Corinne's little boy drowned."

They went out onto the back porch, which felt even thicker with heat after the refrigerated air they'd just left. Buck turned on the ceiling fan, and Junior sat in one of the wicker rockers that had been there when Buck moved in. Buck said, "It must be strange, coming back to the place you grew up and seeing other people's stuff there. Well," he corrected himself, "some of our stuff, anyway. We haven't made a lot of progress furnishing the place. It's a big house."

Junior replied noncommittally, "It's nice to see it filled with people again." He gestured toward the wooden play set, complete with swings, a slide, and a small fort, which occupied one corner of the yard. "Now, that's nice. We would've loved something like that as kids."

"It came in a kit. Took me two weekends to put together, and that was with help from some of the guys at work."

Willis called from the yard, "Hey, Buck, watch this!"

Buck and Junior both watched as Willis tossed a wobbly ball toward Thor, who leaped for it, missed, and bounced the ball off his nose. "Good effort!" Buck called back. "A little more practice."

"Thor needs to work on his eye-mouth coordination," Willis observed sagely, and ran to retrieve the ball.

"Now I see why you took this job," Junior said, amused. "A boy that smart is going to require a first-class education. My sister and I both went to college on the city's dime."

Buck took the rocking chair opposite Junior's and angled it so he could keep an eye on Willis. "I won't deny that was a factor," he admitted. One of the most appealing parts of the benefits package he had been offered was a college scholarship to any state school for his children, including stepchildren, after five years of employment. After ten years, the scholarship expanded to include four years at any public college in the country. "The contract the city came up with was pretty hard to turn down."

"Yeah, it would have to be," Junior murmured, and then, as though surprised to realize he had spoken out loud, he took a quick drink from the bottle.

Buck said, "You said you went to school with Zach Whitley. Is that where you met him, in college?"

Junior shook his head. "Zach and I have been running together since grade school. I guess I spent more time at his house than my own, growing up."

Buck was surprised. "Is that right? I'd think Hollowgrove would be in a different school district."

"I'm sure it is," Junior said. "But Zach's mother was Jarrod Whitley's second wife. She divorced him and moved to town when Zach was just a little thing. She used to work at the bank." He sipped his beer. "Passed away a few years back, I hear."

"I was out at Hollowgrove today," Buck said. "Quite a place."

"That it is." Junior's expression grew shuttered, and he lifted the beer bottle to his lips again. "Zach mentioned some kind of commotion out there. Something about an old graveyard?"

"Something like that," Buck conceded. "Did you spend much time out at Hollowgrove as a kid?"

Junior hesitated, and Buck got the impression he wanted to pursue the reason for Buck's visit to Hollowgrove. After a moment, Junior shrugged, and replied, "A few weekends and holidays. Zach didn't like to go by himself. His dad was a real dick, if you'll pardon me for saying so."

"He still is," Buck said, and Junior smiled a little.

Buck turned his attention to Willis, who was earnestly trying to explain to Thor the mechanics involved in catching a ball. Then he looked back at Junior. "So," Buck invited amiably, "what really brings you back over here today?"

Junior smiled a little, his eyes on his beer bottle. "My daddy used to do that. You never could fool him either."

"It's a cop thing," Buck replied.

Junior glanced at him. "The truth is, I wanted to apologize to that nice Miss Eloise, and to your wife. I'm afraid I offended them this morning when I wouldn't come in, or firm up dinner plans."

"Jolene thought you might not have been comfortable seeing Black people living here," Buck said, watching him.

Junior sighed, looking embarrassed. "Yeah, I realized after I left that's what she probably thought. Nothing could be further from the truth. The fact of the matter is..." He paused and took a sip of his beer. "I don't have great memories of growing up here. Seeing the house again brought up some stuff for me. I didn't mean to hurt any feelings."

Buck waited for him to go on, but that was apparently all Junior was going to say on the subject. Buck said, "I wondered if there might be some hard feelings about Billy not leaving the house to his children."

Junior gave a short, surprised laugh. "This old white elephant? The only hard feelings would be if he *did* leave it to us." He took another sip of his beer. "This house was the least valuable part of the Aikens estate, so don't feel bad about that. Daddy left my sister and me—and our kids and grandkids, if it comes to that— well taken care of. It was my sister's idea to turn the place over to the city all those years ago. Thank God she was able to talk Daddy into it. Believe me, no regrets there. Enjoy it in good health."

"Still," Buck pursued, "It's a little odd, the way he stipulated the house had to be used to house the chief of police. It made me think he expected you to take over the job."

Junior gave a grunt of completely mirthless laughter. "Then he was paying less attention than I thought. I've made a lot of mistakes in my life, but following in my father's footsteps was not one of them."

Junior took a long draw on his beer. "I never thanked you," he said abruptly, staring straight ahead, "for catching the guy that killed my dad. I know my sister sent a note, and it was supposed to be from both of us, but it wasn't. I should have called."

Buck replied, "I was just doing my job." He watched Thor nosing the ball across the ground while Willis raced to the swing set. "And solving his murder doesn't make him any more alive."

Junior drank again but didn't meet Buck's eyes. "Yeah."

Buck said, "I really liked your dad. I thought we'd have a lot more time together. I guess you did too. I'm sorry about that."

Junior said nothing at all.

Buck went on carefully, "It must have been a shock, the way it happened. I mean, you just don't expect that kind of thing in a little town like Mercy."

Junior's lips tightened, but it didn't take long for him to lose the battle with what he was trying not to say. "Matter of fact," he replied briefly, "it wasn't a shock at all. I'd been expecting it."

He drew hard on the beer, and just when Buck was about to ask him to explain himself, Junior turned to look at him. "Look," he said, "you seem like a decent man. Good cop, from all accounts. You probably think what happened with my dad, what you found and what you went through, was the worst you're ever going to see. Believe me when I tell you you haven't even scratched the surface. There's something about this town that's..." His nostrils flared as he sucked in a breath and seemed to search for the word. "Wrong somehow. Twisted. It's like..." Again, he seemed to struggle to give his thoughts life. "I don't know. Tainted. A long-term corruption that you can't even see. Just like that river." He lifted his bottle to indicate the glint of still, dark water in the distance. "Picture perfect to look at, but beneath the surface there are things you don't even want to know about." He shrugged and drained the last of his beer, and with that motion seemed to rouse himself from his musing.

He looked at Buck, and he said, "I guess what

I'm saying is, don't believe everything you see around here. But I'd say you're smart enough to know that already."

"Hey, Buck!" Willis cried. He was on the swing now, pumping his legs for all he was worth. "Look how high I can go!"

"Man, you are flying!" Buck called back. "Hold on with both hands or you might end up on the moon!"

Willis's laughter rang out over the lawn, and the clock in the Methodist church on the square chimed the hour. Six bells, followed by the carillon playing "Holy, Holy, Holy." It was a Mercy tradition, four times a day.

The two men sat easily until the last bell of the hymn had died away, then Junior smiled and placed his empty bottle on the wicker table beside his chair. "Well, I'd better not keep Cousin Corinne waiting." He stood. "Thanks for the beer, and I do want to take you all out to eat one night before I leave. To kind of make up for the misunderstanding."

"We'd like that." Buck stood, too. "I'll have Lydia text you my number."

"You don't have to see me out," Junior said. "I'll just cut across the yard to the driveway."

Buck chuckled. "Yeah, I guess you know your way."

Junior opened the screen door, then looked back. "By the way, I meant to ask... those bones at Hollowgrove. I don't suppose there's any way you could tell who they belonged to. I mean, no ID or anything in the grave."

"Afraid not," Buck said. "I left before the medical examiner got there, but I should have a preliminary report tomorrow."

"Of course," Junior added, "people have been living out there and burying their dead out there for almost two hundred years. There's no telling how long ago those kids died."

Buck nodded noncommittally. "Like I told the family, I'll let them know as soon as I find out anything."

Junior smiled and extended his hand. "Well, it was nice talking to you, Buck."

Buck shook his hand. "Thanks for stopping by, Junior."

Junior went down the back steps, calling, "Goodbye, Willis!" as he crossed the lawn.

Willis called back, "Goodbye, Mr. Aikens!"

Buck watched Junior go through the gap in the hedge to the driveway, wondering how Junior had known the bones belonged to children. Buck was sure he hadn't mentioned it.

He stood on the porch, sipping his beer, until he heard Junior's car start up. Then he went outside to push Willis on the swing until it was time for dinner.

CHAPTER
TWENTY-TWO

O ne of the first things Buck had done after they moved in was to install a two-person hammock chair on the balcony outside the master bedroom so that he and Jolene could sit out there and watch the legendary sunsets over the Blood River. As the sun sank behind the moss-covered trees and the sky took on shades of bold purple and blood red, the temperature dropped a few degrees and a vagrant breeze rising from the river made the outdoors almost bearable. Buck sat in the swing and sipped a beer, watching Willis play with Thor on the dusky lawn below. The days seemed to go on forever this time of year, and he remembered what it was like to be a boy wanting to squeeze every ounce of fun out of each and every one of them.

"That's quite a boy you've got there," Billy said. He turned from gazing out over the river to look at Buck, leaning back against the railing. "It's good to see him out running and playing like that. Most kids these days have got their eyes glued to some kind of screen and their thumbs punching a game controller."

"His mother is pretty strict about things like that," Buck said.

"Good for her."

Buck smiled and lifted his beer to him in a small salute. "Good to see you, Billy. It's been a while."

Billy shrugged, returning the smile. He did look remarkably like his son, but older, firmer, and a little more solid somehow. "Not from my point of view."

Buck took a sip of the beer. "I guess that's right."

"So," Billy said genially. "Settling in, are you? Getting to know folks, finding your way around?"

"More or less. Work keeps me busy." He thought about it for a minute and added, "Miss Corinne is a pain in the ass. I don't know how you put up with her."

Billy chuckled. "You two just need some time to get used to each other. She doesn't trust you yet, just like you don't trust most of the people on your force."

Buck frowned. "You can't blame me, after half of them turned out to be criminals."

"And you can't blame her," Billy pointed out, "after you practically burned her town down trying to root out that so-called crime ring."

Buck's frown deepened. "That's not what I did. Anyhow, we've got an understanding now."

"Do you, though?" replied Billy mildly, and Buck shot him a quick, curious look. "Miss Corinne is a complicated woman," Billy went on. "Not nearly as bad as you think, but a long way from being good, that's for sure. You just stay on your toes around her. You'll be fine."

Billy turned his attention back toward the yard, and the boy and dog playing there. "You need to get yourself a boat," he said, "take the boy downriver a bit to the good fishing holes."

"I'm looking for one," Buck agreed. "Maybe a fourteen-foot jon boat with a trolling motor. Fiberglass."

"Nah, the roots and sand bars in this river will tear a hole in fiberglass. You're better off with aluminum."

"Did you ever try to launch from here?"

"Sure. All you need to do is clear out some of the bushes by the water and a flat-bottomed boat will slide right in."

Buck said, "Not that it looks like I'm going to have much time for fishing anytime soon."

"With the Fourth of July coming up and you short-staffed?" Billy shook his head in sympathy. "You got that right."

Buck shot him an accusing glance. "You didn't exactly leave me in fine shape when it comes to that, Billy."

Billy said, "You're a church-going man, aren't you, Buck?"

Buck replied uneasily, "I try to be."

In truth, that was just another one of the things he was trying to adjust to. Jolene and Eloise had embraced the church that Baker's family went to, which was ninety percent Black. The people were great, and Buck liked the preacher, but he couldn't get used to being the only white face in the congregation most Sundays. Truth be told, if it hadn't been for Willis, he probably would have begged off and stayed in bed Sunday mornings.

Billy went on, "You remember that story from the Bible about this fellow—name escapes me—that started out with an army of over 30,000 soldiers. By the time he got rid of the cowards, the lazy, and the incompetent, all he had left was 300 men to go up against an army of 135,000."

"Sounds like the set-up for a massacre to me," Buck observed.

"They won the battle," Billy informed him, and Buck gave a grunt of surprise. "I always wondered if that's where the Marines got their motto from," Billy added. "Sometimes all it takes is a few good men."

"Or at least," clarified Buck, "good enough that they won't get you investigated by the Attorney General."

Billy chuckled again, and they were quiet for a time, easy in each other's company. Then Billy said, "I hear you've got yourself a mess out at

Hollowgrove."

Buck frowned a little. "Yeah. What the hell is going on out there, anyhow? Those people are weird as shit."

"You're telling me. Always have been. The less I had to do with them, the better. I'll tell you what, though, Buck. You'd better keep an eye on that fellow Carter. He's no more fit to run a security force than that little boy of yours is, and you know how people like that are when you give them a tin badge and a gun."

"Yeah," agreed Buck. "But he doesn't worry me as much as the daughter, Geraldine. She looks like she'd shoot a man just for crossing on the wrong side of the street."

Billy chuckled. "I've met her. And she would. Like you said, they're all strange. Too much inbreeding, if you ask me."

Buck took a sip of his beer. "What do you suppose Carter meant when he said his security guards' job was to protect the women? I didn't see any women, except Geraldine and that girl, Marina. And what are they protecting them from?"

Billy said, "Those farm laborers can be a pretty rough crew, I reckon. A bunch of men, all cramped in together like that."

"That's for sure," Buck agreed. "I've seen better conditions in prison camps." He looked again at Billy. "Where do you suppose those bones came from?"

"Could be anything," Billy said. "My first thought would be an illegal burial from the worker's camp. Some kid got sick and died, or had an accident, and they couldn't afford a real funeral. But it's been a lot of years since any kids lived out there. Aside from the Whitley children, that is." He shook his head, his thick white hair glistening briefly with the setting sun. "It's a puzzle."

Buck added, "Nothing like a thirty-year-old mystery to spice up the holiday weekend."

"Well, you know what they say," Billy replied. "A mystery is just a question we haven't asked yet."

Buck said, "I never heard anybody say that." He added, "Junior said he was friends with Zach Whitley."

"Yeah, they used to run around together as kids. Zach was a pretty decent boy. The only one of that lot worth anything, if you ask me."

Buck sipped his beer in silence for a while, watching the shadows of boy and dog move across the lawn, listening to the sound of happy barks and muffled laughter. After a time, he said, "I think I've figured out why I keep dreaming about you. It's because of my dad. He died while I was in college, I told you that. It was real sudden. We used to have talks like this, work things out that were bothering me. I guess I miss that."

Billy said, "Well, I'm happy to oblige. The only thing is..." His eyes twinkled. "Are you sure it's a dream?"

Buck was not amused. "What happened between you and Junior, Billy?"

The twinkle faded, and a veil seemed to come over Billy's eyes, though whether it was from grief or bewilderment Buck could not say. Perhaps it was a mix of both. "Why, I'm not sure I can tell you, Buck. Kids grow up, lose touch..." His voice trailed off, and his gaze wandered back over the railing to the little boy playing on the lawn.

"It seemed like more than that," Buck prompted carefully. "He said he hadn't been back here since he left for college. He didn't even want to come in the house. Said it had bad memories."

Billy, gazing down at the lawn, didn't answer for a long moment. Then he said, "You better keep an eye on that boy. He's getting awful close to the river."

Buck lurched upright in the swing, but something was weighing him down. He muttered, "What the..."

Jolene said, "Shh. Don't you dare wake him up."

Buck blinked in the dim light as Jolene's face swam into view. "Hey, sweetheart," he murmured. "When did you get home?"

"A little while ago." She gently extricated Willis from Buck's arms and lifted the sleeping boy onto her shoulder.

Willis murmured, "Hey, Mama," without opening his eyes, and draped his arms around her neck. "We had peanuts in the salad and ice cream for dessert. Then we read Harry Potter and watched the bats. It was fun."

"Go back to sleep," Jolene whispered and kissed Willis's cheek. She turned a puzzled frown on Buck. "What bats?"

"Shh," Buck replied. "He's sleeping."

Jolene carried Willis back inside, and Buck put the book he had been reading to Willis on the table beside the swing. Personally, he thought Willis was too young for stories about little orphan boys who were sent off to mean relatives and forced to live in a closet under the stairs, but what did Buck know? His mother had read him stories about wolves that ate grandmothers and then dressed in grandma's nightgown while waiting to dine on little girls.

Buck reached for the beer he had been drinking but it turned out to be Coke, and the can was empty. He'd dreamed the beer, just like he'd dreamed Willis had been playing on the lawn below and wandering too close to the river. In fact, it was raining, and had been since shortly before dusk. He and Willis had come up to the balcony to watch the bats swoop down and devour the mosquitoes that swarmed in advance of the storm and then had read a chapter from the Harry Potter book while the rain rolled in. It was a gentle, velvety rain that brought with it a cooling breeze and the occasional muted rumble of thunder, and the little boy had easily fallen asleep under the spell of its soothing rhythm. So, not much later, had Buck.

The door of the bedroom opened and Jolene came out, a glass of chardonnay in one hand and a glass of bourbon in the other. Before he met Billy, Buck rarely drank anything but beer. His new appreciation for Billy's expensive brand of bourbon seemed the least significant of all the changes he'd undergone in the past few weeks.

Jolene was wearing a long caftan in a sensuous, silky material, and her hair was undone in a braid over her shoulder. Her feet were bare. Buck smiled as she handed him the bourbon and sank into the swing beside him. "Reason Number 680 that I married you," he said, lifting his glass to her in a salute.

She swung her legs over his knees and settled back into the curve of the swing. "You're almost out of bourbon," she told him.

"I'll have to ask Lydia if she knows what brand it was." The house had come with a fully furnished study and a nearly full decanter of bourbon, just the way Billy had left it. Buck had never seen the bottle.

"Probably too expensive for ordinary folks," Jolene observed.

"Nothing ordinary about us, baby." He grinned and tickled one of her toes. She jerked her foot away.

Jolene asked, "So why are we sitting outside when we have air-conditioning?"

"It's not so bad out here now," he said. "And the

rain is nice. It reminds me of home."

Jolene didn't reply. Home, for him, would always be the Smoky Mountains. Home, for her, had always been wherever she happened to find herself. That was one of the many things they did not have in common.

Buck took her chin in his fingers and turned it toward the light from the bedroom, searching until he found the faint purple bruise there. He kissed the mark gently. "This guy who hit you," he said. "I want his name, address, and phone number."

She gave a small grunt of amusement. "So you can go beat him up? My hero."

"Beat him up, hell." Buck sat back and sipped his bourbon. "I want to hire him."

Jolene laughed at that, then took a sip of her chardonnay. "So, what's the brick doing on our foyer table?"

"Somebody tried to throw it through our window."

She lifted an eyebrow. "Anything broken?"

"The glass in your grandmother's photograph. But he missed the window."

"Well, that's good. Some of these windows are leaded glass. A pain in the ass to replace."

They were quiet for a time, swinging gently back and forth, listening to the hiss and pop of the rain. Buck caressed the slippery fabric that covered her thigh. "Junior Aikens came by," he said.

"Oh, yeah?" She glanced up at him. "What for?"

Buck took another sip from his glass. "I'm not sure. Maybe to throw a brick at the window?"

Both her eyebrows rose toward her hairline. "Any idea why?"

He shrugged. "None whatsoever. But the timing was suspicious, and he had a really lame excuse for stopping by."

"The historic plaque on the foyer table beside the brick?"

Buck nodded. "And he said he wanted to apologize for being rude this morning. He wants to take us out to dinner. On the other hand, he's the one who made the phone call to get our AC working again."

She lifted her glass. "In that case, we should definitely be the ones taking him out to dinner."

"There's something weird going on with him and Billy," Buck said thoughtfully. "With him and the whole town, really. I can't quite figure it out. It was like he was trying to warn me about something, but I don't know what it was."

Jolene said, "Any word on your missing infant?"

He shook his head and filled her in on the investigation at Hope House. "But we've got a lead on the birth mother, and Frankie is following up on it now," he concluded. "Hopefully we'll have some answers by morning." He glanced at her. "What are ombre nails, anyway?"

"Ombre is dark at the top and light at the

bottom. Sometimes they have designs painted on them, like flowers or stars."

"Expensive?"

"Depends. If you're some rich chick who has time to go to the salon every week for the upkeep, it wouldn't matter. Otherwise, it could mount up." She stifled a sigh. "I was going to have nail art done on my nails at the spa on the cruise ship. Then I was going to have my hair braided and beaded in the Bahamas."

Buck refused to take the bait. They had been forced to cancel their honeymoon cruise when he took the job in Mercy, and Jo wouldn't let him forget it. What she didn't know was that he had already rescheduled and re-ticketed the cruise for the week after Christmas, and nothing would get in the way this time.

He said, "I had lunch at Hollowgrove Plantation today. A construction crew found some old bones on the property while digging a swimming pool."

"Good lord," Jolene said. "Every time you tell me about your day, I'm glad I've got my job instead of yours."

He glanced at her with a deliberately straight face. "So let me ask you something. You teach sensitivity and de-escalation, right? How did you end up getting punched in the face?"

She frowned uncomfortably. "It was a role-playing exercise."

"Which went terribly wrong."

She elbowed him in the ribs. "Shut up. How was

lunch?"

"The whole place creeped me out, to tell the truth," he replied. "The old man is a racist asshole, and nobody deserves to be that rich. Everybody else is just plain messed up. They keep a bunch of immigrant workers in a trailer camp behind a padlocked chain-link fence."

"Jesus." She sipped her wine. "What about the bones?"

"The least of my problems," he told her. "The crazy thing is that it's Geraldine Whitley, the daughter, who was seen picking up our injured birth mother from the hospital."

Jolene lifted an eyebrow. "No such thing as a coincidence."

"Yeah," he agreed, "but I've got to admit, this one has got me stumped."

He put his arm around her shoulders, and she settled against him. The rain plopped gently on the railing and a breeze blew a gauze of damp air across their faces. She said, "Mama said you had Willis all fed, bathed, and ready for bed when she got home. I don't like to say this much, because I don't want it to go to your head, but I appreciate you."

He kissed her hair lightly. "I told you, I'm good at this."

"Who knew?" she conceded mildly.

"And," he informed her, "that's the second compliment I've gotten from a woman today. Miss Corinne told me she thinks Billy made the right decision hiring me. Although," he admitted, sipping his bourbon, "in her case, I think the compliment was more like a threat."

"It usually is," agreed Jolene.

Buck said, "Jamar Baker told Willis that my ancestors used to own his ancestors. I'm not sure I handled it right."

He felt her stiffen against him, but her voice was even. "What did you tell him?"

"The truth," he admitted. "That Jamar was right, and that what happened was wrong. But I don't like other kids talking to Willis like that. I wonder if I should have a conversation with Baker about it."

"No," she said flatly.

"I don't want anybody to make Willis feel like he's less than he is."

She took a sip of her wine. "Baby, the world is full of people who are going to try to make Willis feel less than he is. Our job is not to stop them. It's to make sure Willis doesn't believe them."

He guided her face toward his with the palm of his hand and felt the tension leave her shoulders as he kissed her. "I'm glad you're home," he said.

He felt, rather than saw, her smile. "Me, too."

"Jo," Buck said after a moment, "are you happy here?"

She thought about it for less time than he had expected. "Yeah," she said. "I am. I like this house. It makes me feel like I can unpack for the first time in my adult life. I like the yard and the garden and the street with all the magnolias, and the river. I like living here with you and Mama and Willis. We're starting to get to know folks. I even like the town, what I know of it." She glanced up at him. "I like being married to the chief of police. Didn't think I would, but I do. So yeah, all things considered, I'm happy. Why?"

"Oh..." He sipped from his glass again. "Just thinking about those crazy people at Hollowgrove, and something scaring a woman so bad that she'd abandon her baby and run barefoot across a field hours after giving birth, and the way Billy died..." He fell into a short, but heavy, silence, and Jolene did not interrupt. "Junior said something," he went on, "about there being a kind of ugliness here I haven't begun to uncover. He said the town was tainted. It got to me, I guess."

"'By the pricking of my thumbs/something wicked this way comes'", Jolene murmured. "Macbeth, Act Four, Scene One."

He smiled down at her. "There you go throwing your liberal arts degree in my face again."

She looked at him. "Are you happy here, Buck?"

"I'm happy with you," he answered, "and Willis and your mom. I'm starting to like the job. Everything else," he admitted, "is going to take a while." Then he added, "I'm going to put up a fence in the backyard."

"That'll be cute," she agreed. "White pickets, so Mama can plant more trailing roses. Better check with Miss Corinne first, and the Historical

Society."

"We can do whatever we want with the back," he pointed out, "as long as it's not visible from the street. I just can't figure out why Billy didn't do it before. He had kids, and an unfenced yard is a safety hazard this close to the river."

There was a muted buzzing, and Jolene fumbled in the oversized pocket of her caftan for a phone. "It's yours," she said, handing it to him. "I got it out of the drawer for you."

"Thanks, babe." Although in truth, he wasn't all that sure he was grateful. The evening had been a lot more pleasant with the remnants of the office stashed away in a drawer.

He glanced at the phone, expecting an update from Frankie. He was surprised at what he saw. "It's a major crimes alert from the county."

He frowned as he read the text, and Jolene sat up straighter, watching his face.

"They just found a woman dead in her partially burned car near the marsh about six miles west of Mercy," he said when he looked up at last. "Shot to death. They think she's been dead less than twenty-four hours."

"Good God," Jolene said.

Buck kept reading, his expression growing ever grimmer. "There was an employee parking sticker still intact on the windshield." He looked up at Jolene again. "It's from Hope House."

Jolene looked at him in the dimness, her eyes big and still. Then she said softly, "Something wicked."

CHAPTER TWENTY-THREE

Buck changed clothes before leaving the house because, as his wife informed him, the chief of police did not go to a crime scene wearing cargo shorts and a faded Mickey Mouse tee shirt. He forgot, however, to bring a rain jacket, and the drizzle beaded in his hair and crawled uncomfortably down the neck of his cotton shirt as he stood outside his car and watched his chief detective approach.

He had parked on the spongy grass shoulder behind a string of emergency vehicles, their lights pulsing blue and red streaks across the wet pavement. Frankie pulled her car in a few feet behind his, drawing the hood of her rain jacket over her hair as she got out. She saw him and ducked back into the car, re-emerging in a moment with a folded umbrella in her hand.

"Emergency equipment, Chief," she said when she reached him, and handed him the umbrella. "We sometimes get two or three of these showers a day this time of year."

"Thanks." He pushed a hand through his wet hair, squeezing some of the moisture out, and opened the umbrella. "And thanks for coming out. I hope it doesn't turn out to be a waste of time."

"It won't," she returned, and he knew she was right. In a county this size, two police incidents involving the same place in one day could not be a coincidence.

They walked together up the line of squad cars and crackling radios toward the rescue vehicles that were barricading the road. Buck said, "Any luck with Geraldine Whitley?"

"No, sir. She wasn't at her residence or the plantation office, and the security guard who followed me around like he thought I was going to rob the place said he didn't know when she'd be back. I waited around for an hour, then decided to try again in the morning. If," she added grimly, "I can even get back in. Those folks don't seem overly fond of law enforcement."

"Yeah, I got the same impression," Buck agreed.

Sheriff Tyler walked out of the foggy lights toward them, hands in the pockets of his jacket and shoulders hunched against the rain, his face grim. He was a round-faced man in tortoiseshell glasses whose demeanor—a least what little Buck knew of it—was usually genial. He could not have looked more miserable than he did tonight.

The two men shook hands wordlessly, and Buck said, "You know Detective Moreno?"

The sheriff nodded to her. "Frankie." He blew out a breath that steamed on the wet air and jerked his head back toward the swirling red lights of the fire and rescue trucks. "Hell of a mess. The Chief here says this might have some connection to a case you're working?"

"It looks that way," Frankie said. "Mind if I have a look?" She was already pulling on gloves.

"Go ahead." He added, "If you've got a mask in your pocket, you'll want it. The smell is..." He swallowed hard. "Bad."

Frankie glanced at him for just a moment of hesitation, then moved on through the rain.

Tyler gestured to Buck and the two of them followed her at a slower pace. "Female victim," Tyler said, "mid-thirties, three gunshot wounds to the chest. Looks like a nine-millimeter to me, but the body's not in great shape. Looks like she was killed here, in the car, and the perp tried to destroy the evidence by pouring gasoline over the car and setting it on fire. He didn't do a very good job of it though. Most of the gas was on the outside of the vehicle, so it just burned the paint off and blew out the back windows. The fuel tank was almost empty, so no combustion. The body itself was partially burned, but still intact. Passers-by called us."

"Any idea how long ago?"

Tyler shook his head. "Before the rain. We got the call about two hours ago, and the car was still smoldering when we got here. Hell, Buck, my people deal with gas station robberies and deadbeat dads. This is way out of our league."

He took a moment. "The M.E. is here. He might be able to tell us more." He looked at Buck through rain-speckled glasses, his expression bleak. "Listen, I appreciate your call. Like I said, we don't have a lot of experience dealing with something like this, and if you've got anything that can help, I'll take it."

Rain plopped on Buck's umbrella and dripped off the plastic covering of the sheriff's hat. The odor of charred metal and spent gasoline, mixed with the faint undertone of something vaguely sickening, grew stronger as they approached the site. Buck said, "You said she had a parking sticker from Hope House. We've got a woman we think ran away from there this morning, and her newborn is missing."

"Right," Tyler murmured. "Our boys were on the lookout." He nodded toward the confluence of lights and trucks just ahead. "There's a baby seat in back."

Buck closed the umbrella, pulled on gloves, and braced himself as he approached the crime scene barrier. He showed his badge to the deputy standing guard and ducked under the tape.

It didn't take long to understand why no one had noticed a burning car from the road until the fire was almost out. The Ford Escort was about twenty feet from the roadway, down a small incline, half in and half out of the marsh. Anyone noticing the smoke from the road might have assumed a small brush fire. In fact, had the front quarter of the vehicle not been lodged in swampy water, the brush fire would probably have been real. Tire tracks, glistening in the mud, showed where the car had left the road. Another set of tracks, made by a slightly bigger vehicle like an SUV or pickup, dug a path on the shoulder of the road and left black marks on the asphalt about twenty feet beyond where it had returned to the road.

Buck caught the attention of one of the deputies and said, "The people who reported the fire—did they drive down here?"

The deputy shook his head. "Not that I know of. They were in a little Civic, probably would've gotten stuck if they'd tried."

"Did anybody else drive down since you got here?"

"Too wet," the deputy said. "But there were footprints, work boots, where somebody left the scene, and slide marks from the same boots going downhill. We got photos."

Buck suggested, "Y'all might want to get photographs of these tire tracks, too."

Buck continued toward the blackened Escort, slipping a little on the downward slope. A crowd of uniforms surrounded the vehicle, most of them with their hands in their pockets, doing nothing but looking uneasy. The M.E.'s team had a gurney and a body bag ready. A police photographer was taking measurements and flashing his camera. Buck walked around the vehicle, shining his flashlight on the long dent along the driver's side. When he bent close, he could see black paint transfer.

Both doors of the vehicle were open, and Frankie was leaning into the passenger side. She straightened up when she saw him and removed her face mask, then quickly replaced it. Buck understood why when he reached her. He tried to protect his nose and mouth with the back of his arm, but his eyes watered with the fumes.

"Most of the fire damage was to the back," she told him, her voice muffled by the mask. She pointed her flashlight toward the gruesome figure in the driver's seat. "Three shots, close range. A lot of blood on the driver's seat, dry now. There's a baby seat in the back seat, and what looks like it might've been a diaper bag. Not much left of her purse. It was too badly burned to get an ID, phone melted. The back of the vehicle took the worst of the fire, but it looks like there might have been some luggage and one of those folding playpens or cribs. Forensics might be able to piece together an ID from that, but I understand the sheriff is running the tags now." She gave her report matter-of-factly. Frankie had come to Mercy from Miami-Dade and had no doubt seen worse than this.

Buck handed her the umbrella and took her flashlight. He tried to hold his breath as he ducked inside, focusing the flashlight beam on the passenger seat first, then the front windshield, which was cracked with heat and spattered with dried blood, and finally on the corpse. He avoided the blistered features and blackened limbs, and shone the light on the torso, confirming what both Frankie and the sheriff had said. Three shots, close range. Blood spatters on the steering wheel and driver's door. She had been facing the passenger seat when she died. He swung the flashlight to the backseat, where the melted remains of an infant car seat were still visible. It was facing backward, and correctly installed. Nothing on the floor except the safety glass that had shattered from the heat.

Buck backed out of the car, covering a coughing fit in his elbow. He gestured to Frankie to move uphill, and she returned the umbrella to him. He took a deep breath of rain-soaked air which, tainted as it was with the fumes from the car, still felt fresh to him, and said hoarsely, "Three shots at close range. Amateur. He could have killed her with one. Fire burned out before the evidence was destroyed. Amateur. He thinks he's smarter than he is. By a lot."

He coughed again, this time longer, and Frankie looked concerned.

"Are you okay, sir?"

Buck lifted a reassuring hand. "Fine," he managed. Not everyone knew that the same shooting that had mangled his leg had also taken part of his lung, and he didn't advertise the fact. "Listen," he said when he could, "the shooter was in the passenger seat. I think he ran her off the road and left his own vehicle to come down here and shoot her. He had to open the passenger door and get inside to shoot from that angle. He's bound to have left DNA that wasn't destroyed by the fire. The fire came later. Tire tracks say he came back not long before the rain started and set the car on fire. It couldn't have burned long before the rain put it out."

Frankie said cautiously, "Is this our case, Chief?"

Before he could answer a man spoke behind him. "We're ready to transport if y'all are about done here."

Buck turned to see the medical examiner, Dale Weatherstone, standing a few feet away. He had only met the doctor once, at a welcome lunch the Local Law Enforcement organization had given for Buck soon after he arrived in Mercy, but the man was not easy to forget. Standing six and a half feet tall, with a bushy gray mustache and a fierce gaze, Dale Weatherstone was rarely mistaken for anyone else. His height and his dour demeanor had earned him the unsurprising nickname of Lurch, but no one ever called him that to his face. He did not seem to be the kind of person who'd be amused by the reference.

Weatherstone stuck out his hand to Buck and said gruffly, "Lawson, right? Out of Mercy. What're you doing out here this far from home?"

Buck shook the other man's hand. "We think there might be a connection to a case we're working."

Weatherstone turned his dark, ruminating gaze from Buck to the vehicle, then back again. "Trouble will find you, I guess," he said. "You got everything you need from the scene?"

Buck saw the sheriff standing at the edge of the road, checking something on his phone. "You'll have to check with the sheriff on that," he said. "We're just visiting."

The three of them started up the slope toward the sheriff, who greeted them with, "The vehicle is registered to a Marianne Martindale, 213 Colonial Way, Apartment C-3, Mobile Alabama." He looked at the medical examiner. "Are you going to be able to get fingerprints?"

"Partials, maybe," replied Weatherstone. "There's a lot of swelling. It'll take a while."

Buck said to the sheriff, "You should try to lift prints from the passenger side of the car, since that's where the perp shot her from. The fire didn't do much damage to the passenger door, so there might be some prints left on the door handle."

"Good thing your perpetrator wasn't a very good arsonist," observed Weatherstone.

Frankie said, "Chief." She looked up from her

own phone. "I just double-checked my notes. Giselle Martindale's sister's name was Marianne, and her last known address in Mobile was 213 Colonial Way." She glanced down at her phone and added, "Apartment 3-C."

"Damn." Buck scowled, annoyed with himself for not recognizing the name immediately. "That would make her the aunt of our missing newborn." He glanced back at the car, remembering the baby seat. "And she was working at Hope House."

"Yes, sir," Frankie said. "She was the R.N. who was on duty last night when the baby was born."

Sheriff Tyler said, "Do you think maybe she had the baby you've been looking for this whole time?"

"Maybe," Buck agreed. To Frankie, he said, "We need a local address on Marianne Martindale."

"On it." She took out her phone and glanced up at him. "Do you think the baby might be at her house?"

Buck thought about it only briefly. "Unlikely. The luggage, the diaper bag, the crib...looks to me like she was on her way out of town with the baby. But as soon as you get a location, take a couple of uniforms and see what you can find." He looked at the sheriff. "If that's okay with you."

The sheriff said, "Hell, I'll supply the deputies if you need them."

Buck said, "We'll let you know what we find."

Frankie said, "Yes, sir." She started to walk away, working her phone.

Weatherstone asked the sheriff, "You ready for us to load up?"

"Yeah, go ahead," replied Tyler unhappily. "How soon can we have a preliminary?"

"It'll be a couple of days," he replied. "I've got two victims from that traffic accident last night, and an unattended death in Gray ahead of you." He glanced at Buck, "By the way, I was going to call you in the morning about your victims from Hollowgrove."

Frankie, overhearing, stopped and looked back.

Buck said, "I don't want you to prioritize them over this. Whatever happened to them was too long ago to be called urgent now."

"Maybe," agreed Weatherstone. "But homicide is homicide, and we've got to treat them the same."

Buck stared at him. "What are you talking about?"

"My team was able to recover all the remains," Weatherstone reported. "That's the good news. Two males between ten and twelve years old. One presented with a broken hyoid bone, indicating strangulation. The other had a blunt force trauma to the left temple resulting in a skull fracture and probable brain hemorrhage. These are just preliminary observations, nothing I'm ready to put on paper, but I doubt I'll find anything to change the probable cause of death. Not with what I've got to work with."

Buck frowned. "Can you tell how long ago it

happened?"

"Thirty years ago, at least," he said. "We found some remnants of clothing that might help us narrow it down further. I'll let you know."

Buck said, "What about race? Can you do DNA testing or anything on the skeletal remains?"

Weatherstone's heavy brows lowered even further in thought. "We can," he admitted, "but that would take a lot of time and a lot of money. We'd have to farm it out to a forensic anthropologist. There aren't too many of those around, and the ones there are are backed up for years."

"Yeah," Buck said thoughtfully. He doubted very much that the mayor would consider something like that a prudent expenditure of police department funds. "Thanks."

Weatherstone turned to go back down to the crime scene, and Sheriff Tyler said, "Sounds like you've got your hands full."

"Yeah," Buck agreed. "That's the job description."

Tyler said, "I'm thinking I'd better call in the GBI on this one. If I don't, it's still gonna be hanging around to haunt me at my retirement party, and that's the last thing I need."

"Maybe not," Buck said. "Give it a day or two, let me track down some leads. The victim's sister is still at large, and she might be able to give us all the answers we need. We need to talk to her employer and coworkers, take a look at where she lived, plain old-fashioned footwork."

Tyler asked, "Are you volunteering to take the lead on this case?"

Buck hesitated. "I'm volunteering to do what I can. I'll have Frankie keep your investigators up to date on what we find."

"Good enough."

They shook hands, and Buck trudged through the soggy ground to where Frankie was waiting a few feet away. She looked unsettled.

"I heard you talking," she said.

"Yeah?" The rain had eased to a mild mist, so Buck collapsed her umbrella and returned it to her. They walked toward their cars.

"It's probably nothing," she said. Her features were drawn into a troubled frown. "I mean, I don't see how it could be anything. But do you remember Jeff Gilford telling us that he'd heard about Hope House from a lawyer he'd met at a retreat or corporate function of some sort? Well, I interviewed that lawyer this afternoon, and it turned out he met Gilford last year at a hunting party weekend at Hollowgrove Plantation." She glanced up at him uncertainly. "Coincidence, right?"

"Right," murmured Buck, slowing his step. "Because we see so many of those in our business."

The two of them locked gazes for a moment, acknowledging the improbable, and parted to get into their separate vehicles. The case had just gotten a lot more complicated.

CHAPTER TWENTY-FOUR

Every morning between 5:00 and 6:00 A.M., Jolene ran the loop from their house on Magnolia, through the deserted downtown area for two blocks, and down Riverside Drive, where the mayor lived. All the streets in the historic district were toney—including the one in which Jolene lived—with wide, beautifully landscaped yards surrounding spacious Victorian-era mansions that overlooked the river. But the ones on Riverside Drive were set back further from the street, with deep views of the misty river between houses. At the end of the street was a small private park with a bench for enjoying the wide river vista, and a footbridge that led back to Magnolia. The loop was a little over three miles, and at that time of morning, it was cool enough, and bug-free enough, to enjoy the run.

She started out in the dark, and as she ran along the silent downtown sidewalks the day gradually lightened to gray. The only traffic she ever encountered was the occasional police cruiser, and when one passed the driver would flash his lights in acknowledgment or roll down his window and call, "Morning, Miz Lawson!" She had resigned herself to the fact that no one on Buck's force would ever remember she had not taken her husband's name when she married, and that old-fashioned mindset had its own kind of charm. She would always lift her water bottle in a returned greeting, even though most of the time she had no idea who the person behind the wheel was. She didn't think even Buck had had time to learn everyone's name yet.

She ran in biker shorts and a loose, low-necked tee shirt with a .38 tucked into a holster inside her sports bra beside her phone. If she had been in a gym, she wouldn't have covered up with a tee shirt, but she was the police chief's wife and as such she felt a certain amount of decorum was necessary. She was an attractive woman and she knew it, but, aside from a college education, courtesy of her early pageant days, the only thing being beautiful had gotten her so far was trouble. In the military, she had learned how to fight off would-be rapists, and in law enforcement, she'd learned how to quell leers and dirty jokes with a single hard look. Mercy was a quiet town, and the streets were empty. But she carried a gun because she was an attractive female, and she would be a fool not to.

By the time she reached Riverside, the mist that floated above the water had taken on a pink hue, and as she came closer to the footbridge, she would occasionally catch glints of gold morning light playing off the still water. It was a beautiful run, and even though she wasn't the kind of woman to indulge in pointless emotion, she couldn't deny a little thrill of wonder every time she looked up at the graceful mansions and the still, black river. One minute she was in Afghanistan with an M16 slung across her back, the next she was living in an antebellum mansion in a quaint Southern town with a Confederate statue in the park, going to church suppers and watching the sun rise over the river. How in the world had she gotten here? How could this be her life?

The lights in the mayor's house went on every morning at precisely 5:45, and it amused Jolene to know that fact, as though she was privy to some top-secret information. She liked to imagine the mayor going to the toilet, washing her face, making her eggs, and choosing her Chanel suit for the day, just like an ordinary person. Somehow, she always fell short on the "ordinary person" part, though. Whatever else Mayor Corinne Watts was, she was not ordinary.

The yellow squares of light from the mayor's house were half a block behind her when Jolene heard a vehicle turn onto the street. She couldn't help being surprised. There were only a dozen residents on Riverside Drive, most of them retired and none of them, with the exception of the mayor, were accustomed to being out of their homes before dawn. In all the time she'd been running this route she'd never met a car, either coming or going. She glanced over her shoulder as she moved away from the edge of the sidewalk and caught a glimpse of the headlights of a red Jeep Wrangler coming up behind her. The Jeep drew abreast and had almost passed her when the window rolled down and she heard the explosion of automatic gunfire.

Jolene dived for the cover of a boxwood hedge, drawing her pistol, crouching into firing position. Her breath roared in her ears and her heartbeat sounded like a train piston, but just as she steadied her aim on the back window of the passing vehicle, she heard the whoop of laughter coming from inside. That was when she realized the sound she'd heard had not been gunfire. It was firecrackers.

And yet her finger was on the trigger of her weapon, ready to squeeze.

Jolene drew in an audible gasping breath and sank back into the shadows of the hedge. She engaged the safety and re-holstered her gun. Her knees were shaking. Sweat dripped into her eyes. Vaguely she was aware of more lights coming on from houses up and down the street. Tires screeched as the jeep made the U-turn at the end of the road and started back toward her. Jolene's nostrils flared and she whipped out her phone.

"Go home, bitch!" the driver shouted when he passed her.

She snapped his photo.

"We don't need your kind here!" He hung his head out the window and shouted over his shoulder, "Go back to Africa!"

Jolene got another photo of the kid and a perfectly clear shot of the license plate before he rounded the curve, and she took it. She waited until the taillights disappeared before she resumed her run. And she was chilled all the way home.

Buck had just finished shaving when Jolene burst into the bathroom without knocking and plopped her cell phone down on the vanity top in front of him. "I want you to arrest this punk," she said. Her breathing was tight, her eyes hard. "Illegal use of fireworks within the city limits. Making terroristic threats. Public nuisance. Desecrating a historic zone. And..." she drew in a single, harsh breath, her eyes glittering. "Violation of the noise ordinance."

If there was one thing Buck had learned over the years of working with Jolene, and eventually marrying her, it was that when she ratcheted up, his only rational response could be to bring the temperature down. Doing so was automatic to him these days. Buck wiped the remaining shaving cream off his chin with the towel that was draped around his neck and picked up the phone. He examined the photo of a leering teenager hanging his head out of the driver's side window of a red jeep.

He said calmly, "Where and when?"

"Riverside Drive," she returned tightly. "About 5:50 this morning."

He asked, "What happened?"

"The stupid asshole threw live firecrackers out the window of his vehicle as it passed me on Riverside Drive." Each word was a sharp, staccato note, like stones being thrown at a window. "He turned around at the park and when he passed me again, he yelled at me to go home, or go back where I came from, something like that."

A police officer of Jolene's caliber did not mistake details or use words like "something like that." Buck pressed, "Which one? 'Go home' or 'go back where you came from?'"

"Oh, for God's sake, Buck, what difference does it make?" Jolene hugged her elbows tightly, her voice shrill. She dragged in a breath that ended in a choking sound. "I almost shot him," she said. Her eyes were suddenly bleak. "I had my gun out and… I almost shot that kid."

Buck felt his gut clench, and all he wanted to do was draw her into his arms and tell her everything was okay. He also knew that was the last thing she wanted or needed. He gave her a moment, and then he said, "Did you get the license plate?"

She reached forward impatiently and swiped to the next picture. He enlarged the photo and saw a perfectly clear Georgia tag number: Whitly4. His jaw tightened.

"What did he call you?" he said. "When he yelled out the window. Did he use the C-word, the B-word, or the N-word?"

She stared at him. "Oh, for God's sake, Buck, I'm not trying to open a federal hate crime case! I just want you to drag in a dickhead kid and put the fear of God into him!"

His voice was cold as he repeated deliberately, "What did he call you?"

She returned his stare, nostrils flaring breath for breath, and then she snatched the phone from him. "Bitch, okay?" she snapped. "The driver called me a bitch and told me to go back to Africa."

Buck made his shoulders relax with a concentrated effort. "Okay," he said. "E-mail me the photos. I'll take care of it. You take a shower and calm down before breakfast."

"Don't tell me to calm down," she shot back, her thumbs busy on the phone as she forwarded him the photos.

"Baby," Buck said, and waited until she looked up. What he saw in her eyes was more than anger, more than righteous indignation and runaway adrenaline. It was disappointment. She liked it here. She had felt safe here. She wanted to call this place home. She thought she was welcome. Now she was no longer sure, and it broke his heart.

He took her face between his hands and kissed her gently. "I'm sorry this happened. But we knew we were going to run into racist idiots here. After all, what do you expect from a town with—"

"A Confederate statue in the park," she supplied, looking frustrated and angry. "I know. But I've got a right to be pissed, don't I?"

"Absolutely." He gave her a moment. "But if it makes you feel any better, I don't think it was personal. There's a good chance it's related to this Whitley case. And I've got it, okay?"

After a moment, her features lost some of their tension. She took a breath and nodded. Then she frowned. "What are you doing up so early? You were up half the night working on that homicide."

He turned to pull on his shirt. "7:00 roll call."

"The police chief doesn't go to roll call," she pointed out.

"Yeah, well," he replied, "today I'm not the police chief." There was an edge to his voice as he checked his appearance in the mirror and straightened his collar. "Today I'm a cop."

He cupped her face with his palm, kissed her lightly once again, and left.

CHAPTER TWENTY-FIVE

Buck got a cup of bitter-tasting coffee from the break room and stood at the back of the call room while Sully briefed the day shift. A dozen officers were gathered there in folding chairs with notebooks and cups of stale coffee like the one he had, and the smell of the place—sweat and gun oil and testosterone—was as familiar to him as an old shoe. It felt like home, and it didn't.

In fact, this was only the third time Buck had been on the second floor, which housed the officers' lockers and squad room as well as the training room and break room, and he was annoyed with himself for that. He had gotten into the habit of keeping the same 8:00 to 5:00 schedule that Billy had, confining his role here to the first-floor administrative offices. But this was where he belonged. This was the heart of the building, the place where the people that he sent every day into harm's way worked, and he didn't like feeling like a visitor there.

Sully took the lectern at the head of the room and noticed Buck come in. Buck had updated Sully at midnight via email on the events of the night before, and Sully knew why he was there. He acknowledged Buck with a nod and proceeded with his shift briefing.

"Okay, folks, listen up." The murmuring and scraping of chairs subsided. "The holiday rush has hit early, starting with a three-car pile-up with injuries on Highway 127 at Poole Road. Marsky, Reynard, you relieve B shift at the scene as soon as we're done here. Traffic accident Number Two, the intersection of Pine and Windward, DUI with minor injuries. Deland, assist with clean up. Everybody else, stand by." He rested his gaze on Buck. "Chief?"

Buck made his way to the front of the room, aware of a certain tensing within the ranks as he passed. The last time he had addressed them all like this it had been to inform them that ten of their members had been fired for gross violations of department policy.

Buck nodded his thanks to Sully as he took the lectern. "First order of business," he announced, "is a new coffee maker in the break room." He grimaced and lifted his cup. "Seriously, I don't know how you all drink this shit."

There was nervous laughter throughout,

breaking the ice a little. Buck gave it a moment to die out, and he sobered. "Sometime yesterday a young woman named Marianne Martindale, a nurse at Hope House Women's Center, was shot to death at close range inside her Ford Escort with a nine-millimeter pistol. The perpetrator apparently then set her vehicle on fire and left it —and the body—to burn in the marsh off Peabody Road outside of Mercy. There was an infant seat securely fastened in the back seat of her vehicle."

There was some murmuring and shifting of bodies in their seats. This was not the kind of news they got every day. And it was not the kind of news they needed to hear two days before the busiest holiday weekend of the year.

Buck said, "Fortunately, yesterday's rain worked in our favor and the attempt to destroy evidence wasn't as successful as it could have been. The victim is identified as the sister of Giselle Martindale, the woman who encountered Officer Miller's vehicle about this time yesterday on Glenhaven Road. We believe Giselle Martindale to be the mother of the missing newborn, and that she gave birth a few hours earlier at Hope House. This is why I've volunteered the Mercy Police Department to assist the county sheriff with the homicide investigation of Marianne Martindale."

Buck glanced over the rows of faces until he found that of Trish Miller. She sat beside Baker, her back straight, her gaze intent, her expression perfectly still. A smear of color highlighted each cheekbone, otherwise, her face was perfectly white.

He went on, "We got security footage from her apartment complex showing the victim arriving at her home around noon. She left again at 2:15 and turned left out of her complex. She appeared to be followed by a black pickup truck, windows tinted, license plate obscured."

There was a rustle of movement as the officers took notes, glanced at each other, and shifted restlessly in their seats. Buck went on, "According to the evidence at the scene, the victim's vehicle may have been forced off the road and into the marsh. The killer then opened the passenger door, shot her three times at close range, and later returned to the scene and attempted to set the vehicle on fire. We don't know what became of the infant."

Again, there was uneasy movement in the ranks.

"I'm telling you all this, even though it's Detective Moreno's case, because we need to get this killer off the streets, and we need to do it now. We're looking for a black Durango with damage to the passenger side and possible traces of blue paint. Keep your ears open for talk about anyone with an unexpected newborn, and check the grocery stores, dollar stores, any place that sells baby supplies. As of this time, we don't have prints, but you all know who the bad guys in this county are. You'll be working with the sheriff's deputies to track them down and check them out. We're looking for a nine-millimeter handgun that might still be in the killer's possession, or it might have been tossed anywhere along Peabody Road. You'll be assisting in that search as well. This means most of you will be pulling doubles through the weekend."

He started to add "I'm sorry" but then he caught the expression in his officers' eyes. Determined, focused. This was what they had signed up for. This was what *he* had signed up for. Not traffic tickets and school crossings; not budgets and duty rosters. They weren't sorry. They were eager. So was he.

Maybe Billy was right. Maybe all it took was a few good men.

He said, "We're going to get this guy." He corrected, "*You're* going to get this guy." He glanced at his second in command. "Captain."

Sully stepped forward again. "All right. In addition, we have a report of a Peeping Tom at the Evergreen Campground. Johnson, you caught it. Site Number 52, a Caroline Nicholson complaining. Garrison, I need you at 428 Marshview to take a burglary report. Abe and Jill Eller came home from vacation to find their TV and two laptops missing. All this, and most folks haven't even finished their cereal yet. You can count on things getting worse."

He looked up from his notes. "The rest of you have your patrol assignments on your phones.

Keep your eyes and ears open. It's going to be a busy day." He closed his tablet.

"Finally, I'd like to welcome the newest member of the Mercy PD, Patrice Miller. She's a native of Mercy and comes to us with three years' experience under her belt from the Orlando PD. She'll be riding with Officer Baker for six weeks of field training. Let's all make sure she knows she made the right decision coming home. Miller, stand up."

Trish Miller got to her feet with a blush that was visible even from where Buck stood fifteen feet away. Every head swiveled to look at her, and her cheeks flamed even brighter. She ducked her head and sat down quickly.

Sully said, "Okay, you heard the boss. Hit the streets. Updates will be forthcoming. Eyes and ears."

As the room was filled with shuffling feet and scraping chairs, Frankie came in and pushed her way toward the front against the crowd. Buck caught Baker's eye and beckoned him forward as well.

"Sorry I missed the briefing," Frankie said, reaching them.

She was a little breathless and looked even more disheveled and rumpled than usual. Her clothes appeared to have been slept in, except that the dark circles under her eyes suggested she hadn't slept at all. Her hair was a rat's nest of tangles and her face puffy with exhaustion. Buck frowned when he saw her.

"Detective," he said, "you're no good to us if you're running on fumes. Did you get any rest at all last night?"

"Yes, sir," she replied distractedly. "I mean No, sir, not much." She pushed a hand through her tangled hair in a vague attempt to neaten it. "I stayed with the crime scene people until they finished up at Marianne Martindale's apartment. The place looked like it had never been lived in —no personal items, no clothes or mail. But," she added with satisfaction, "there was a newborn-sized diaper in the trash, and a receipt from a Dollar Store for infant formula and bottles. They got plenty of prints and DNA, although," she admitted, "I don't know how helpful the prints will be, given the condition of the body."

Buck nodded somberly. He had received updates from her throughout the night and knew most of this already. "Did Sheriff Tyler notify her parents?"

"Yes, sir. I understand they're on their way. He didn't say anything about Giselle," she added. "I asked him specifically not to. I thought it would be better if we all had that conversation together. And maybe by then we will have located Giselle—and the baby."

Buck said quietly, "She was the baby's aunt. Whatever happened between her and her sister, whatever agreement they did or didn't have, she was just trying to take care of her niece. She didn't deserve this."

A respectful silence followed. This was the part they always glossed over in training classes and police reports. The loss of innocent life. The survivors. The breaking of the bad news. The people who had to go on living after the worst day of their lives.

After a moment Buck said, "So we know the baby was with its aunt for at least part of the past twenty-four hours. But where is it now?"

"I don't think it would be a bad guess to say that whoever shot Marianne Martindale took the baby," offered Sully.

Frankie said, "I'm on my way to Hope House to see what I can find out, and I still have to talk to Geraldine Whitley. Meantime, I spent a couple of hours going through Hope House's financial records. Most of it was pretty straightforward, nothing to draw the attention of any accrediting agency or the IRS, at least that I could see. But there was one expenditure that kept showing up over and over, going back as far as ten years. Two or three times a year, sometimes more, there were payments of as much as $50,000 to Aegis, Incorporated. Aegis is the parent company of South Forty Farms, which is a branch of Hollowgrove Plantation Enterprises."

Buck frowned deeply and Sully said, "That's no small change. Any idea what the payments were for?"

Frankie shook her head. "But I'll find out. If

there's one thing I can't stand, it's a mystery."

"A mystery is just a question we haven't asked yet," Buck murmured.

Frankie shot him an odd look. "Yes, sir. Billy used to say that."

Buck forced a smile. "Probably where I heard it."

Baker had come up in time to hear most of this, accompanied by Trish Miller. She hung back a little, looking uncertain about where she was supposed to be.

Buck said, "Okay. Frankie, good work. Talk to whoever you have to at Hope House but bring that Summerfield woman back here for questioning. If she gives you any trouble, charge her with obstruction. She's in this up to her ass, and if she doesn't know where the baby is, she knows who does."

"What about Geraldine Whitley?" Frankie said. "She's our best lead on finding the birth mother."

Buck said, "Leave her to me. I've got to go out there sometime today to talk to the old man, and I'll see what I can find out from Geraldine then. Right now, I want you full-time on the Marianne Martindale case."

"Yes, sir."

"I'll ask the sheriff to station a deputy at Martindale's apartment," Buck went on, "just in case Giselle shows up. I'll text you whatever comes in from the M.E.'s office. Also..." He glanced at Sully. "Can you put somebody on the phone to call around and find out who does ombre nails around here? With art details," he specified. "You know, little flowers and designs and such. Giselle was probably a regular customer, and if she was, they've got credit card info on her, maybe even a contact number."

"Ombre," Sully repeated, and took out his notebook. "How do you spell that?"

Miller cleared her throat. "Um, sir?"

Buck looked at her.

Miller shot a quick glance at Baker and said, "That salon we were at yesterday, the one where we arrested that kid?"

Baker nodded impatiently, encouraging her to go on. She looked back at Buck.

"The manicurist wasn't on duty yesterday, but the salon owner said, when I interviewed her about Paulo—that's the kid we arrested—that they hired him to sweep up after he quit his last job, which was driving the shuttle for Hollowgrove Plantation. That's why she wasn't worried about references, because she figured the Whitleys had already cleared him, and she was really shocked that he had drugs because she knew Hollowgrove was really strict about their employees."

Baker made an impatient spinning motion with his finger, and she flushed. "The point is, sir," Miller hurried on, "the salon owner said Paulo would drive a group in from Hollowgrove every two weeks to have their nails done."

Baker frowned. "I thought all they did out there

at Hollowgrove was shoot birds."

"Not all," Frankie said. "I went to a wedding there one time, and I think they have corporate events and things like that."

"So, the shuttle the kid was driving, it was to take guests into town to have their nails done?" said Sully.

"I assume so, sir," replied Miller. "The owner said the ladies came to her salon because her manicurist was the fastest in the county with nail art."

Buck said, "You told Officer Baker you thought this Paulo recognized the photo of Giselle, and that's why he ran."

She straightened her shoulders. "Yes, sir. That was my impression."

Sully said to Buck, "That might explain how Giselle knew Geraldine Whitley. If she was a guest at Hollowgrove or had been."

Buck replied thoughtfully, "Maybe. But it doesn't explain why he ran." He added, "It's worth tracking down that manicurist and seeing what she can tell us about Giselle Martindale. Baker, you and Miller are on it. I'll talk to this Paulo character myself. He's still in our jail, right?"

Sully glanced at his watch. "Scheduled for transport to county at 3:00."

Baker said, "Anything else for us, Chief?"

Buck said, "Yeah. Yesterday somebody threw a brick at my house with the message 'back off' written on it. This morning somebody threw a string of live firecrackers at Jolene while she was running on Riverside Drive."

Buck saw Baker's expression darken, as he had known it would.

"We got a complaint from the mayor about the noise violation," Sully said. "B-shift took the report."

"Here's your perp." Buck took out his phone and brought up the photographs Jolene had taken.

Sully looked at it first, and Buck turned the phone to show Baker and Frankie. He thumbed over to the photo of the vanity license plate, Whitly4, and Sully nodded. "Yeah, I thought he looked familiar. Zach Whitley's oldest."

"The air conditioning guy?" Buck said.

"Right. Nate, I think his name is. A real smart-ass. We picked him up a couple of times for misdemeanors—vandalism, underage drinking—but somebody was always here to take him home before we even finished booking him. Far as I know, he never even went before a judge."

Buck put his phone away. "Well, he's not going home with daddy this time. Let's see what a couple of nights in jail does for his attitude."

Sully looked both amused and skeptical. "We can charge him with a fireworks violation, but as soon as we do his folks will bail him out. So, what are we holding him on?"

"I'll let you know," Buck replied. "I've got forty-eight hours to decide."

Sully grinned crookedly. "You got it, boss. I'll

put the word out to patrol."

"No," Buck said, unsmiling. He met Baker's glowering gaze. "This one is Baker's."

Baker nodded sharply, his hands resting on his gun belt. "Yes, sir."

"The kid is probably still in town," Buck said, "but you are authorized to go as far as necessary to bring him in." He paused, aware that his instructions could be taken more than one way. He might have clarified, but all he said was, "I want that kid in my jail before the end of the day."

Baker replied, "You got it, Chief."

Buck nodded. "All right everybody, thanks. Let's get to work."

CHAPTER TWENTY-SIX

The three officers started toward the stairs when Buck said, "Miller, hold back five seconds."

Trish cast a quick alarmed looked at Baker, who said simply, "Meet you at the unit." She walked back to Buck and Sully, shoulders tensed, chin high.

Buck said, "I'm sorry we didn't get to our welcome interview yesterday." He smiled, trying to put her at ease. "Seems like we threw you in the pool head-first."

Her shoulders relaxed a fraction. "Yes, sir. I mean, that's what I'm here for, sir."

Buck gestured her forward, indicating she should accompany them as they walked toward the elevator. The stairs in the old building were steep, and Buck did not entirely trust his injured leg with them at this hour of the morning. That was probably another reason he didn't visit the second floor often.

"I read Baker's first-day assessment of you," he said.

She said quickly, "I'm working on it, sir. I'll get better."

He glanced at her with a mildly raised eyebrow. "It was entirely positive."

She swallowed hard and clasped her hands behind her back. A wine-colored stain spread across her cheeks.

Buck said, "Law enforcement is not easy on female officers. There've been a ton of studies that show females have faster reflexes, sharper instincts, and are ten times better at conflict resolution than male officers are. But it looks like most of us haven't gotten the memo on that yet. The chances are you're always going to be underestimated, underappreciated and underutilized. I apologize in advance."

She glanced at him quizzically and he went on, "I want you to know that here at the Mercy PD, every officer is an essential part of the team. Hell, we're way too understaffed not to take full advantage of every single resource. So I'm going to need you to give us everything you have, even if it means fighting off a few assholes in the process. Okay?"

Her shoulders relaxed, and she smiled. "Yes, sir. I've fought off a few in my time."

He returned her smile. "So, what brought you back to Mercy? Just to be with family?"

They had exited the meeting room and were walking down the hall, which by now was mostly empty. She took a moment before replying. "No, sir. I mean," she amended quickly, "Yes, sir, but not entirely. I'm glad to be home, naturally, but the reason I wanted to work for you was... well, you fired a third of the officers in your first week here because they weren't good enough." She drew a breath and straightened her shoulders once again, looking him in the eye. "I wanted to be part of a team where only the ones that were good enough got to stay."

Buck stopped walking and looked at her for a long moment. "Good answer," he said at last and started walking again toward the elevator. "You only need three things to work for me," he went on. "Honesty, commitment, and courage, in that order. I'm impressed with what I've seen from you so far, Miller." They had reached the elevator. Buck stopped to put his barely touched cup of coffee on a table by the elevator door and turned to offer his hand to Trish. "Welcome to the Mercy PD, Officer Miller. Keep up the good work."

She shook his hand firmly, her expression glowing. "Yes, sir. Happy to be here."

Sully pushed the elevator button and the door opened almost immediately. Buck stepped inside. Trish stood there uncertainly for a moment, then gestured toward the elevator. "Should I, um...?"

Sully caught the door just before it closed. "Take the stairs, Miller," he said.

She scurried off, and Sully stepped inside the elevator.

"Good hire," Buck observed as the doors closed.

"Yeah, I think so," Sully agreed. "Listen," he said as the elevator lurched downward, "I figured I better check on what you wanted to do about Hobo for the Fourth."

Buck stared at him for a moment, unblinking. "Hobo," he repeated. "The alligator?"

Among the town's many eccentricities was a 75-year-old alligator, completely toothless, who had been named the town's mascot. He wore a red collar to advertise his status as a protected animal and wandered the streets, parks, and fountains of Mercy with impunity. There were humorous signs all over town warning folks of the town ordinance that set a $3000 fine for anyone found harming or harassing the alligator. Buck was not a fan of either the ordinance or the alligator.

"That's right," Sully said. "I know you're not that crazy about the old dude, but he's a real tourist draw. Lots of folks come back every year just to take selfies with him. On the other hand, having him wandering loose like that with so many strangers in town can be a problem, so Billy used to put up a temporary fence around the fountain in the park to keep him enclosed and out of the way. People can still pet him, bring him scraps from their lunches, take pictures and all, but he's not holding up traffic or knocking over toddlers with his tail."

Buck murmured, "Right."

"Of course, we have to station an officer with him around the clock," Sully added, "and being short-handed and all…"

An active murder investigation, a missing mother and newborn, a thirty-year-old double homicide, and a pet alligator taking up police resources on the Fourth of July. Such was the nature of keeping the peace in Mercy, Georgia.

Buck said, "How are you going to get him in the pen?"

"A couple of guys, a raw chicken, and a pickup truck," replied Sully confidently. "To tell the truth, I think he kind of enjoys the ride."

The doors opened on the first floor. "You're officially in charge of Operation Hobo," Buck said. "Carry on as always."

"Yes, sir. Have you given any more thought to the parade?"

"Still thinking."

They walked past the receptionist's desk and Buck greeted her, "Morning, Stephanie."

"Good morning, Chief. Captain Sullivan." She reached quickly for her phone, no doubt to alert Lydia to their imminent arrival.

Buck went on, "Listen, Sully, do me a favor, will you? Give ICE a call and find out what kind of complaints they've had about Hollowgrove in the past few years. They're trying to hide something out there besides old bones, and I need to figure out what it is. That'll at least give me a place to start."

"Yes, sir, boss. I know one of the regional agents. It shouldn't take him too long to look it up. In the meantime…"

The way he paused made Buck look at him, waiting.

Sully said, "We wrote fourteen citations yesterday for speeding and traffic light violations, most of them on 127 between the elementary school and Savannah Road. We responded to three multi-vehicle collisions without injuries and two parking lot fender-benders. Today and tomorrow are the two biggest traffic days leading up to the Fourth. I'm afraid if our boys get caught up working a bad wreck—which is bound to happen if we pull them off patrol—there's not going to be anybody left to work these two major investigations."

Buck grimaced and pinched the bridge of his nose. He had studied the numbers until his dreams were haunted by them, and he knew it took every one of Mercy's police officers to cover the major holidays and the summer tourist traffic. The problem was that, thanks to him, the number of officers was now reduced by thirty percent. The mayor was right. He'd thought he was doing the right thing, but this one was on him.

He said, "Yeah, okay. Put a couple of unmanned vehicles with lights flashing at the intersection of

Savannah and 127, and again at the elementary school. Maybe that'll slow people down. I'll try to get us some extra help from the state patrol."

"Yes, sir. Sounds like a plan."

"And Sully."

Sully glanced at him as they pushed through the metal door that led to the administrative offices.

Buck said, "I'm sorry about this. I thought recruitment would go faster. I thought," he clarified, "we'd get more qualified candidates."

"Billy was more of a warm-bodies kind of man when it came to hiring," Sully admitted. "Small town like this, he figured if it could walk and shoot and drive a car, that's all he needed. Turns out, that didn't work out so well."

"But he had enough men to handle Fourth of July traffic," Buck pointed out unhappily.

"Who knows?" Sully said. "Maybe the Marines got it right. Maybe a few good men are all it takes."

Buck glanced at him, surprised. "You're the second person who's said that to me."

Lydia was coming down the hall toward them. She looked surprised and disapproving, but perfectly put together as always in a figure-hugging white sheath splashed all over with red and blue flowers, her hair done up in a neat bun, her earrings tiny replicas of the American flag. She had her notebook and the day's schedule with her, but no coffee. "Chief Lawson," she said, "you're here early."

"So I am," he agreed. "You look stunning today, Lydia."

"I think that's probably a workplace-inappropriate comment," she replied, walking with them toward the chief's office.

"I think you're probably right. And I like your earrings."

"Thank you, sir. But..."

"Before I forget," he interrupted, "we need a new coffee maker in the upstairs break room. Get something nice that makes decent coffee. And speaking of which..."

"Yes, sir." She made a note. "We're making a fresh pot." She slid a look toward him that was mildly accusing, as though he had a nerve to ask for coffee when he wasn't even due in the office for another ten minutes. She went on, "I'm compiling last night's reports for you now. Here's today's schedule. Don't forget you're the guest speaker at the League of Women's Voters' luncheon tomorrow. Your speech is on your computer. I've updated the template Billy always used with today's statistics, but of course, you'll want to modify it to suit your style. Also, the mayor called. Good morning, Captain Sullivan."

"Good morning, Lydia."

Buck glanced over the schedule as the three of them walked toward his office. "I'm in the middle of a homicide investigation," Buck said, "two missing persons investigations, and a town full of Fourth of July tourists. I don't have time for a luncheon."

Lydia slowed her step, fixing him with a hard look. "Sir, it's the League of Women Voters." She said it with the same distinct emphasis she might have given the words "it's the *pope*."

"I understand, but—"

She interrupted, "The Chief of Police always addresses the League of Women Voters at their July luncheon. It's tradition."

Sully said nothing, but Buck could sense his amusement.

"The mayor," Lydia added deliberately, "will be there. And the paper always covers it."

It took little more than a glance to assure Buck that there would be no arguing with Lydia on this point. "One hour," he said, scowling. "I can give them one hour."

"Yes, sir," replied Lydia. Her tone was crisp and professional. "Also..." They had reached the closed door of his office. "Mr. Gilford is waiting in your office."

"Good," Buck said, gesturing for Sully to accompany him. "I want to talk to him." He paused before opening his office door. "Say, Lydia, do you know what brand of bourbon Billy drank?"

"Yes, sir," she replied, making a final note. "It was Hollowgrove's special label. Mr. Whitley sent him a case every Christmas. Shall I call out there and order you some?"

"No," Buck said. He glanced at Sully and murmured, "All roads lead to Hollowgrove."

Sully lifted an eyebrow and inclined his head in agreement. "Starting to look that way."

Jeff Gilford was sitting on the edge of the blue velvet sofa, but he stood immediately when Buck opened the door. He said, "Chief Lawson. I'm sorry to bother you this early."

"It's no bother. You remember Captain Sullivan?"

The two men nodded a greeting and Buck glanced around the office. "Where's your wife, Mr. Gilford?"

Jeff Gilford smiled and smoothed his hands on the front of his khaki trousers. He looked both nervous and excited, and very anxious to be on his way. "She's in the car," he replied, "with our little girl. That's why I'm here," he rushed on. "We're dropping our complaint. We have our baby, and we're on our way home."

CHAPTER TWENTY-SEVEN

Buck moved behind his desk and gestured for Jeff Gilford to be seated. Gilford remained standing and went on in a rush, "Mrs. Summerfield called late yesterday and left a message explaining how the birth mother had changed her mind—again—and returned her baby to Hope House. Our baby. Our baby, our little girl, had been cleared by their pediatrician and was ready to go home with us. Of course, on the advice of counsel we weren't taking her calls but how could we ignore that? Anyway, long story short, we called her back, she explained everything, and we ended up driving back down here last night. Beth cried all the way down, afraid it was going to be another disappointment, but it wasn't."

He paused and smiled and pulled an envelope from his jacket pocket. "Mrs. Summerfield met us at the door with baby Arabella in her arms. They were even nice enough to put us up in one of their guest suites overnight. Here's the pre-adoption form. The final papers won't come from the state for a month or so, but I thought you'd want to see this."

He handed the envelope across the desk to Buck. "Chief Lawson," he said sincerely, "I'm truly sorry for the trouble this has caused. My lawyer said I should be sure to officially withdraw my complaint before we left town, so that's what I'm doing. Mrs. Summerfield also said she'd be in touch with you this morning."

Buck sat down and withdrew the papers from the envelope, murmuring, "I'm sure she will be. We have a detective on the way to talk with her now."

Jeff Gilford looked deflated. "Oh. Again, I'm sorry for the trouble."

Buck took his time finding a pair of reading glasses in his desk drawer, unfolding the papers, and reading through them. Sully, meantime, stood by the door, busy on his phone—texting Frankie, Buck hoped. Finally, Buck looked up from the document and smiled at Gilford. "Arabella," he said. "I like it."

Gilford said, "It was my grandmother's name. We picked it out years ago." He added, "Would you like to see a picture?"

Buck said, "I would."

While Gilford was bringing up the photo on his

phone, Buck punched the intercom button. "Lydia, would you step in here for a moment?"

Jeff Gilford came around the desk to show Buck the photo, and Buck couldn't help smiling at the screwed-up little face wearing a pink headband with a bow atop her bald head, nested in a bed of pink and white lace. "She's a cutie all right," Buck said, and Gilford looked both proud and abashed.

"I know I'm acting like a dopey dad," he said, putting the phone away. "I don't seem to be able to help myself."

"Mr. Gilford," Buck began, and was glad when the connecting door between his office and Lydia's opened, delaying what he had to say.

Lydia set a steaming mug of coffee on Buck's desk and glanced at Gilford. "Mr. Gilford, may I bring you some coffee?"

"Oh, no, thanks," he said quickly, "my wife is waiting in the car, and I really have to get going."

Buck said, "Actually, this might take a few minutes." He passed the adoption documents to Lydia. "I need a copy of this," he said, "and can you please get me the Gilford file from Frankie's desk?"

"Right away, sir."

Lydia started to leave, but Buck held up a delaying finger. He looked at Gilford. "Are you sure about that coffee?"

The other man glanced at his watch. "I'm sorry, we need to get on the road. Do you think you could speed this up?"

"I'm afraid not." Buck looked past Gilford to

Sully. "Captain, do you mind going out to the parking lot and asking Mrs. Gilford to come in? There's no point in her waiting in the car in this heat."

"Oh," said Jeff Gilford quickly, "She won't bring the baby inside. Germs, you know."

"She and little Arabella can wait in the detectives' office," Buck assured him. "There's no one there and we have plenty of hand sanitizer and face masks." He glanced at Lydia. "Lydia, maybe you can find one of the staff to sit with Mrs. Gilford and make sure she has everything she needs."

"Absolutely, sir." She turned to Jeff Gilford and added, "Cream and sugar?"

Jeff Gilford looked completely confused. "Yes, thank you. I mean, I really don't have time..."

But Lydia was already leaving, and Sully was gone.

Buck said, "Sit down, Mr. Gilford." This time it was not an invitation.

Gilford sank uneasily to the edge of the sofa, and Buck leaned back in his desk chair. He picked up his coffee cup, but it was still too hot to drink. He set the cup down and took a moment to choose his words.

"I'm really glad this worked out for you and your wife, Mr. Gilford," he said. "And I hope everything continues to go well. But things have gotten a little complicated since we talked last time, and I think it's only fair that I bring you up to date. But first, I need to ask you some questions."

Gilford rubbed his hands together nervously. "I don't understand."

"I know you don't." Buck genuinely felt bad for the guy. He took out a legal pad and a pen. "Mr. Gilford, what time did you say you received the call about the baby from Ms. Summerfield?"

He barely hesitated. "Yesterday, around 4:00 p.m. It came to my office, through my secretary. Like I said, I wouldn't have returned the call, but she left the message."

Buck made a note. Marianne had been murdered, by best estimate, between 3:00 and 5:00 p.m. "So, you were at work. Where was your wife?"

"She was at a DAR meeting. Daughters of the Revolution. She helps place wreaths on the graves of soldiers every Independence Day."

Of course, she does, thought Buck, and he felt like a jerk.

"What time did you get to Mercy?" Buck asked.

"Around 10:00 last night. We Facetimed with Ms. Summerfield, saw the baby, called our lawyer, and then we just left to drive down here. We didn't even pack toothbrushes."

By 10:00, Marianne Martindale had been dead for hours, and Buck himself was investigating the scene.

Buck said, "Do you own a handgun, Mr. Gilford?"

The other man looked both horrified and outraged. "Are you serious? Absolutely not! We're baby-proofing our home, for God's sake!" His eyes narrowed in sudden suspicion. "Wait. What is this about? Why are you asking?"

Buck took off his glasses and put them on the desk, leaning back in his chair. "You told my detective that you were recommended to Hope House by a lawyer you met at a shooting party at Hollowgrove. Is that the same lawyer who's representing you now?"

Gilford shook his head, looking worried. "No. No, the man I talked to was just somebody that does business with my company. Doug Evans. I gave his contact info to the detective. My attorney is Dale Richter." His brows drew together anxiously. "Do I need to call him? Is something wrong?"

Buck shook his head. "No. You're not in trouble, and as far as I can tell the adoption seems to be in order. This is just part of an ongoing investigation that I hope you might be able to shed some light on."

Gilford appeared to relax, and Buck said, "How did you happen to be at Hollowgrove when you met Mr. Evans? Are you a member of the hunting club?"

"No," Gilford said, "but my company has a membership. Hastings Enterprises," he supplied. "Maybe you've heard of us? One of the largest manufacturers of paper products in the southeast."

Buck pretended to be impressed. "So do you come down often?"

"No, it was just that once. A corporate retreat." He looked mildly abashed. "To tell the truth, guns and hunting and shooting aren't really my thing, but you know." He shrugged. "You've got to go along to get along. Fortunately for me, the weekend turned out to be more about drinking and networking than killing things."

Buck said, "And Mrs. Gilford? Was she there?"

Gilford shook his head. "No. We've had other corporate retreats where the wives come, but my understanding was that wives weren't allowed at the quail shoot."

Buck lifted an eyebrow. "Any idea why?"

Gilford looked uncomfortable. "I heard some of the men say wives are a distraction at a hunting party, but if I'm honest, I don't think that was it."

"No?"

The other man hesitated, chewing his inner lip. "Look, I'm not saying anything for sure. I probably shouldn't say anything at all, because I don't really know." He fell silent.

Buck picked up his mug again and took a sip of his coffee. "That's okay. Why don't you just tell me what the weekend was like? I've never been on one of these hunting weekends." He smiled. "I like to shoot quail, but something like Hollowgrove is way out of my price range. So how was it?"

He answered carefully, "There were twelve of

us, just the Senior VPs, and a few of our best clients with their people, like that lawyer, Doug Evans. We each had private rooms, either in the house or in one of the cabins on the property, but all our meals and social events were in the main house. It was damn nice, I'll tell you that, but it should've been for what they charged."

The door opened and Lydia slipped in, placing a coffee cup and a bowl containing sugar and creamer packets on the end table next to Jeff Gilford, then leaving the file folder and the copies Buck had requested on the desk. Buck said, "Thank you, Lydia. Is Mrs. Gilford settled in the detectives' office?"

"Just now, sir," she replied. "Hannah is sitting with them. She has a little one of her own."

"Good deal," Buck said. He opened the folder and glanced through it. "Ask Sully to join us when he can, will you?"

"Yes, sir."

Lydia closed the door as she left, and Buck looked up with an encouraging smile to Gilford. "I know your family will be more comfortable here than in the car. Now, you were saying?"

Gilford returned a strained smile and stirred sugar into his coffee. "I just hope this doesn't take long. We should have been on the road already."

Buck prompted, "You were talking about Hollowgrove, and your weekend there."

Gilford emptied a packet of creamer into his cup and cleared his throat. "Well, like I said, it was nice. And pretty much what I expected the first day. We had a tour, got settled in our rooms, had lunch. There was an orientation on gun safety and hunting protocols in the afternoon, then cocktails and dinner. Everyone was assigned a hostess, like a cabin steward on a ship, you know." He continued to stir his coffee, not meeting Buck's eyes. "Her job was to make sure you had everything you needed." He paused. "But I, uh, got the feeling that went beyond just bringing extra towels and refilling your wine glass at dinner."

Buck couldn't help thinking about the pretty Marina, so attentive, so skilled. *I'm your hostess*, she had said. He said, "Like how far beyond?"

Sully came in quietly and stood by the door. Buck glanced up from the note he was making on the legal pad, but Gilford barely seemed to notice Sully's entrance.

Gilford started to pick up his coffee cup and then set it down again, deliberately, on the coaster. Finally, he met Buck's eyes. "Look," he said. "I need to be clear. This is not something I participated in. I have no direct knowledge of anything."

Buck nodded reassuringly, and Gilford went on, "I mean, at the place Beth and I were in, after everything we'd been through, do you think I'd jeopardize my marriage for a weekend?"

Buck said, "I don't, not for a minute. I'm just trying to get to the truth, here. Anything you can tell me about what went on at Hollowgrove that weekend will be a big help." He picked up his coffee cup again. "The hostesses. They were attractive? Young?"

Gilford nodded. "But in a classy way. Their hair, their nails, the way they dressed and moved... even their perfume. They were all... what's the word? Understated. More like one of the trophy wives you'd see at the country club than..." He stopped and picked up his own coffee cup, taking a sip.

"Than call girls?" Buck supplied.

He nodded, and even seemed relieved to hear it said out loud.

Buck made another note. "So, are you saying the men on the retreat paid to have sex with these women?"

Gilford looked at him. "I think that was the point. At least from the talk I heard. But the guests —the guys on the retreat— didn't pay anyone. The word was that the women were all part of the 'premium package.'"

Buck turned a page in the report on his desk. "And that was on November 13 of last year?"

"That's right. But I really don't see what this has to do with..."

Buck said, "I'll need you to make a list of everyone who was there that weekend before you leave town."

Gilford stiffened his shoulders. "Look, I've answered your questions. I've been as polite as I can. But I'm leaving now." He put his coffee cup down and stood. "If you need anything else, contact my lawyer. I gave his number to your detective."

Sully took a subtle step in front of the door, and Buck said, "We can do that, of course. But that's not going to get you back to Atlanta any sooner."

Gilford stared at him. "What are you talking about?"

Buck said, "Mr. Gilford, a young woman was murdered last night, and we believe it was related to an attempt to kidnap your baby." At Gilford's horrified expression, Buck held up a calming hand. "The investigation has just begun. But until we know more, I can't let you leave town."

Buck could see the thoughts racing across the other man's eyes, and it was a moment before Gilford could speak. "But, of course, we're leaving. We have a home, and a nursery, and a life back in Atlanta. You can't keep us here!"

"Actually, I can," Buck replied apologetically. "I'm taking you all into protective custody. Don't worry, we'll put you up in a nice hotel and make sure you have everything you need, all at our expense. It shouldn't be more than twenty-four hours. Believe me, this is the simplest way. You don't want to get the APD involved."

Gilford's tone, and his expression, were stunned. "This is a nightmare."

"I understand." Buck nodded to Sully. "Why don't you take Mr. Gilford to his wife while I make arrangements for them to stay overnight?"

Sully gestured Gilford toward the door, and Gilford jerked out his phone, suddenly roused from his stupor of shock. "I'm calling my lawyer."

"Give him my number," replied Buck.

He punched the intercom button as Sully left with Gilford, the other man scrolling furiously through his phone. "Lydia," Buck said, "call the Holiday Inn and make a reservation for the Gilfords for the weekend. Put it on the city's tab. They'll probably say they're full but mention the mayor's name."

Buck was sipping his coffee and tapping his pen thoughtfully on the open file folder before him when Sully returned.

"Those are two very unhappy people," Sully reported, tilting his head toward the office down the hall where he had left the Gilfords.

"They'd be a lot less happy if we let them leave here with a baby they might not get to keep," Buck replied.

"It's a mess, all right," Sully agreed. Then, "You don't really make Gilford for the killer, do you?"

"Not a chance in hell," Buck replied. "I really don't even peg him for co-conspirator, but until we're sure..." He shrugged. "The Gilfords stay put. Did you get in touch with Frankie?"

"She's at Hope House now," Sully said. "Do you want to call off the search for the baby?"

"Let's wait to hear from Frankie," Buck said. "We don't have any proof that the Gilfords' baby is the same one Giselle Martindale gave birth to. There's no identifying information on the adoption form."

Sully nodded, then said, "So, hookers at Hollowgrove? Again, can't say I'm surprised. Are we opening an investigation?"

Buck finished his coffee, closed the folder, and stood. "I think we already have," he replied. "I just can't figure out which one. I'll be in the basement," he added. "Text me if you hear from Frankie."

CHAPTER TWENTY-EIGHT

The truth about detective work, as Frankie tried to explain to anyone who thought she led an exciting life, was that it was mostly routine. You asked questions, you got answers. Sometimes those answers led to other questions, which you asked and got answered. Sometimes the questions ran out, and your case went completely dead. That was an outcome Frankie tried very hard to avoid.

Yesterday had been an exercise in frustration, with far more questions than answers. Today, with much more at stake, would be different.

She arrived at Hope House at 7:55 and stopped in front of the small gatehouse. A uniformed guard was walking toward one of the cars parked in a small gravel lot a few feet away, while another, spotting her from inside the gatehouse, waved her forward. Frankie ignored him and got out of the car.

"Excuse me!" she called to the guard who was walking toward his car. He turned around and she held up her badge. "Detective Moreno, Mercy Police Department," she said as she approached. "Are you Charles Levitz?"

He was a man in his late fifties with graying hair and middle-aged spread, most likely a retired cop. He waited until she got close enough for him to read her badge, and then extended his hand. "I reckon you're here about the kidnapping yesterday, or whatever it was. Guess you heard it all turned out okay. They brought the baby back yesterday afternoon."

Frankie said, "Who brought the baby back?"

"That Whitley woman. The same one who checked the expectant mother in this winter."

Frankie tried to hide her surprise. This was made easier when the other guard opened the door of the gatehouse and looked out curiously. "Hey Charlie," he called. "Everything okay?"

Charlie lifted his hand in assurance and, after another moment, the other guard went back inside the shelter.

"George Upton," Charlie explained, "my day relief. I guess you talked to him already."

Frankie nodded. "Yesterday morning. He wasn't able to be of much help, since he wasn't here when the incident occurred. I tried to reach you all day yesterday."

He nodded, unsurprised. "Earplugs. I sleep during the day, you know."

She said, "You said Ms. Whitley brought the baby back to Hope House yesterday. What time?"

"Well, it was before I came on shift, but the log checks her in around 3:30," he confirmed. "That was a relief to hear, I can tell you. I was afraid something had happened to the kid. I heard it was only a couple of hours old."

Frankie said, "There's only one guard on duty at night?"

"That's right. I mean, it's not like we ever have any trouble out here." He frowned. "Or at least we didn't."

"Tell me what happened the night the baby was taken."

The frown cleared. "Well, like I say, not much happens here during the night, so when something does happen, it gets your attention. The midwife came through about 1:00 a.m. and said one of the girls was having her baby. So, when the monitor for the east door went off at about 5:00 a.m., I figured it was the midwife leaving. Still, you know, I checked my screen to make sure and that's when I saw somebody carrying a baby across the parking lot. That's never supposed to happen, not at that hour anyhow, so I zoomed in to get an ID. I mean, if it was a medical emergency of some kind a doctor would have been called in, or an ambulance. There are really strict protocols about that kind of thing."

Frankie prompted, "Did you recognize the woman carrying the baby?"

He bobbed his head up and down firmly. "Sure did. It was one of our nurses. One of the sweet ones—Marianne something, I think. She used to stop at the bakery once or twice a week and bring pastries for the break room. Always remembered to leave a bag of donuts at the guard shack."

Frankie brought up the driver's license photo of Marianne Martindale that the sheriff's office had provided. "Is this her?"

He nodded. "Sure is. She's new, only worked here about six months, but everybody liked her. I wasn't all that worried at first. Curious, is more like it. But then I saw the other woman with her, and it just didn't look right. I decided to check it out."

"Who was the other woman?"

"One of the clients. The expectant mothers. I see them around sometimes, and you get kind of familiar with them."

Frankie showed him the picture of Giselle, and he frowned. "Yeah, that's her. She looks bad in that photograph. But she's okay now, right?"

Frankie put her phone away. "So you left the guard house to check out what was happening in the parking lot?"

"By that time all the security lights had been triggered," he said, "so it wasn't hard to see something was wrong. They looked like they were arguing, Marianne and the little mother. I'm sorry,

I don't know her name. Mrs. Summerfield could probably tell you."

Frankie prompted, "What made you think they were arguing?"

"Well, for one thing, the girl was in her nightgown, no shoes, like she'd just gotten out of bed to follow Marianne outside. Marianne was moving real fast toward her car, and she kept looking over her shoulder, saying something to the other girl, whispering it, really. The girl looked like she was crying. A couple of times Marianne tried to grab the girl's arm but she pulled away. Then Marianne opened the back door of her car and put the baby in, like she was fastening it into a car seat, while the other girl just stood there, kind of wringing her hands and looking scared. That's when I shouted out to them."

"How far away were you?" asked Frankie.

"About thirty feet. I was running, but..." he made a wry face. "You might've noticed, I'm no spring chicken. There was no way I could keep them from driving away if that's what they had a mind to do, and when I shouted for them to stop, Marianne looked me straight in the eye and then grabbed the other girl and tried to force her into the car. That's when I took out my weapon and fired a shot into the air. Just to scare them, you know. To stop them."

He shook his head regretfully. "I know it was stupid. I shouldn't have done it. The mother looked terrified. She turned and ran into the woods, and Marianne screamed after her. Then she got into her car and drove off with the baby, so fast she damn near ran me down."

He drew a heavy breath. "I called Mrs. Summerfield and told her what had happened. That's procedure. I said I was calling the police, but she said she'd take care of it. I searched for the girl, the mother, until she got here but..." he shrugged. "One man, one flashlight, in that tangle of bushes..." He nodded toward the wood line that was clearly visible at the edge of the parking lot. "No chance.

"Anyway," he added, looking relieved, "I hear it all turned out okay. They found the mother, a little bruised and scratched up, and took her to the hospital. But she's going to be fine. And like I say, Ms. Whitley brought the baby back." He shook his head sadly. "I just don't know what got into that sweet Marianne. What in the world could she have been thinking?"

Frankie said, "Do you have any idea how the baby came to be in Ms. Whitley's possession?"

"Now, that I couldn't tell you," he admitted. "I asked myself the same thing."

Frankie glanced down at her notes. "You said she'd checked the expectant mother into Hope House?"

"Sure," he replied. "She brought in quite a few of the girls. I heard she works with some kind of charity or such that, you know, takes care of that kind of thing."

Frankie kept her expression neutral. "Do you keep a copy of the security footage on your monitors here in the guard house?"

"No, ma'am," he said, "that all goes through the main office. I'm sure Mrs. Summerfield will be able to bring it up for you."

Frankie smiled and put her notebook away. "Thank you, Mr. Levitz. You've been very helpful."

"You should really talk to Mrs. Summerfield," said Charlie. "She's the one in charge."

"I know," Frankie replied, "and that's exactly what I intend to do."

CHAPTER TWENTY-NINE

The manicurist, whose nametag read "Kiki," had a pierced nose, multiple gold studs outlining her ears, and a colorful tattoo of a rose garden on one arm. Her nails were painted aqua and were so long it was difficult to imagine how she managed to hold a nail polish brush, much less produce the kind of intricate artwork that had been evident on Giselle's nails.

She didn't recognize Giselle's photo at first, but when Trish zoomed in on a close-up of one hand, Kiki said immediately, "Oh, sure, I do her. Daisies. It's always daisies. Sometimes roses," she admitted, "but mostly daisies. Suits me, because roses are a pain to get right."

Baker said, "When was she in here last?"

Kiki screwed up her face in thought. "Well now, that I couldn't tell you for sure. I don't think she had her hair done here. They have a stylist out at the plantation that does that."

Baker and Trish exchanged a quick glance, but Kiki went on, "It was before she got knocked up, I know that. So I'm gonna say...Thanksgiving maybe?"

Trish said, "That's not possible. Her nails looked freshly painted, not a chip on them."

"That's because they were," replied Kiki smugly. "I did them myself at Hope House last week. Say, did she have her kid yet? She looked ready to pop when I saw her."

Baker said, "So you're saying she came here for her manicure first, then you went to her at Hope House?"

Kiki nodded. "Sure. A bunch of them come in from that plantation every other week or so with this older woman, kind of mean-looking. She never gets anything done, just kind of stands and watches. But she always tips in cash for everybody, and she's not stingy, either."

"And the boy who used to sweep up here, Paulo," Baker said, "he's the one that drove them, right?"

She shrugged. "I only work here three days a week. I don't socialize much."

"But the women he brought in," Baker persisted, "were they staying out at the plantation or what?"

"You mean like guests?" She shook her head. "No, these were the staff, at least that's what I heard. You know, waitresses and stuff. They get to live on the place, get all their meals, *plus* hair and nails. Pretty sweet deal. I tried to get on out there myself, but no dice." She shrugged. "Probably just as well. I got a boyfriend, and he wouldn't like me being gone at night."

"So, let me understand this," Baker said. "You met Giselle when she was working at Hollowgrove, and she came in with some of the other employees to have her nails done. And when Giselle went to Hope House, you started going there to do her nails?"

"Not just hers," replied Kiki. "I'm out there every Monday. Those girls from the plantation, they always stay looking sharp, even when they're as big as a balloon."

"Girls?" said Trish. "Do you mean there's more than one girl from Hollowgrove at Hope House?"

Kiki shrugged. "Sometimes. Say, what's this about, anyway?"

Baker said, "Who paid you to do Giselle's nails?"

"Here at the salon, it all goes on a corporate credit card. At Hope House, they pay in cash."

Trish said, "Did you ever talk to her? Giselle?"

"Nah, none of those girls had much to say. I figured most of them didn't speak enough English to make conversation, but the daisy girl—that's what I called her—she just seemed sad. Plus, the woman that runs the place—Hope House, I mean —she's always in there when I'm working, talking my ear off." She added, "Is she in trouble? The daisy girl? 'Cause I kind of liked her, even if she did look sad."

Trish said, "We hope not. Right now, we just want to talk to her, so if you see her can you give us a call?"

It was Baker who handed Kiki his card, which she glanced at and put aside. "Sure," she said. "Only," she added, "I don't think that was her name."

Trish and Baker had started to leave; now they looked back. "What do you mean?" Trish said.

"What you keep calling her," replied Kiki. "Giselle? I heard that woman—the older chick—say her name one time, and that wasn't it."

Baker frowned. "What was it?"

Kiki shrugged. "I can't say for sure. Some kind of drink, I think. But it wasn't Giselle."

"Brandy." The young man who sat across the table from Buck managed to look both eager and scared to death, and he nodded his head vigorously when Buck showed him the picture of Giselle. "Yes, that is her. I can go now? I say what you want?"

"Brandy," Buck repeated. "You're sure?"

"That's what they call her, yes. Brandy."

The Mercy jail was on the basement level of the police station. The antique brick walls were painted industrial green, the sealed concrete floors were bare, and the strong scent of disinfectant barely disguised the musty dampness that seemed to seep like a fog from the old mortar. The buzz of the fluorescent lights that flooded the place was a constant background noise, day and night.

The jail consisted of a small intake area, three old-fashioned cells constructed of iron bars, each with two cots and a steel toilet, and one slightly larger holding cell that could accommodate up to ten prisoners in an emergency. So far, there had never been such an emergency. The jail was manned by two police officers; one at the front desk and one who oversaw the prisoners. Since Mercy rarely held a detainee for more than forty-eight hours, jail assignments were considered easy duty.

Buck met with the teenager, Paulo, in a windowless room that might once have been a storage closet, barely big enough to accommodate the table and two chairs it held. Paulo was handcuffed to the metal ring on the table across from Buck which, given their relative sizes and the scared look in Paulo's eyes, was probably overkill.

Buck said, "Who calls her that? Brandy."

"The others, at the farm. I drive them in the van sometime. Tiffany. Jewel. Scarlett. Others. The girls."

"You mean the girls that work at Hollowgrove," Buck said.

"Live there, work there." He shrugged. "No difference."

"Why did you run away when the officer tried

to show you her picture?" Buck asked.

Fear darkened the boy's eyes, and he gave one tight shake of his head. "I cannot go back there. To the farm. I cannot."

"Why not?"

He just shook his head, his lips tight.

"How long have you worked at Hollowgrove?" Buck asked.

Paulo held up two fingers on his cuffed hand.

"Two years?"

Paulo nodded.

"Where were you before that?"

Paulo hesitated. "I tell you this, and I can go?"

Buck said, "Where will you go when you leave our jail?"

He said eagerly, "My mother's brother. He plants flowers for rich white people in Florida. That is where I go. Where we all go when we leave Guatemala. My mother, my sister, me. We walk a long way, and when we get to the border men with guns try to drive us away. There are many others like us, and not much food. We hear of a place we can go, get papers, work hard, earn money enough to go to Tío James. At night, the trucks come. They take the boys, the young and the strong, and the pretty girls. *Mi madre...*" He flinched with the memory. "She is pushed away. *Mi hermana*, my sister..." He shook his head. "I do not know. I am in the truck. Very dark, very hot, many people. We go a long way." He paused. "Some of them, with the heat, no water... they die. *Morte.*"

He fell silent. Buck prompted, "What happened to the bodies?"

Paulo just shook his head. "When the truck stopped and we all got out, they were carried away."

Buck said, "When the truck stopped, where were you?"

Paulo replied simply, "Here. In the farm."

"Do you mean Hollowgrove Plantation?"

"Yes. That is it. We plant potatoes, we dig onions, do other things. Me, I have license to drive. Miss Geraldine, she comes to say I can drive the van with the girls. I do this for a time, but it takes me no closer to my *tío* in Florida. I must have money. So last time I drive the girls to town, when Miss Geraldine takes the keys and goes inside the shop, I leave the van and I hide."

Buck said, "Didn't they pay you for working at Hollowgrove?"

He shook his head. "We get food, we get mattress to sleep on, sometimes..." he held his thumb and forefinger close together and brought them to his lips, imitating holding a joint. "To smoke, yes? But no money. The nice lady at the hair shop, she gives me $10.00 an hour to sweep and clean the machines and carry away the trash. Very soon I have enough for Florida."

"Why didn't you leave before?" Buck asked.

Again, he shook his head. "Big fence, hard to climb. Some have tried but the men with guns..." He arranged his arms as best he could to indicate holding a rifle and made a rat-a-tat-tat motion that imitated the firing of a machine gun.

Buck said, "They shot people who tried to leave?"

He nodded solemnly. "This I hear. No one tries to leave. We are too afraid. But when I drive the girls, no men with guns come with me. So I go and I hide where they cannot find me."

Buck said, "Do you have any idea where Giselle... I mean, Brandy, might have gone after she had her baby?"

Paulo shook his head. "They go away, they come back."

"Do you mean the girls?"

"Yes. The girls I drive."

"How many times," Buck asked carefully, "have girls gone away to have babies since you've been at Hollowgrove?"

He shrugged. "Four? Six? But," he added sadly, "they always come back. Always."

CHAPTER THIRTY

The doors to Hope House were opened for her before Frankie even pressed the buzzer. Eliza Summerfield waited for her in the reception room, smiling.

"Detective," she said. "I was just about to call you. You heard we had a happy conclusion to the Gilford's situation?"

"I did," Frankie agreed, not returning the smile. "Can we talk in your office?"

"Of course." She gestured the way with her open palm, her expression pleasant and professional.

Frankie followed the older woman into the pretty pink and green office she had visited yesterday, but she did not take the seat she was offered.

She said, "Mrs. Summerfield, what's your relationship with Aegis, Incorporated?"

Mrs. Summerfield did not blink, but a pink flush crept from her neck toward her chin. She moved behind her desk, smoothed the skirt of her powder blue suit, and sat down before answering. "I'm sure I don't know what you're talking about."

"That surprises me," replied Frankie, "since at last count..." She consulted her notes briefly. "Hope House has issued payments to them in excess of one million dollars."

The other woman's jaw knotted. "That's a bookkeeping matter. I wouldn't know anything about that. And I can't imagine what any of that has to do with the Gilford adoption—which, may I remind you, was successfully concluded."

Frankie said, "Do you have an employee by the name of Marianne Martindale?"

There was just the slightest flicker of unease in the woman's eyes before she answered, "Why, yes. She's an R.N. on the night shift. Obviously, she wasn't on duty when you interviewed the staff yesterday."

As a general rule, Frankie did not bring her emotions to work. Doing so was unproductive and unprofessional. But fatigue and frustration had ground her patience down to a wire. She said shortly, "She wasn't here yesterday because she was dead."

Eliza Summerfield sank back in her chair, color draining from her cheeks. Her gaze was frozen on Frankie. "What?"

"She was murdered," Frankie said, "by the same person who stole the Gilfords' adopted baby out of her car. And she might well be alive today if you hadn't lied about what happened to that baby and erased the security tape that showed Marianne taking the infant from this facility in full view of the child's mother. Did you know Marianne Martindale was the baby's aunt?"

The shock in Summerfield's eyes deepened. "What? I—what are you talking about?"

"You knew Marianne Martindale took the baby," Frankie pressed on, "because your own security guard reported it to you. But instead of calling the police you called Geraldine Whitley. Why? Because you had already promised her $50,000—half of the Gilford's adoption fee—for Giselle Martindale's baby and now there was no baby. No baby, no money. Is that about right, Mrs. Summerfield?"

Frankie watched the color return to Eliza Summerfield's face in the form of an angry flush. She said coolly, "I think you should leave, Detective." She swiveled her chair toward the phone on her desk and reached for the receiver. "You are way out of line and I'm calling my attorney."

Frankie said shortly, "You can call him from the police station. Get up, Mrs. Summerfield. You're coming with me."

CHAPTER THIRTY-ONE

Baker tossed the keys to Trish Miller while he took out his phone to text Frankie the results of their interview with the manicurist. "You're driving," he said.

"Yes, sir." She looked more pleased than the situation warranted as she slid behind the wheel. "Are we going to pick up the Whitley boy now?"

"We're going to look for him," replied Baker absently, typing. "You remember the license plate?"

"Whitly4," she replied. "Red Wrangler."

"Good for you." He did not look up from checking his messages.

Trish drove in silence for a time, heading back toward town. Then she said quietly, "I never thought I'd be involved in a murder case my second day on the job. Actually," she amended,

"I guess it started yesterday, when that woman Giselle ran out in front of my car."

Baker said, "It's not really our case. We're just helping out the county."

"Still, a woman is dead."

"And she'd be just as dead with or without you. It doesn't pay to take these things personally, Miller."

"Yes, sir."

Baker put his phone away just as Trish turned into the Dairy Queen at the intersection of 215 and Post Road just outside of town. He started to question, but she drove purposefully down the row of parked cars to a red Jeep Wrangler and stopped behind it, blocking the car in. The license plate read, Whitly4.

"Good eyes, Miller," he remarked.

"Not really, sir." She put the unit in park. "This is where I used to hang out as a kid during the summer. I figured nothing much had changed in the past few years."

They got out and stood beside the car for a moment, their gazes sweeping the parking lot and surrounding area. There were a couple of weathered picnic tables to the side of the building toward the back, shaded by a big magnolia. A group of teenage boys had gathered there, along with a couple of girls in short shorts and demi-tanks. Some were sitting on the table, smoking or vaping, others had cups of ice cream and sodas. Nate Whitley grinned and nudged the boy next to him when he saw Baker and Miller pull up, and after a moment, the others turned to watch them. None of the kids looked particularly nervous to see the cops, which told Baker nothing illegal was going on. At least not at that moment.

Baker walked around the Jeep and peered in the passenger side window. There on the floorboard was an open box of firecrackers. He beckoned Miller over and pointed out his find. The kid watched them from the picnic table, murmuring something to his companions that made them laugh. Baker rested his hands on his gun belt and watched them. "This is going to be fun," he said.

They walked over to the kids. Nate Whitley sat at the end of a bench, resting his forearms on the table, still grinning as he watched them approach. He said, "Morning, Officers." One of the girls giggled.

Baker said, "Nate Whitley?"

"That's me."

Baker nodded back toward the parking lot. "Is that your red Wrangler parked there?"

"It is," he agreed genially. "Beauty, isn't it? But don't you worry, Officer. You keep going to work every day, being a good cop, driving your little beat, and in twenty or thirty years you might be able to afford one just like it." He cast a grinning glance around the table, encouraging his friends to laugh, and they did.

Baker stared them down. To Nate, he said, "Are those your firecrackers on the floorboard of the vehicle?"

"It's the Fourth of July, dude," he said. "No law against having firecrackers on a national holiday." Again, he glanced around his group and got a few smiles, though not as many as before.

Baker said, "Officer Miller, maybe you could inform this young man of the City of Mercy's position on setting off fireworks within the city limits."

"Yes, sir," she replied. "City Ordinance Number 143: deployment of fireworks within the city limits without a permit lawfully obtained from the Mercy Police Department shall be punishable by a fine of $500 or up to three days in jail per incident."

Baker said, "And isn't there something about a noise violation in there somewhere?"

"Yes, sir. City ordinance number 216 restricts excessive noise within the city limits between the hours of 11:00 p.m. and 7:00 a.m. Such noise may be described as, but is not limited to, that produced by machinery, construction, vehicles, gunfire, human voices, barking dogs, electronics, musical instruments and..." a slight pause. "Fireworks."

"In other words," said Baker, watching the kid, "the mayor likes her beauty sleep."

The smile on Nate's face turned into a smirk. "Yeah, well, real interesting, bro, but I got places to be." He pushed up from the table. "So how about moving that rat trap cop-mobile of yours? It's blocking me in."

The minute he stood up, Trish moved a step closer. So did Baker. Only Baker's steps were longer than hers, and he was now practically nose-to-nose with the young man. Baker said in a low, very controlled tone, "You made a couple of mistakes this morning, punk. First, you pulled your little prank right across from the mayor's house. Not smart. Not smart at all. Second, you threw those firecrackers at an officer of the law. That's assault on a police officer, and that's a serious criminal offense. Put your hands behind your back."

The sneer on the teenager's face didn't waver. "Man, I don't know what you're talking about." He jerked his head over his shoulder to the kids who were watching. "Come on, guys, let's bounce. This place is starting to smell."

He started to push past Baker, bumping his shoulder hard against Baker's. Baker grabbed his arms, spun him around, and slammed him to the concrete patio. Before Nate could even get enough breath to yell, Baker jammed his knee into the small of the kid's back and twisted his wrists into handcuffs.

The other kids jumped to their feet, startled. Two of them whipped out their cell phones and started recording. Some of them shouted, "Hey!" and "What the hell?" Trish moved toward them, one hand raised in a warning, the other hand on her taser. Nate bucked beneath Baker's weight and yelled, "Get off me, asshole!" To his crew, he screamed, "Are you going to let this stupid black motherfucker treat me like this?"

Baker grabbed a handful of the kid's hair and jerked his head back. He was within half a second of slamming the boy's face into the concrete, hard, and maybe not just once, when Trish Miller gripped his arm. "Sir!" she said sharply.

Baker took a moment for the red haze to clear, breathing hard through his nose. Still, he couldn't resist giving the kid's hair one last twist, yanking his head back almost to his shoulders as he hauled him to his feet. Nate Whitley screamed like he was being scalped. "Are you getting this?" he yelled to the girls who were holding up their phones. "Are you getting this?" To Baker, he said, "You have no idea what a pile of shit you just stepped into, dickhead!" He swiveled his head back around and shouted, "Somebody call my dad!" Then he spun around and spat on Baker's uniform.

It took all the self-restraint Baker had—and one look at his alarmed young rookie's face—to keep from backhanding the kid across the mouth. Instead, he grasped the back of the kid's neck with one hand and his shoulder with the other and, without saying another word, marched him toward the patrol car.

CHAPTER THIRTY-TWO

Buck said, "So it's like we figured. Marianne Martindale took Giselle's baby and tried to take Giselle, too, according to the security guard's statement. But why?"

He listened to Frankie's report while sipping his second cup of coffee and enjoying a selection of pastries from the bakery across the street. One of the administrative staff brought them in every morning and left them in the coffee room, a fact of which Buck had been unaware until recently. All things considered, he had probably been better off not knowing.

Frankie said, "Giselle Martindale was a teenage runaway. I think Marianne tracked her sister down somehow and got a job at Hope House to be close to her. In my opinion, it wasn't so much a kidnapping as a rescue."

"Except it sounds like Giselle didn't want to be rescued."

"Yes, sir," admitted Frankie. "It sounds that way."

"Did you get anything else from Summerfield?"

"No, sir, and we're not likely to. I'll try questioning her again when her lawyer gets here, but right now all we've got her on is lying to the police and obstructing a homicide investigation. If we bring in Geraldine Whitley, though, I think we can make her accessory to murder."

Buck shook his head. "Geraldine Whitley didn't kill Marianne Martindale. I saw her yesterday at Hollowgrove close to 1:30, and again about an hour later. There's no way she could have gotten to Marianne's apartment, then twenty miles further east to the place she was killed, and back to Hollowgrove again in that time frame."

"We need to talk to Giselle Martindale," Frankie said. "I'm pretty sure she's at Hollowgrove. Baker said the manicurist told him she worked there."

"And that kid Paulo said he knows four or five girls from Hollowgrove who've gone to have babies at Hope House," Buck said. He pushed the plate of pastries toward her. "Here, have one. My wife would kill me if she knew how many of these I've eaten. I ought never to skip breakfast."

"Thanks." Frankie took a bear claw and a paper napkin from the stack by the plate. "Would you like to hear my theory?"

"That Hollowgrove is keeping women prisoner,

forcing them to work as prostitutes, and then selling their babies when they get pregnant?"

Frankie nodded with the pastry midway to her mouth. "If you think about it, the profit margin has got to be higher selling babies than running prostitutes."

"That's pretty damn sick." Buck reached absently for a cinnamon roll, leaning back in his chair, and took a bite. "What I don't understand is why didn't Giselle just get in the car with her sister and her baby."

"Then," supplied Frankie, "they'd both be dead, wouldn't they?"

Buck's brow knit. "Yeah."

Sully rapped lightly on the frame of the open door. "Excuse me, boss," he said, "but I thought you'd want to know. I just got off the phone with my guy at ICE."

Buck waved him in. He saw Sully eyeing the plate of sweets and he said, "Help yourself."

"Thanks, Chief." Sully selected a Danish and took one of the duck-printed guest chairs. "He found four investigations had been opened at Hollowgrove Plantation and Farms in the past eight years," Sully went on. "All involved harboring or employing undocumented aliens." He took a bite of the Danish and added, "All investigations closed with no action taken."

"Which means," Buck concluded, "somebody shut down those investigations. Somebody with a lot of power."

"Yes, sir," agreed Sully. "That'd be my guess."

Buck remembered the photographs on the wall at Hollowgrove. Corinne Watts saying, *Every one of these men owes Jarrod Whitley a favor.* Jarrod Whitley had dominated this part of the state for decades. Making a few ICE investigations go away would be child's play for him.

"My man Paulo claims nobody is paid for working at Hollowgrove," Buck said. "Immigrants are picked up at the border and trucked here. Some of them don't make it alive. He also claims," Buck added deliberately, "that people who try to escape are gunned down on the spot."

Sully paused in the process of taking another bite. "What do they do with the bodies?"

"I don't know," admitted Buck. "But they made an awful fuss a few years back when archaeologists wanted to dig up the old slave graveyard. And it looked to me like the place had been used a lot more recently than the nineteenth century."

"If what the kid says is true," Frankie pointed out, "it might explain why Giselle didn't just get in the car with her sister. She was afraid to leave."

Buck summarized for Sully what Frankie had learned from Hope House that morning. "So," he concluded, "We've got them on human trafficking, running a prostitution ring, labor law violations, unlawful detention…"

"Illegal disposal of human remains," Sully put in.

"Not to mention murder or conspiracy to commit murder," Frankie said. "I need to question Geraldine Whitley. She's the one who returned the baby to Hope House an hour after it was taken from a murdered woman's car. I'd like to see her try to explain that."

"We'll be talking to Ms. Whitley, all right," Buck assured her, frowning. "but I'd prefer to do it while she's behind bars. Anybody who can get out of four ICE investigations without missing a step is not going to stand still while we go on a fishing expedition. She'll have a story ready for anything you accuse her of, and she'll have a dozen witnesses to back her up. Right now, your best bet is to get that Summerfield woman to turn on her. What we need is hard evidence, and a lot of it."

"Yes, sir," said Frankie. She wiped her fingers on the napkin. "I'll go back out to Hope House and see what else I can gather."

"We might try talking to Giselle Martindale," Sully suggested. "She's got to be at Hollowgrove, and she doesn't even know her sister is dead. Not officially, anyway."

Buck was about to reply when he was interrupted by a knock on the door that separated his office from Lydia's, followed almost immediately by the opening of that door. "Excuse me, sir," Lydia said. "You have a visitor."

Buck glanced at his watch with a brief frown of annoyance. "I don't have any appointments," he said. "And we're kind of in the middle of something here."

"Yes, sir," Lydia replied. A corner of her lips twitched with something closely resembling a smile as she stepped back from the door. "But I think you're going to want to see this young man."

The shaggy brown head of a big dog peered around the corner of the door, followed almost immediately by the boy holding the leash. "Hi, Buck," he said.

CHAPTER THIRTY-THREE

"**W**illis!" Buck sat up straight, surprise sharpening his voice. He got up and came around the desk, glancing around for Eloise. "What are you doing here? Where's your grandmother?"

"She's at home," Willis replied, "measuring for curtains." He came into the room, extending his hand politely first to Frankie, then to Sully. "Hello, Sergeant Moreno. Hello, Captain Sully. Have you met my dog, Thor?"

Sully and Frankie, both grinning, returned Willis's greeting and made a fuss over the dog while Buck stared at his stepson, the shock slowly settling in. "Willis," he said carefully, "did you walk all the way downtown by yourself?"

"Yes, sir," replied Willis. "Mama Eloise said Thor was getting underfoot so I took him for a walk. Next thing I knew, here we were." He smiled proudly. "It wasn't far," he assured Buck, "and I pressed the button at the traffic light and waited for the green walking man like you told me."

It was a moment before Buck could speak. Sully glanced up from petting the dog with a wryly raised eyebrow, and Lydia said, "Should I call your mother-in-law, sir?"

Buck started to answer when his phone buzzed in his pocket. He saw the caller ID and told Lydia, "No, that's okay." He answered the phone, "Miss Eloise, don't worry. He's with me at the station."

"Oh, thank you, Jesus!" He could tell she was trying not to cry. "I don't know what happened. I swear, I turned around and he was gone! I looked everywhere, and I was afraid... the river..."

"Yes ma'am," Buck said, working hard to keep his voice calm. "I know. But everything's okay now. We're on our way home."

Buck put his phone away and looked sternly at Willis. Willis returned his gaze innocently. Lydia retreated quietly back into her office and closed the door. Sully and Frankie got to their feet.

"Looks like you've got your hands full here, Chief," Sully said. "Why don't we pick this up on the flip side?"

Frankie said, "I'll be at Hope House." Then she turned to Willis with a smile. "It was good to see you again, Willis."

Sully ruffled the little boy's curls as he left and added, "Catch you later, kiddo."

Buck knelt before Willis, eye level, and looked at him while he chose his words. Willis said solemnly, "Am I in trouble, Buck?"

Buck replied, "Yes, sir. I'm afraid you are. You know you're not supposed to leave the house without telling someone."

Willis admitted, "I guess I forgot."

"And you're not allowed to leave your yard without permission."

Willis said, "Oh."

"And you never, ever cross the street by yourself."

Willis replied, "That's a lot of rules, Buck."

"Maybe," Buck replied, "but rules are made to keep people safe—you, me, Mama Eloise, Thor... think how you'd feel if Thor just up and took off and you didn't know where he was."

The child's eyes widened. "I wouldn't like it a bit," Willis admitted. "That's why he always wears a leash."

"Which is a rule," Buck pointed out, "to keep him safe. Do you understand?"

Willis nodded vigorously.

"Tell me the rules," Buck said.

Willis ticked them off on his fingers. "No leaving the house without telling someone. No leaving the yard without permission. No crossing the street by myself. No walking Thor without a leash."

Buck couldn't help smiling. "Good fellow." He stood and took Willis's hand, walking toward the door. "Was there anything in particular you wanted to see me about?"

"No," replied Willis easily, "I just thought I'd stop by." He thought about it for a moment and said, "Well, maybe there was just one thing."

"What's that?"

"Can I get my picture taken with Hobo?"

"Absolutely not."

"Jamar says everybody does."

"Jamar is wrong."

"Maybe," suggested Willis hopefully, "I'll ask Mama."

"You be sure to tell her I said absolutely not."

His expression fell. "Yes, sir."

Buck said, "You scared Mama Eloise half to death, you know. You're going to have to apologize."

"Yes, sir."

"And I imagine your mom will have a thing or two to say about all this when she gets home."

Willis sighed. "It didn't seem like such a big deal when we started out," he admitted to Buck, "but it's sure starting to sound like one now."

"A lot of things in life tend to go that way," Buck assured him. He stopped by Lydia's office as they passed it. "I'm going to take this renegade home," he said. "I'll be back in half an hour."

"Yes, sir, no problem. And," she added as they turned toward the employee entrance and parking lot, "if I may suggest, it would probably be faster to walk. Traffic is already backed up through town."

He saw what she was talking about when they came out of the front door of the building and into the blasting heat of the sidewalk. Traffic was bumper-to-bumper in both directions. Every parking spot on the street was filled and there were more people on the sidewalks than he had ever seen at one time. Already two men were arguing as one of them tried to back out of a parking space into the street and the other blocked him in. In this heat, it was only a matter of time before that dispute, or one like it, turned violent.

Buck took out his phone and dialed Sully. "Don't move," he told Willis, and when Sully picked up, he said, "We're going to have to pull a couple of men off patrol to manage traffic downtown. It's not even lunch yet and things are a mess."

"Yes, sir," agreed Sully, "I was afraid of that. We usually implement the holiday traffic management schedule starting today, but what with everything else, we just don't have the manpower."

Across the street, Buck saw the manager of Aikens Department store come out onto the sidewalk, hands on hips, looking angry and red-faced. He spotted Buck and beckoned him over impatiently. Buck raised a hand in acknowledgment. "I know," he told Sully, frustrated. "Get some people in from D Shift to cover. In the meantime, is there anybody in the building who can come out here and break up a fight that's about to start in front of Tina's Boutique?"

"Yes, sir, boss. On it. Also," Sully said, "Baker just got in with your suspect, Nate Whitley. I thought you'd want to know."

"Good," Buck said briefly. "Put him in the interrogation room until I get there."

"Which will be?"

"Not anytime soon," Buck replied.

"He's already squawking for a lawyer."

"Tell him I'll call one as soon as I get a chance."

"What about his dad?"

"He's old enough to be questioned without a parent present," Buck said. "Dad can wait in the lobby."

Sully sounded amused. "Yes, sir, you got it."

When Buck put his phone away Willis said eagerly, "Do you think we should stay and watch the fight, Buck?"

"I do not." He took Willis's hand and the dog's leash and led them down the street toward the crosswalk, trying not to think about what might have happened if one of these impatient motorists had tried to jump the light while Willis and Thor had been crossing the street a few minutes ago. Back in the small mountain county where he had been sheriff, Buck had had to deal with traffic problems, domestic disputes, drug abuse, and the occasional major crime, often all at the same time.

He had thought it wouldn't be much different transferring those skills here. Now for the first time, he wondered if he had been wrong.

The manager of the department store met them as soon as they crossed the street, fuming. "Chief Lawson," he demanded, "you've got to do something about this traffic! Folks can't get in and out of my store! They're double-parking out back, blocking deliveries! It was never like this when Billy was alive!"

Buck urged Willis to keep moving. "We're working on it, Mr. Dotson."

"You better do more than work on it!" He called after them. "I'm trying to run a business here!"

Buck lifted his hand in acknowledgment and continued down the street, holding the dog on a short leash as they wove their way in and out of tourists, sidewalk displays, and Fourth of July decorations. Willis said, "That man sure was mad, huh, Buck?"

"Yeah, he was," Buck agreed. He was thinking about Billy, who never would have agreed to take on a murder case that happened outside of city limits, who would have classified the Gilford's complaint as a civil case within the hour, and who, he was quite sure, would have closed the file on Giselle Martindale as soon as she checked herself out of the hospital. Billy knew how to run a town like Mercy. He kept the traffic moving and the budget balanced. He didn't get in over his head. He was a good police chief.

Eloise was waiting for them on the front porch when they got home, hands pressed together, looking anxiously up the street. She swept Willis up into a fierce embrace and said, "I should skin your hide! Don't you ever do that again! You scared me out of ten years' growth!"

Willis looked at Buck helplessly over his grandmother's shoulder, and Buck encouraged, "Tell your grandmother where you've been."

"Well," replied Willis, who had obviously been preparing his story all the way home, "it all started when I was watching this television show about this boy that had a dad that was sheriff, and how he used to go to the jail to see his dad all the time, so I thought maybe that would be something I could do. Don't worry, Mama Eloise," Willis assured her as she set him carefully on his feet, "the show was on your approved list."

Buck met his mother-in-law's horrified gaze, trying to hide his own amusement. "That may be," he told Willis, "but that television show was a long time ago, and I think the streets of Mercy are a little busier than the streets of Mayberry."

"Oh," said Willis.

"Go on," Buck said.

"So anyway," Willis continued, squaring his shoulders, "I got Thor and put on his leash, and we walked down to the crosswalk and pushed the button and waited for the green walking man. Then we walked across the street and down to the police station. We went inside and this nice lady said could she help us, and I said I was there to see my stepdad, Chief Buck Lawson, so she picked up the phone and in a minute Miss Lydia came out and took us down the hall to Buck's office. I got to shake hands with Detective Moreno and Captain Sullivan, and then Buck said I shouldn't ever do that again. Come to the police station without permission, I mean. I'm real sorry to worry you, Mama Eloise," Willis concluded earnestly. "I was going to bring you flowers but Buck said we shouldn't pick them out of other people's gardens."

By this time Eloise's hand was clutching her throat as she looked at her grandson in muted astonishment, shaking her head. "You are a sight in this world," she said.

"Yes ma'am," agreed Willis.

"Tell Mama Eloise the rules," Buck advised, and Willis obediently recited the newly memorized rules as they walked into the house.

Eloise sent Willis to the kitchen for cookies and milk, and said as he scampered off, "I should be sending him to his room to wait for a spanking." She pressed her lips tightly together and closed her eyes. "When I think of what might have happened…"

"Well, it didn't," Buck said firmly before she could let her imagination take her to the far side of panic. "Willis is a handful, but we're all having a little trouble adjusting to our new jobs here, even Willis."

She managed a smile and dug into the pocket of her slacks for a tissue. "I guess you're right."

"Besides," Buck added, "he's a good boy, you know that. He always does the right thing, as long as he knows what the right thing is. So let's not be too hard on him, what do you say?"

She sniffed and wiped her nose. "Maybe a little less Andy Griffith and a little more Ninja Turtles."

Buck chuckled. "Maybe." He turned his attention to the big box under the foyer table. "What's this?"

"Oh." Eloise stuffed the damp tissue back into her pocket. "The box was delivered an hour or so ago by a messenger service."

Buck knelt to drag the box out from under the table. It was heavy, and it was printed all over with "Special Label Hollowgrove Plantation Bourbon Triple Distilled." Buck remembered what Lydia had said about Jarrod Whitley sending a case of bourbon to Billy every Christmas, and he wondered if that might be one of the reasons four ICE investigations were closed without action. He wondered how many other complaints of criminal behavior from Hollowgrove had been ignored over the years, and his jaw hardened.

"Well, I hope that messenger didn't get too far, because this is going straight back," he said. "Jarrod Whitley needs to know this administration doesn't accept bribes."

"Oh," said Eloise, surprised. "But that's from Mayor Watts. At least, that's what the card says."

Buck turned the box until he saw the card taped to the top. In fancy script, it read: "Compliments of Mayor Corinne Watts."

"Well, in that case," he murmured, mostly to himself. He picked up the box, more puzzled than pleased, and turned to take it into his study across the hall.

"And before I forget," Eloise added, "I found some old high school yearbooks up in the attic that I thought the young Mr. Aikens might like to have. I think they belonged to his dad. I put them on your desk for the next time you see him."

"Thanks, Miss Eloise. I'm sure Junior will appreciate it."

She hesitated on her way to the kitchen, still looking anxious. "Buck," she said, "I'm so sorry you had to come home from work for this. Can I make you a ham sandwich or something? You didn't have any breakfast."

Buck thought guiltily of the empty plate of pastries and replied, "No, thanks, I'm good. I need to get back, but I'll check on Willis before I leave."

The study was a mahogany-paneled, coffered-ceiling cliché of a gentleman's retreat from the 1850s, complete with floor-to-ceiling bookshelves and a giant marlin mounted on one wall. It was the only room that had been completely furnished when Buck moved in, and it was here that the memory of a man he barely knew had lived so vividly that it had sustained him through the turbulent first days of his tenure as police chief. He could still feel Billy's presence here and suspected he always would. As much as he loved his new family, there were times when he just needed to be here, stretched out on Billy's sofa, sipping Billy's bourbon, alone with his thoughts. Fortunately for him, his wife understood that. She might not like it, but she understood.

Buck placed the case of bourbon in the cabinet beneath the bar and texted Jo. *Got a minute?*

While he waited for her reply, he flipped open one of the dusty high school yearbooks Eloise had left on the desk. It opened naturally to a class photo, and Billy was easy to spot. The tallest one in the class, center back row, as handsome as ever with his big, friendly grin and thick blond hair. In front of him was a gorgeous girl who had to be Corinne Watts: perfectly styled, long blond hair, immaculate makeup, a smile that didn't show too many teeth, her chin lifted just so to make the best of her profile. Her eyes were shifted slightly to the right, as though she was looking at the boy next to her. Buck frowned over that. Who *was* he? And why did he look so familiar?

His phone buzzed, and he answered, "Hey, babe."

"I have five," she replied. "What's up?"

Buck sat down in the leather desk chair, stretching out his legs. "Willis had a little adventure."

She stifled a groan. "Is this something I need to know about right this minute?"

"Nope," he assured her. "This is just a cover-my-ass call for when you ask me why I didn't tell you."

She sighed. "Okay. I'll deal with it when I get home."

"No need. Already dealt with."

"Have I told you lately how much I love you?"

"I could hear it again."

"This much," she said, and Buck smiled.

"Yeah, don't go all sentimental on me," he said. "I'll think I've got the wrong number. Also, I wanted you to know we've got your suspect in custody."

"Awaiting the rack and thumbscrews, I presume?"

"You got it." He paused. "Jo, can I go over something with you? Tell me what I'm missing."

She listened as he detailed, as succinctly as possible, the newest developments in the Hope House case.

"Jesus, Buck," she said when he was finished. "This sounds like more of a RICO case than something a small-town police department should be handling. If these people aren't the definition of organized crime, I don't know what is."

"You're probably right," he said. "But it landed in my lap, and I've got to deal with it. What gets me is how brazen they are about everything. Marianne Martindale was murdered in broad daylight. They take their hookers to town to get their nails done. Knowing that every cop in the county is looking for Giselle's newborn, they steal it from its aunt and calmly take it back to Hope House to be sold. It's like they don't even care if they get caught."

"It's not that they don't care," Jolene pointed out, "it's that they don't think it's possible. Baby, they've been doing this for 200 years—buying and selling humans, keeping them in captivity to work their fields and clean up their messes, burying them in unmarked graves. It's a way of life for them. They think they're unstoppable, and so far, they've been right. What I don't understand is why they even bothered to call the police when those two skeletons were found, especially when they had to know what was going on at Hope House."

"Yeah, I've wondered the same thing," Buck murmured, his frown deepening. "Except..." He turned the yearbook around and looked again at the class photo, Corinne Watts—formerly Corinne Mercer— looking at the boy in the row next to her. "They didn't call the police." He followed the caption until he found the name. Donald Estes. That was why he looked familiar. He was the same Don Estes who managed Hollowgrove Plantation. "They called the mayor."

"Hoping she'd cover it up, no doubt."

"Maybe," Buck said doubtfully. Except, of course, she hadn't covered it up. Instead, she had called Buck, wasting his time on a thirty-year-old crime when she must have known he had more urgent things to deal with.

Jolene was silent for a moment, an indication that she had no more ideas than he had. Then she said, "I've got to get back to class, babe. I'm sorry I don't have any answers for you. But you know who does, don't you? That punk kid that's sitting in your jail right now."

Buck gave a startled grunt of surprise. "You may be right."

"Of course I am. And good news—I'll be home by six. You want to go out to eat?"

"Honey, there's not a restaurant in town that has a free table tonight," he replied. "How about I pick up a pack of steaks and let's see if we can find that grill?"

"Steaks, huh? There goes our food budget for the month."

"We're worth it," he said, grinning. "See you tonight. And listen," he added, "don't come through town. Traffic's a mess. Take the back roads."

"I'm not worried," she said, "I know the police chief."

CHAPTER THIRTY-FOUR

Two officers were stationed at each of the town's main intersections, directing traffic against the lights and helping people get in and out of parking spaces. The traffic was better than it had been, but Buck could practically feel the mayor glaring at him from her office across the street as he entered the police station. Billy would have never let this happen.

His undershirt was damp and his hair was dripping when he passed the receptionist's desk; the air conditioning raised chill bumps on his skin. When he'd first seen the police chief's office he'd wondered why there was a private shower. He didn't anymore.

Stephanie smiled at him as he passed. "Everything all right at home, sir?"

"Just fine," he replied. "And if you should see

a boy matching my stepson's description in this lobby in the future, do me a favor and call the fire department, not the police."

She chuckled and turned back to her computer. "Yes, sir. I'll be sure to do that."

He saw Leon Baker coming down the stairs as he was turning to go to his office, and Buck caught his eye. Baker joined him and they walked toward the administrative area together. "I hear you brought the Whitley kid in," Buck said, pushing through the metal door that led to the offices. "Did he give you any trouble?"

"Some," admitted Baker, looking uncomfortable. He brought out his phone.

Buck slowed while Baker brought up the website and pushed "play." He watched the video of Nate Whitley, screaming obscenities and threats, being thrown to the ground and handcuffed, without comment. He paid particular attention to the part where Trish Miller had stepped forward to intervene.

"Ten thousand views," Baker said. "I think that's what you call 'going viral'."

Buck smiled tightly and returned the phone to him. "Congratulations. I never had a viral video in my life." He added, "It all looks according to procedure. Assuming your body cam backs it up, you're good."

"Yes, sir."

Buck started toward his office, but Baker hesitated. Buck looked back.

"It's just," said Baker, looking uneasy, "I was wondering... was this a test? Because I've got two reprimands for excessive force on my record already this year, one of them put there by you. One more and I'm out of the running for detective. So, I thought maybe you wanted to see how I'd handle somebody like this Whitley kid. And if that's it, how'd I do?"

Buck felt his back teeth clench, almost entirely outside his will. He wanted to tell Baker that yeah, that was it, a test, and he'd passed with flying colors. All was well. But a rush of guilt rose to his throat as he remembered the morning, and the look of desolation in Jo's eyes, and he said, "No. It wasn't a test. I was hoping the kid would act out, and I was hoping you'd beat the shit out of him."

Baker nodded slowly. "Yeah," he said, "I thought so. You play cards with a man for a couple of months, you learn to read his tells." He added warily, "But... if it had gone south like you thought... you would've had my back, right? Acting under orders and all that?"

Buck hesitated just a moment too long. "I always have my officers' backs," he said, "as long as they're acting within the law."

He saw the curtain come down on Baker's eyes even before he finished speaking. Baker straightened his shoulders and turned for the exit. "Yes, sir, understood." He looked back, his expression opaque. "I was thinking," he said, "maybe we shouldn't play cards anymore."

Buck had no answer for that, so he said nothing. He just stood there, cursing himself and this case and the whole damn Whitley empire, while Baker strode out the door and back to work.

Buck was not in a very good mood when he opened the door of the basement interrogation room for the second time that day. Nate Whitley was sprawled in the chair there, sipping a bottle of water, looking cool and comfortable and vaguely bored, completely unconcerned. He might have been playing video games for the past hour.

Buck turned on the video recorder and pulled out the chair across the table from Nate. He opened the boy's file on the table and said, "State your name for the record, please."

Nate grinned. "Johnny Longdick."

Buck leaned back in his chair, regarding him in expressionless silence for approximately thirty seconds. When the cocky grin started to waver a little, Buck said, "If that's the way you want to play it, I've got nothing but time. And you're sure as hell not going anywhere."

Nate's grin was gone now, replaced by a belligerent scowl. "I'm entitled to a fucking lawyer."

Buck turned a page in the file. "You people use Ken Jefferies, right?" That made sense. Jefferies was not only the mayor's lawyer, but the city attorney as well. The Whitleys would have only the best. "He's in Maine with his family for the next two weeks. I can call his associate, but he's in court until 5:00. He can probably get over here sometime tomorrow though."

The boy sat up angrily. "I'm not spending the night in fucking jail! My dad is on his way. I told my friends to call him. He'll get me out of here!"

"Oh, yeah?" Buck took out his phone and brought up the video Baker had shown him. "Your dad's a big fan of Tik-Tok, is he? Because this is what your friends have been busy doing." He turned the phone to face Nate and let the video play out. "Don't think they did you any favors, Johnny, old man. I particularly like the part where you spit on Officer Baker's shirt. Makes you look like a real upstanding citizen. The kind of fellow judges love."

Nate folded his arms across his chest and glared at Buck. Buck put his phone away. "Want to start again? Name."

After a long time, the boy replied, "Nate Whitley."

"Age?"

"Twenty."

"Occupation?"

"I'm a fucking waitress at a fucking topless bar," he shot back. "Can we get this over with and get me the hell out of here?"

Buck finished making his notes on the blank sheet in Whitley's file and looked up. He said, "Here's how this goes. You're not charged with anything. You're entitled to have your lawyer with you while you're being questioned. I'm entitled to keep you here for questioning for forty-eight hours without charging you. Once charges are brought, you'll go before a judge to have bail set and then maybe—just maybe—you pay the bail and go home. Or you can answer my questions now and maybe be home for supper. What's it going to be?"

The boy's belligerent stare did not waver. "That's bullshit."

"I know that's not the way things usually work for you," Buck admitted, flipping back through the file at the kid's previous charges. "But..." He looked up with a thin smile. "There's a new chief in town."

Nate unscrewed the top of his water bottle, sprawled out even deeper in the hard wooden chair, and took a drink. "Ooh," he said. "I'm scared."

Buck stared him down for exactly sixty seconds, then closed the file folder and walked to the door. "Oh, by the way," he said just before he opened it, "you know that judge I mentioned? The one who's going to set your bail? It's a holiday weekend and he won't be in until Tuesday. Enjoy your stay with us."

He opened the door and told the jailer who was standing outside, "Take him to holding." The jailer moved past him into the room and Buck added to Nate, "Of course, the bad news is we're starting to fill up our little jail, it being a holiday weekend and all, so we're probably going to have to ship you off to county. There's a shuttle leaving this afternoon. I'll be sure to let your lawyer know where to find you." He shook his head in mock sympathy. "You picked a hell of a time to show your ass, kid."

"Hey!" Nate's chair scraped the floor as he bolted out of it, and the jailer rushed forward to push him back down.

Buck turned to look at him, one eyebrow cocked in the mildest expression of interest. The kid glared back at him furiously, wresting his shoulder from the jailer's grip. When the jailer moved to restrain him more forcefully, Buck lifted a staying finger.

"Did you change your mind?" he inquired politely.

Nate's nostrils flared with several angry breaths, then he said, "What do you want to know?"

Buck dismissed the jailer and took his time returning to the table, settling down, opening the file, reading through the pages. Finally, he took out his phone and brought up a photograph. He showed it to Nate. "Is that your car?"

The boy scowled. "So what if it is?"

Buck thumbed to the next picture. "Is this you behind the wheel?"

He said reluctantly, "Yeah, okay. Looks like me."

"Where were you at 5:50 this morning?"

"Ah, come on, man." Nate gave a half laugh as he sank back into his chair again. "Is that what all this is about? Me setting off firecrackers in front of the mayor's house?"

Buck said, "So you admit you threw lit fireworks out the window of your car toward a jogger on Riverside Drive at or around 5:50 this morning?"

Nate unscrewed the bottle and took another sip. "I admit I set off a string of firecrackers to celebrate the Fourth of July. If that's what you're going to charge me with, get it over with. And while you're at it, you might as well bring in every other person in town under thirty."

Buck said, "Did you throw a brick at my house yesterday afternoon?"

The faintest flicker of caution crossed his eyes, and he paused before taking another sip from the bottle. "Why would I do that?'

"You tell me."

After a moment, Nate gave a small smile and a shake of his head. "Look, man," he said, "I get that you're new here. But you're messing around in things you don't understand, and that's not going to turn out well for anybody, okay? So just back off."

"Back off," Buck repeated thoughtfully. "Back off from what?"

"Just stay out of our business is all I'm saying," Nate replied impatiently. "What goes on at Hollowgrove has got nothing to do with you."

Buck said, "But I guess you know everything that goes on out there."

His mouth turned up in a smirk. "Of course I do. I'm going to be running the place one day."

Buck nodded. "So what can you tell me about a girl named Giselle Martindale? You probably know her as Brandy."

A shutter came down over Nate's eyes, but not before Buck caught a flicker of surprise there. Or maybe it was alarm.

Nate said cautiously, "What am I supposed to know?"

"Does she work for Hollowgrove?"

"Maybe." He shrugged. "We've got almost a hundred employees. I don't know all of them."

Buck brought up her picture on his phone. "Maybe this will jog your memory."

Nate stared at the photo without expression. Buck got the feeling he was one of those people who had developed an expertise at evading the truth from an early age.

"She had a baby recently," Buck prompted, "spent a few months at Hope House and gave up her baby for adoption. Your aunt Geraldine checked her out of the hospital yesterday. Did she come back to Hollowgrove?"

"Maybe," said Nate diffidently. "Sounds like something Aunt Geraldine would do. She takes good care of the household staff."

Buck said flatly, "She runs a prostitution ring and you know it. You know everything that goes on at Hollowgrove, right?"

Nate unscrewed the top of his water bottle

without blinking and took another drink. He held Buck's gaze throughout, which was a mistake because Buck could see the shadow of unease behind the carefully maintained contempt there. "That," said Nate, "is bullshit."

Buck tapped over to Marianne's driver's license photo and showed it to Nate. "What about this woman? Have you seen her before?"

He barely glanced at it. "What, is she supposed to work for us too?"

"No," replied Buck calmly, "she's Giselle Martindale's sister, and she was murdered yesterday."

The boy was surprised, Buck was sure of it. But all that showed in his voice was anger as he replied, "What the hell does that have to do with me? I don't know the chick, never seen her before. Why are you wasting my time with this shit?"

Buck checked his watch and closed the file again. "Well," he said, rising, "speaking of wasting time, I've got a busy day. Busier day tomorrow, so it'll probably be Saturday or Sunday before I get back to you. "

"Hey!" Nate said as Buck walked away. "Hey, wait!"

Buck did not turn around.

"Listen to me!" There was real desperation in the kid's voice now. "I've answered all your damn questions, I've done what you said, let me out of here!"

Buck kept walking.

"Because if you don't," Nate cried, his voice hoarsening, "if I'm still here this time tomorrow, all those people are going to die and it will be on your hands, do you hear me? On your damn hands!"

Buck turned around slowly. "What people?"

CHAPTER THIRTY-FIVE

Junior took the old Cottonfield Road entrance to Hollowgrove, which he saw had been paved and widened. Puddles left over from last night's rain splashed beneath his tires and a low, steamy morning mist rose up from the marshy fields on either side of the road. Tendrils of fog drifted across the road like greedy, seeking fingers before evaporating over the hot asphalt. It was all different now, of course. And so terribly familiar that it made his gut clench with a kind of visceral, completely inarguable dread.

There was the twisted sycamore, its gnarled branches stretching low over the road, almost meeting the row of live oaks on the opposite side. Junior had fallen out of that tree as a kid and sprained his wrist. Of course, the road had been dirt back then. He probably would have broken it on asphalt. Not too far ahead, an easy bike ride for a couple of adventurous boys, was the track that used to lead off through the weeds to the old tool shed—a shack, really—where Junior and Zach used to go to smoke cigarettes and sometimes, if Zach could sneak into his older brother Trey's stash, more interesting things. That was, at least, until they found out the other things that were going on in that shack.

His mind had drifted, and with it, the car. He jerked the wheel back toward his own side of the road as one of Zach's Whitley Heating and Air vans passed him and lifted his hand in an abashed greeting. The driver wasn't Zach, but Junior hadn't expected it to be.

A few hundred yards later he made the turn into the gravel parking lot of Whitley Heating and Air. A small modular office with a faux cedar façade had been erected in the center of the lot, with ten or so service vans and a couple of big cargo trucks around back. To the side was an enormous metal warehouse, bay doors closed. There were two vehicles parked in front of the building: Zach's pick-up, which Junior recognized from their meeting yesterday, and a deep blue Mercedes. Junior parked next to the Mercedes and went around to the steps that led to the office. He paused to glance back at Zach's truck, then went up the stairs.

The lights were on and the door was unlocked, so Junior went in. The desk in the small reception area was empty, and he started to call out to announce himself. He stopped when he heard voices in the private office just behind the reception area. The door was open, and he could see Zach standing beside the desk, frowning at his father.

"Look, I ain't got time to stand here arguing with you," Jarrod Whitley said. "I just stopped by to let you know Nate's taking care of the shipment. He's got the keys, should be here by sunrise. You just make sure none of your boys are around when it comes in."

Zach said, "Damn it, Daddy, I told you I don't like Nate being involved in this. He's just a kid."

The old man grunted out a laugh. "He's man enough to pull his weight around here. Besides, what the hell else has he got to do with his time except get high and get into trouble? At least he's got an appreciation for the family business."

Junior cleared his throat and stepped forward. "Morning, y'all," he said.

The elder Whitley turned his head sharply and sucked in his breath. "Holy shit," he said, staring.

Zach said, "Junior! I didn't expect you."

The shock on Jarrod Whitley's face transformed into a sly grin. "Well, I'll be damned, boy. For a minute there I thought you were your old man, come back from the grave." He stepped forward and shook Junior's hand. "How the hell are you, anyway? Been a year or two. What brings you out this way?"

Junior shook his hand, once again the twelve-year-old boy being polite to a man he detested. "Good to see you, sir." Then, because he wasn't twelve years old, he withdrew his hand and turned to Zach. "Sorry to barge in on you, man. I thought I'd try to catch you before you headed out for the day."

"Yeah, sure." Zach tried to sound enthusiastic but there was confusion in his eyes. "You just caught me. Half day because of the holiday. My secretary isn't even coming in. I'm taking the wife to the beach, you know. Come on in. I think I've got some coffee left."

Jarrod looked from one to the other of them, a keen skepticism in his eyes. "Well," he said, "I'll let you boys catch up." He glanced again at Zach. "Don't forget. Tomorrow morning."

Zach gave a discouraging frown but did not reply. They both were silent until they heard the front door close firmly behind Jarrod Whitley.

"He hasn't changed much," remarked Junior when they were alone.

Zach shrugged uncomfortably. "You know. Thirty years older and about that much meaner." He turned to the coffee pot that sat atop a low file cabinet on the other side of the room. "All I've got is powdered creamer. That okay?"

Junior said, "Do you think he knew?"

Zach shot him a sharp look but said nothing.

"What Trey was up to," Junior clarified. "Do you think he knew?"

Zach brought Junior a Styrofoam cup of coffee, his expression guarded. "What're you doing here, Junior?"

Junior went over to the coffee stand, added powdered creamer to his cup, and stirred it absently. "I'm not sure," he admitted. "Just wanted to see the place again, I guess."

The two of them were silent for a moment, then Zach said, "You know, if you shaved the beard and put a little color in your hair, you wouldn't look like him that much at all. I mean, you never even liked your dad that much. Why would you want to go around looking like him?"

Junior shrugged. "I've got my issues, I guess. We both do." He glanced around the room, looking for conversation, and came up with, "What happened to your truck, man?"

Zach shrugged, not meeting his eyes. "One of the guys backed into it with a van. These kids, fresh out of tech school, they know their way around a compressor but can't drive worth shit."

Junior sipped his coffee. "I hear you."

Zach leaned one hip on the edge of the desk, watching Junior carefully. "Looks like the police got all they needed yesterday. You know, from the site. Daddy said construction started up again this morning."

Junior nodded without comment.

"I mean," Zach went on, "it was thirty years ago. Not like anybody's interested now, right?"

"Right," Junior murmured, gazing into his

coffee.

"I've been thinking," Zach went on with more confidence. "And what I think is that they'll probably send the bones to some out-of-state lab somewhere that does that kind of thing—you know, identify old bones—but what are they going to find? A couple of kids with no relatives, no public record, nothing to link them to anybody alive today. I mean, it's stupid really. I don't know why I panicked."

Junior nodded again, not looking up from his coffee. "You know, it's funny. Looking through all of Daddy's old things, remembering stuff... realizing how much I don't remember. I mean, there are pictures of us, me and Julia and Mama and Daddy, when we were happy. Daddy and me, catching fish on the pier. Camping down in Kissimmee. Birthdays and shit. But that day changed everything. It made me forget the good things."

Zach said quietly, "Don't go down that road, Junior. Nothing good ever comes of it."

Finally, Junior stopped stirring his coffee and looked up at him. He said, "We bullied those kids. They worshipped the ground we walked on, and we treated them like dogs. No, worse than dogs. Like slaves. Making them do our chores, pump up the tires on our bicycles while we sat in the shade, holding bets on which one of them could eat the most bugs..."

"Come on, Junior," Zach said uncomfortably,

"that was just being kids. Besides, there were lots of times when it wasn't like that, when we just hung out, the four of us. You know that."

"Sure," Junior agreed. "After they got old enough to steal cigarettes from the Magic Mart for us without getting caught, take the blame for pranks we pulled, sneak booze out of your dad's liquor cabinet… we had a great time hanging out. The thing is, it all seemed so normal. The white kids and the 'little spics.' Isn't that what your daddy used to call them?"

Zach's face was tight. "You don't have to make it sound like that. We were friends, you know we were."

"Yeah," agreed Junior thoughtfully. "At least they thought we were. But all the time, we were just setting them up." He looked at Zach steadily. "So yeah," he said, "I think your daddy knew. He was feeding those kids to Trey like baby chicks to a snake. And so were we."

"Jesus, God, Junior!" Zach slammed his coffee cup down on the desk, spilling most of it, and stood abruptly, his face haggard. "Do you think I don't think about it every damn day? Do you think I don't have nightmares just the same as you do? But what good does it do to keep going over and over it? Why can't you just let it stay—"

"Buried?" suggested Junior, and the faintest hint of a mirthless smile twitched his lips, then faded. "Because these things never do, do they?"

Zach pushed a hand through his thinning hair

and sucked in a breath as though for a reply, then released it wordlessly.

Junior looked down at his coffee cup and his eyebrows knit briefly. Without looking up, he said, "So, to answer your question, I guess I came out here to see if anything had changed. But it hasn't, has it?" He put the cup aside with a small grimace of distaste and stood, fixing Zach with his gaze. "After everything that happened, all these years, you people are still doing the same old shit."

A thread of fear crept into Zach's eyes. He tried to disguise it with a nervous chuckle.
"What are you talking about?"

Junior said, "He bought you. All of this..." He made a brief gesture to include the building, the warehouse, the vehicles outside, and beyond. "Your nice house with a view of the marsh, even the kids' education, I'm betting. Payment in full. And all you have to do is look the other way."

Zach licked his lips nervously. "You don't know what you're talking about, Junior." He moved behind the desk, almost as though for protection against his old friend. "I built this business myself, it has nothing to do with the plantation, or with family money."

The look Junior gave Zach was pitying, and he did not reply. Junior opened the door and then looked back. "Do you know how many times I started to tell my dad the truth?" he said. "I wanted to, I tried to, but I kept imagining the look on his face, the disappointment, the-- I don't know, the *revulsion*, I guess-- and I lost my nerve every time. After a while, it got so I couldn't even look him in the eye, and it stayed that way till the day he died. I let the guilt and the shame eat away half my life, but it stops now."

Zach said urgently, "Junior, you can't be thinking about bringing the law into this, not after all these years. You know if Daddy ever finds out the truth it will destroy him. It'll destroy my whole family. Let it go. It's over, done with, forgotten. Just leave it be, can't you?"

Junior looked at him sadly for another moment. "But that's the problem, isn't it? It's not over. It won't be until somebody stops you. And I guess maybe that somebody is me." He turned to leave.

"Junior, damn it..." Zach choked out hoarsely, but Junior didn't stop. "Junior," he said again, "for God's sake, don't do this. You have no idea what you're getting into. I can't let you go to the police. Stop!"

Junior turned around to see Zach standing behind the desk, desperation in his eyes, a handgun clutched between his fists and pointed straight at Junior.

Junior looked at the gun, then at his friend. He said quietly, "I can't believe it's come to this. Put the gun down, Zach. You know you're not going to..."

His old friend pulled the trigger.

CHAPTER THIRTY-SIX

B uck repeated very distinctly, "What people?"

The empty water bottle crackled loudly between Nate's fingers as he crushed it. He clamped his lips together at the same time, looking as though he already regretted the outburst, but Buck did not move.

In a moment Nate burst out, "The workers, okay? We've got a dozen new workers coming in from the border and somebody's got to be there to let them out. It's the holiday and my dad's going to be out of town, so Grandpa gave the key to me."

Buck came back to the table. "The key to what?"

"The truck, stupid!" Nate sounded more frustrated than belligerent now, and there was genuine desperation in his eyes. He went on in a rush, "My dad's box truck, Whitley Heating and Air. The border patrol never searches it, we move parts out of Texas all the time. Don't pretend everybody doesn't do it. Jesus, man, they come here looking for a better life and we give it to them. They're glad to be here! But it's a hard trip, especially this time of year. Grandpa said we're pushing it to get them here alive, and if I'm not there to pay the driver and let them out they won't be, do you hear me? So how about cutting the bullshit and letting me do my job?"

Buck sat down, hiding his expression as he made careful notes on the blank pages inside the folder. "What time is the truck going to be here?"

"6:00 in the morning," he said quickly, "at the warehouse. I have to be there, or else—man, you don't know what my grandpa is like. If he loses any more inventory..."

Buck said mildly, "Inventory?"

"You know, workers. They're paid for already, and it can't be on me if they, you know, if they can't do the job." Nate was starting to sweat. "It can't be on me. This is my chance, man, and I'm not going to blow it over some bogus, trumped-up charge..."

Buck interrupted, "This truck. Do you know the license plate?"

Nate exploded, "How the hell should I know that? It's just a truck, man! A Whitley Heating and Air truck! He's got three of them. Whichever one is missing is the one he sent to Texas, okay?"

Buck was silent, pretending to read over his notes. He could feel his pulse throbbing in his neck. He said, "What time does the truck leave the border?"

"I don't know," he replied impatiently. "Why should I?"

"Do you know where, exactly, it picks up its cargo?"

"No. I told you, my job is just to meet it when it gets here."

"Who else knows what time the truck is arriving?"

"I don't know." The water bottle crackled between his fingers again. "Grandpa. He might have told my dad, but I doubt it. My dad wasn't talking to anybody last night. He was too mad about his truck."

Buck glanced up from his notes. "What truck? The one he sent to Texas?"

Nate shook his head. "No, his *truck*. His pickup. Somebody backed into him yesterday, put a scrape in the side. Listen, have you got enough? Are you going to let a stupid brick and a string of firecrackers stand in the way of all those people getting out alive? I'm sorry, okay? Now let me go."

Buck closed the file folder, keeping his expression neutral. "Okay, Nate," he said. "Let me see what I can do for you. Just sit tight."

Nate sank back in his chair, shoulders relaxing. "Now that's more like it," he muttered as Buck walked toward the door.

The jailer was waiting outside. Buck jerked his head back toward the room, barely breaking stride. "Lock him up," he said. He headed for the elevator.

CHAPTER THIRTY-SEVEN

Buck caught the frame of Lydia's open door with his hand as he passed. "Lydia, can you get..." He broke off when the file clerk, Marion, looked up from Lydia's desk. "Is it lunchtime already?" Marion took over Lydia's desk from precisely noon to 1:00 every day for Lydia's lunch hour. Since Buck usually took lunch himself around that time, he didn't often see Marion.

"Yes, sir," she answered cheerfully. "Can I help you with something?"

"Yeah, get me the regional office of ICE on the phone. I'll talk to whoever answers."

She looked alarmed and uncertain. "Um, I usually just answer the phone until Lydia gets back."

He hesitated, rubbing away the crease between his brows. There was always the possibility the kid had lied to him, but even if he hadn't, Buck would need more concrete evidence before he could expect any urgent help from a federal agency—and that was exactly what any customs official would tell him over the phone. Moreover, there was a good chance he could get that evidence without tipping off Geraldine Whitley that she was under investigation. The Whitley crime empire was established like a set of carelessly arranged dominoes. If one piece fell, the whole would cascade.

Buck said, "Okay, never mind. I need to check something out first anyway. Where's Sully?"

"I think he said something about securing Hobo for the holiday," Marion replied, then added helpfully, "I can try to reach him for you."

"That's okay." He glanced again at his watch. "Just have Roland bring my car around, will you? I'm going out for a couple of hours."

Junior came to with blood dripping from his fingers and a swirl of words fading in and out of his perception, like bad recordings in an old movie. Zach's face floated into view, distorted, distressed, his voice choked. "I'm sorry, man, I'm sorry. I didn't mean..." *Fading.* "Never would have...accident..."

Junior couldn't feel his left arm. That was probably good because when he turned his head, ever so slightly, he could see a small dark hole in his left shoulder from which blossomed an ever-deepening carnation of red. He thought about his wife. She loved carnations.

Junior mumbled, "Zach, what the hell?" He tried

to stand up, grabbing the doorframe for support, but his hand was slippery with blood, and the blinding flame of pain that shot through his shoulder caused him to collapse again, biting back a scream.

When his head cleared again, Zach was still standing there above him, the pistol held loosely in his hand, a helpless look in his eyes. "Damn it, Junior, you don't understand. It's not just the boys, not just Trey... if you go to the police they'll find out, they'll know..." He wiped a shaky hand across his mouth. "Damn it, Junior! Why did you have to come here?"

Junior struggled to keep his voice steady. The pain was throbbing now, pulsing explosions of yellow-orange fire all down his left side. "Zach," he managed, "it's okay. Whatever you did, it'll be okay. This..." He gritted his teeth and tried, once again, to stand up. "It was an accident, like you said. Just—call an ambulance, okay? I need to get to the hospital. I can't... can't get there on my own."

Zach stood there for another moment, still clutching the weapon, looking desperate and uncertain. Sweat sheened his face. His eyes shot toward the phone on his desk. And then, with a single breath, he seemed to find his calm. Resolve came over his face. "No," he said quietly. "I can't do that."

CHAPTER THIRTY-EIGHT

Trish drove. Baker frowned over his phone, just as he had been doing for the last fifteen minutes. He hadn't spoken in at least that long. At last, Trish ventured, "What are you looking at, sir?'

Without glancing up, he replied, "Job opportunities."

Trish cast him an alarmed look. "Sir, if this is about what happened this afternoon, I'm happy to go to the chief on your behalf. The suspect was clearly resisting arrest and I only intervened because..." Here she stumbled.

"Because you thought I was going to bash the kid's brains out on the pavement," Baker supplied, "and you were probably right." After another moment he put his phone away, staring straight ahead. "You acted appropriately, Officer Miller. I've been known to have issues with my temper."

Trish struggled to find a reply. "I, um... Yes, sir." Then she glanced at him. "But in this case, you may have been justified. Nate Whitley is a prick."

One corner of Baker's lips twitched with a small smile. "Yeah, he is." He looked over at her. "I was just joking about looking for a job. The chief is cool. Although..." He turned his gaze forward again. "Maybe not as cool as I thought he was." He frowned. "Where the hell are we, anyway?"

"Broken Bridge Road," she replied. "Eight miles from the city limits."

"What are we doing here?"

"I'm asserting myself, sir," she replied, "just as you advised."

The look he gave her was not amused. "That's out of our territory."

"Yes, sir," she admitted, "but we haven't had lunch yet, and there's a great barbecue place just down the road."

"Hog Heaven," he replied. His frown was less ferocious, but still there. "That's in the middle of damn nowhere. We'll never make it there and back in an hour."

"We will if we take the shortcut," Trish assured him, and made a sharp right turn.

Baker lurched against his seatbelt and Trish gave him an apologetic look. "I thought you might need a break from all the craziness in town," she said. Then she added, "Me, too."

They rode in silence for a minute, and then Baker

said, "So how was your dad when you told him about what happened with your car?"

She hesitated. "I didn't exactly tell him," she admitted. "I said I had a breakdown and called a tow company."

"Yeah, good thinking." He looked over at her. "That was a pretty swanky place I brought you home to yesterday. If you don't mind me asking, what does your daddy do?"

"I don't mind," she said. "He's the president of the Mercy Community Bank." And before Baker could even lift an appreciative eyebrow she added, "My mother is a judge."

Baker said, "Oh, yeah? Around here?"

"Yes. District Court." She cast a quick glance at him. "Judge Warren."

Now he did lift an eyebrow. Both, in fact. "No lie? I've been in her courtroom. She's a real..."

"Bitch?" suggested Trish.

Baker grinned. "I was going to say 'badass'."

Trish grinned back.

Baker said, "And they didn't want you to be a cop?"

She shrugged uncomfortably, the grin fading. "It's complicated."

Baker said, "Well, for what it's worth, they were wrong. You're doing a good job."

Trish cast a quick, shy smile his way. "Thank you, sir."

Baker said, "Look, kid, we're going to be riding together for a while, so it's okay if..."

But that was when the call came in. Baker grabbed the radio mic and hit the lights and sirens almost before the dispatcher had finished speaking. "Unit 32 responding," he said. "Show us six minutes out."

He looked at Trish. "How fast can you drive?"

"Fast," she replied, and pressed the accelerator to the floor.

CHAPTER THIRTY-NINE

There were four vehicles in the parking lot of Whitley Heating and Air when Buck arrived, all parked in front of the office. One was a black Durango pickup truck, and not far from it, a white sedan that looked like a rental car. At the other end of the building, parked crookedly against the curb, were two other black pickups with "Hollowgrove Plantation" stenciled in gold on the door, like the one Don Estes had driven yesterday. Buck turned into the back driveway, away from the office building, toward the warehouse where the service vehicles were parked. He got out of the cruiser and looked around carefully.

From what he could tell, the kid had been right. There were six service vans parked behind the warehouse, but only two box trucks. He snapped a photo of the license plates and walked around the warehouse. The doors were locked, and the place seemed empty. Closing up for the holiday, he suspected.

He left his vehicle where it was and walked toward the office fifty yards away. Sunlight glared off the gravel, sending up a white heat that caused Buck to move to the relative shade of the grassy berm that lined the drive. The black Durango was parked in the last spot in front of the office building, away from the door. The tag read "Whitly6." Even as he approached, Buck could see the damage to the passenger side panel, and he moved to examine it closer. A long scrape and dent ran from the front headlight to the passenger door, and it was unmistakably streaked with blue paint. Buck looked toward the office. The door was partially open, and he could hear angry voices inside. He moved around the vehicles toward the building and noticed a small dark smear of something on the trunk of the white sedan. He touched it lightly, and his finger came away wet and stained. It was blood.

Buck tried the trunk, but it was closed and locked firmly, as were the doors. He returned to the trunk and grasped the handle firmly, shaking it. The vehicle bounced slightly on its wheels, and he thought he felt something shift inside, but he couldn't be sure. Buck looked around again, more carefully. There was blood spattered on the gravel beside the rear panel, and a long smear of it on the bottom steps, as though someone had fallen or been dragged. The voices inside the building grew angrier.

Buck pushed the emergency button on his phone that connected him to dispatch. He spoke quietly, "This is Chief Lawson in need of backup at Whitley Heating and Air on Cottonfield Road. Possible assault in progress, at least one injury." He disconnected quickly, before the dispatcher's reply could give away his position. It would take fifteen or twenty minutes for a unit to reach him out here. Until then, his job was to manage the situation as best he could, and hope it wasn't as bad as it appeared.

He started cautiously up the steps, his hand on his sidearm. He stopped when he reached the door. It was open about six inches, and there was another smear of blood, a handprint, on the doorframe. Buck slid his pistol from its holster and took a quick step back from the doorway, shielding himself from view. His heart was pounding.

The voices, a man and a woman arguing, came to him clearly now. The man sounded nervous. "I told you; it was just one of the technicians coming back for parts. They never come in here."

"And I told *you* to hurry up and get this place cleaned up before somebody does come in. And close the damn door!" That was the woman.

"None of this would have happened if it wasn't for you," returned the man. His voice sounded close to breaking. He didn't appear to be moving any closer to the door, but Buck pressed himself against the wall, just in case.

"I'm not the one who shot my best friend and locked him in the trunk of a car," the woman retorted. "And I'm not the one who took a simple job and screwed it up so badly every cop in the county will be looking for you if they're not already!"

"I told you, that wasn't my fault! All I did was drive the truck! It was Carter that shot that woman!"

"Nobody was supposed to shoot anybody! All you were supposed to do was get the kid back! It couldn't have been simpler! And now we've got another mess to deal with. What the hell were you thinking, Zach?"

Buck adjusted his grip on the pistol, listening without hope for the sound of approaching sirens and knowing that help was not coming. All his officers were in town, directing traffic and trying to keep the tourists from killing each other. They didn't even patrol out here. The entire sheriff's office was out looking on the other side of the county for Marianne Martindale's killer—a killer who was right here, on Hollowgrove Plantation. It didn't matter how many times Buck pushed the emergency button on his phone, he was alone.

The man said quietly, "What are you going to do with Junior?"

She replied matter-of-factly, "Wait until dark and dump him in the river. Wipe down the car and leave it in a parking lot somewhere."

Buck glanced at the white car, the smears of blood. If Junior was inside, likely bound and gagged and possibly unconscious, he couldn't have been there long. In this heat, the blood would have dried within minutes. And in this heat, Junior would not survive much longer than that.

Zach Whitley's voice was shaking with horror. "You can't do that! You can't leave him in the trunk all day! He'll die!"

"Isn't that the point? If you'd had better aim, he'd be dead already!"

"No! No, I just wanted to stop him. I didn't want—I didn't want any of this!"

"Just shut up, Zach," she snapped back. "You knew exactly what was going to happen when you called us. Stop whining."

There was a sound like a broken breath, then, "Just get out of here Geraldine. I shouldn't have called you. I'll deal with this myself. Just give me the keys to the car and get out of here."

"Like hell. The way you deal with things will put us all in prison."

"I said give me the keys!"

"Oh, for God's sake, Zach, put down that gun. Do you think this is a game?"

Buck couldn't wait any longer. He shot out his arm and pushed the door fully open, stepping inside the building in a single swift movement. His eyes took in the scene in one sweep. It was a typical office set-up with the reception area in front, desk and filing cabinets, and a private office behind. There were smears of blood on the gray Berber carpet, and the strong smell of bleach. Zach Whitley stood in front of the desk, leveling a pistol at Geraldine

Whitley. She stood a few feet away from him wearing a pair of yellow kitchen gloves and a furious look on her face.

Buck took in all of this in less than the time it took him to step inside, and he swung his weapon on Zach. "Police!" he said sharply. "Drop your weapon!"

Both Geraldine and Zach spun to face him at the same time. Zach held the gun in both hands aimed straight at Buck's chest, and at this distance he couldn't miss. Neither could Buck.

The look in Zach's eyes was distraught, on the edge of panic, and Buck thought he saw the dampness of tears in the blue circles beneath the other man's eyes. His gut tightened. An unstable gunman was something no law enforcement officer wanted to face. Particularly when the gun was pointed, with unwavering accuracy, at him.

Buck took a small step to the side, getting his back away from the door and keeping both Geraldine and Zach Whitley in sight. The barrel of Zach's gun jerked to follow him. Without taking his eyes off the gunman, Buck said, "Ms. Whitley, I need you to sit on the floor where you are and lace your hands behind your head. Do it now."

"Oh, for God's sake, Zach," she snapped angrily, ignoring Buck, "are you crazy? Put the fucking gun down!"

Buck repeated to her, "*Do it now.*"

Geraldine Whitley shot him a look filled with anger and contempt, then sank on the floor, her gloved hands laced behind her head.

Buck held the gunman's eyes steadily and kept his voice calm. "Listen to me, Mr. Whitley. Zach, is it? Zach, listen. This is not going to end well. I'm only allowed to give you a certain number of warnings before I open fire. Whatever is going on here, we can work it out. But you need to put the gun on the floor in front of you right now."

Zach Whitley gave a short, tight shake of his head. "No. No, I can't. I can't go to prison. I can't do that to my wife, my kids."

"Oh, please!" Geraldine sounded exasperated and infuriated. "You know Daddy's not going to let you go to prison! Not for that girl yesterday, and not for Junior. But you're pointing a gun at a policeman and you're about to get your fool self killed!"

Buck said quietly, "Is that it, Zach? Is that what you're afraid of? Were you involved in the death of Marianne Martindale yesterday?"

"I didn't do it!" Zach cried. "We were just supposed to go to her apartment and take the baby. But Carter said it was too risky, he was afraid of being seen, so we followed her, and I—I ran her off the road, but we weren't going that fast, I didn't think she'd be hurt, or the baby... then Carter had to go all Rambo and run down the hill with his gun out and—and he shot her! There was..." His voice caught. "There was blood on the baby's blanket when I took her out of the car seat."

Buck said, "Okay. We just need to get your statement on paper, and then we'll talk to Carter.

But right now, this is your last warning. Put the gun down."

Out of the corner of his eye, Buck saw Geraldine glance toward the back of the room, where the door was open to the inner office. That was when he remembered. Four vehicles in the parking lot. She had said 'us.' *You wouldn't have called* us.

Buck demanded sharply, "Who's in the back room?"

He didn't have to wait for a reply. A bullet ricocheted off the door casing over Buck's shoulder and Carter Whitley burst out of the back office, his Glock in hand. Buck ducked down behind the heavy oak desk next to Geraldine while Zach swung his gun wildly between Carter and Buck. Stupidly, Carter fired another round, this time straight into the desk. Wood splintered inches from Geraldine's face, and she screamed, diving for the floor.

"Put down the gun, Carter!" Buck shouted. He edged toward the corner of the desk until he could see both men while still blocking a clear shot from either of them. "I'm between you and the door and I'm a hell of a lot better shot than you are. You are not getting out of here. Put down the gun!"

"Not going to happen, my friend!" Carter returned, breathing hard. "You're outnumbered and you know it. And don't think you'll be the first cop to disappear out here."

Carter was still wearing his security uniform, the green pants smeared with blood from whatever role he had played in getting Junior in the trunk of the car. He took a step closer to Zach, lining up a better shot at Buck.

"Yeah, and thanks for throwing me under the damn bus, *bro,*" he told Zach bitterly, taking another step toward the desk. "I ought to shoot you, too, while I'm at it."

Zach looked frightened and confused. The barrel of his gun had dropped, his aim faltering uncertainly. He was not Buck's target. Buck tensed his muscles, tightened his grip. One smooth move, stand, swing, aim for center mass, squeeze the trigger. If his leg held up. If he was quick enough.

And then, unbelievably, he heard the sirens.

The others heard it too. Geraldine hissed from the floor, "For God's sake, it's over! Do what he says! I'm not going to get myself killed because of you two idiots!"

Carter flicked a quick, uneasy glance toward the door, and tightened his grip on his weapon. "Shut up!" he told his sister. "I can handle this. Come out from behind the desk. I can't get a clear shot with you there."

Buck took his eyes off the gunman long enough to flash Geraldine a hard, warning look. Her expression was angry, not scared. He had no idea what she was going to do. If she moved, it might distract Carter long enough for Buck to get off a shot. Or she might try to tackle Buck from behind, and she might succeed.

Buck could see uncertainty creep into Zach's eyes, warring with grief and fear and, finally, a kind of calm resignation. He said quietly, "I can't do this. I can't let Daddy find out what I did. Tell Junior I'm sorry. I never meant for it to turn out this way."

That was when Buck realized the sirens had stopped.

Zach started to lower the gun, and Carter cast an angry, astonished look his way. Taking advantage of that half-second of distraction, Buck prepared to swing into action.

In the moment, it all seemed to happen at once, a blur of noise and blood and movement. But in retrospect, as Buck tried to put events in order for his report, the sequence of events was clear. Buck sprang out from the cover of the desk, his gun aimed at Carter. Baker appeared from the back office at the same moment, his gun thrust into the back of Carter's neck. "Police!" he shouted. "Drop your weapon!"

Trish Miller swung through the front door, her weapon fixed on Geraldine Whitley. "Don't move!" she shouted. "Hands behind your head!"

And while all this was happening, Zach swung the gun upward and shoved the barrel into his mouth.

Buck shouted, "*No!*"

Carter swung his head toward Zach.

Geraldine Whitley screamed, "Zach! No!"

Zach Whitley pulled the trigger.

Buck rushed forward. Blood exploded from Zach Whitley's head, spattering his brother's face with bright viscous fluid and pale tissue. Carter Whitley staggered back, slipping in the blood, and fell to his knees. The gun skittered out of his hand. Buck kicked it out of the way. Baker, spattered with blood, forced Carter to the floor and cuffed him. Trish rushed forward and cuffed Geraldine Whitley. Buck turned to Zach Whitley.

It was, of course, too late.

CHAPTER FORTY

Three hours later the grounds of Hollowgrove Plantation were still covered with law enforcement vehicles. Junior Aikens, having been discovered in the trunk of his own car, bound and gagged with duct tape and bleeding from a bullet wound to the shoulder, was transported to the nearest hospital. Geraldine and Carter Whitley had been taken into custody by sheriff's deputies. Zach Whitley's remains had been claimed by the county medical examiner, and forensic technicians were now photographing and collecting evidence from the scene.

Sheriff John Tyler stood with Buck in the parking lot of Whitley Heating and Air, shaking his head in quiet disbelief. "So that's what this was all about? A baby kidnapping?"

"In a way," Buck said. "Marianne Martindale tried to rescue her sister and her newborn niece from Hope House, which was really just a front for selling the babies that Hollowgrove supplied through their pregnant girls. The problem was that the baby had already been legally adopted—and paid for—by someone else, and they were threatening to investigate. Geraldine Whitley sent her brothers to get the baby back, they got over-zealous and killed Marianne."

Tyler frowned deeply. "Unbelievable," he said. "Here in Corley County. But the baby's all right?"

"She's with her adoptive parents now," Buck replied.

"Sweet Jesus," breathed Tyler with another shake of his head. He looked at Buck. "So, you say it was Carter Whitley who did the killing?"

"That's according to Zach," Buck said, "and I'm inclined to believe him, under the circumstances. Of course, you'll want to run both guns through ballistics, but my money is on Carter."

Tyler wrinkled his brow, puzzled. "Why do you suppose Zach Whitley killed himself? The charges against him weren't that serious if he was telling the truth. Junior Aikens is going to be fine, and Zach didn't do anything but drive the car in the other case."

Buck shook his head, his expression somber. "It's hard to know a man's mind, Sheriff."

The other man extended his hand. "Call me John," he said firmly. "It was good working with you, Buck. You're a man of your word. You said you'd help, and by God, you did."

Buck shook his hand. "Well, it's all yours now, John. Yours and the GBI's, that is. I'll have Frankie send over her notes, and you can take it from here. I'd check out the old slave graveyard, too, if I was you. I suspect you'll find enough to keep you busy there for a few years, and I'm not talking about 200-year-old bones. Oh, and you might want to assign a few deputies to help ICE unload a truck that's due here in the morning. Human cargo."

Tyler looked disgusted. "Good lord. Is there anything these people weren't involved in?"

Buck admitted, "We haven't found any drugs yet. But then, we haven't finished the search."

Tyler gave another heavy shake of his head. "Looks like we've got our work cut out for us."

Buck clapped him lightly on the shoulder. "No offense, John, and I hope you'll understand when I say this, but I'm glad it's you and not me."

Buck drove to the main house and the adjacent office, where the Whitleys' so-called household staff were being interrogated by a mixture of deputies and Mercy police officers. The ladies, with their perfectly styled hair and artistically manicured nails, were dressed in designer jeans and belly tops, short summer dresses or swimsuits and gauzy cover-ups. It looked like a convention of supermodels.

"Good duty if you can get it," Buck remarked to Sully, who was leaning against his cruiser, admiring the view.

Sully straightened up with an abashed grin. "So

far we're not getting anything incriminating," he said, "but I didn't expect to. They all claim they work here as waitresses or housemaids or whatever, and all deny taking money for sex—which is true, I guess, if what Gilford said is right. The guests pay Hollowgrove, not the girls. That one..." He nodded toward Marina, who had been Buck's hostess when he dined at Hollowgrove. She was dressed today in flowing white pants and a fitted white top, with her hair piled atop her head and her eyes carefully watching every interaction between the other girls and the police. "She seems to be more or less in charge. Everybody looks at her before answering. I interviewed her myself. Same story."

Buck said, "Just as well. We're not here to arrest the victims, at least not today. Hell, in a county this size, we don't have the cell space."

Sully agreed heavily, "That's for damn sure." He followed Buck's gaze to the mansion and added, "What about him?"

Jarrod Whitley stood on the verandah of the big house, his arms folded across his chest, his jaw jutting furiously as he watched his empire being dismantled piece by piece. He was flanked on either side by deputies and attended by Dobie Jones, the Whitley attorney's overworked young associate. Apparently, Jones had considered an event of this magnitude worth canceling his afternoon court appearances for.

Buck handed Sully the folded paper he had come to deliver. "Here's the warrant. We've got him on false imprisonment and half a dozen other labor law violations, with more to come tomorrow, and probably more after that. Did somebody tell him about Zach?"

Sully nodded grimly. "He didn't shed a tear. Seemed mad if anything, at all the violation of his rights and invasion of his property."

Buck let out a breath. "That is one sick son of a bitch."

"Yes, sir." Sully looked at him carefully. "Chief, you all right? It couldn't have been easy, you know…" He shifted his eyes back down the road. "Back there."

It was a moment before Buck could reply, and then he said simply, "Yeah." Yeah, it hadn't been easy. And yeah, he was okay. Or he would be.

Sully held up the warrant. "Are you sure you don't want the pleasure?"

Buck said, "I would, but my mama raised me never to kill or arrest a man after I've dined at his table. You take care of it. And Sully," he added as Sully started toward the house. His face was hard. "Be sure to cuff him."

"You got it, boss."

Buck walked over to the grassy area in front of the office, where Frankie was interviewing the woman Buck immediately recognized as Giselle Martindale. She looked considerably better than when Buck had last seen her. Her hair was clean and pulled back with a tortoiseshell clip, highlights glistening in the sun. Her makeup was light and deftly applied, although her eyes looked pink and wet from crying. Nonetheless, she appeared composed in a pale blue linen dress and open-toed pumps, her hands laced together demurely before her. She might have been on her way to a garden party.

Buck caught Frankie's eye but hung back, not wanting to interrupt the interview. Trish Miller came over to him, her young face lined with puzzled distress. He said, "Anything useful, Officer Miller?"

Her brows corkscrewed as she tried to make sense out of her reply. "It's like something out of *The Handmaid's Tale*," she replied. "None of the women I've interviewed admit to taking money for sex. In fact, they don't get paid for anything, but they live better than I do—designer clothes, jewelry, spa treatments, gourmet meals. Some are Russian, most are South American. They've all been here since they were thirteen or fourteen. From the time they get here, they get lessons in English and deportment and..." She flushed faintly. "'How to please a man.' That was a quote, sir." They have an on-site gym and a very strict routine that Geraldine Whitley oversees. On top of that, they actually get rewards for getting pregnant. Not only do they get to live at that posh Hope House until the baby is born, but when they come back here they get their own suite of rooms and three months off from work. They say Miss Geraldine treats them like queens, as long as they do what she says, and nobody wants to leave." The bewilderment in her eyes deepened. "I mean, *nobody*."

"Stockholm syndrome," Frankie said, coming up to join them, "like I suspected. Which means none of them are likely to press charges, and it's going to be even harder to get them to turn state's evidence."

"This is their home," Trish pointed out. "Where would they even go?"

Buck couldn't resist turning to watch the old man, cuffed and cursing mightily, being perp-walked to a waiting squad car. The satisfaction he felt was immense.

He turned back to Trish. "Fortunately, that's not ours to decide. The GBI will be taking over this investigation, with assistance from the county. You did good work today," he added, and extended his hand. "Thank you. Good to have you aboard."

She shook his hand, blushing furiously. "Yes, sir. I um…"

Buck turned to Frankie, putting Trish out of her misery. "As soon as you finish up your interviews," he said, "send everybody back to duty and forward a copy of your report to the sheriff's office. We're outta here."

"Thank God," said Frankie, and Trish looked as relieved as she did. "This whole investigation has given me a giant case of the creeps."

Buck managed a smile for both of the officers, and then went over to talk to Giselle.

"Miss Martindale," he said, "I'm Chief Lawson, Mercy Police Department. First, I want to tell you how sorry I am about your sister."

She looked up at him with wet, hurt eyes. "She came all this way," she said, "even got a job here so she could be near me...but I never asked her to do that. Why would she do that? She kept talking about what we were going to do and where we were going to go after the baby came and some of it sounded good, yeah, but I never said I would. I *never.* She said she wanted to help me and now she's dead and it's all my fault, but I never asked her to come here!" She looked at him helplessly, a fat tear spilling down her cheek. "Why did she do that? *Why*?"

"She loved you," Buck replied simply. "And she wanted a good life for you and your baby."

Giselle shook her head angrily, wiping the tears from her face with a swipe of the crumpled-up tissue she held balled in her fist. "I didn't ask her. *I didn't ask her.*"

Buck said, "I know Detective Moreno already asked you this, but why did you run? Why didn't you get into the car with your sister?"

She shook her head, not meeting his eyes. "I knew I'd be in trouble for leaving Hope House. I was scared, and it was all so sudden. I'd just had a baby, for God's sake. I heard the gunshot and Marianne screamed at me to run and I panicked. I was going to come back to my room as soon as people stopped looking for me. I didn't want to get in trouble. But I got lost in the dark and..." she shook her head wearily. "Everything was so messed up."

Buck said, "I guess the detective told you that your daughter is fine. Would you like to see her?"

She looked at him as though he had suddenly started speaking a foreign language. "What? Why would I?"

He said, "Did you sign the adoption papers willingly?"

Still, there was nothing but puzzled curiosity in her eyes. "Sure, months ago. It's what we do." She added with just a touch of casual pride, "It's my second one, you know."

Buck said hesitantly. "Your second...?"

"Baby," she replied. "I'm good at it."

Buck could do nothing but nod, pretending to understand.

He started to walk away, but then she said, "Her name is Daisy." There was a touch of wistfulness in her voice, and she looked, for just that moment, completely forlorn.

Buck said, "Thank you, Miss Martindale. You've been a big help. I hope everything works out for you."

But somehow he doubted that it would.

He saw Leon Baker a few feet away, finishing up an interview with one of the women. Buck came over to him.

Baker said, "These people are really messed up." His uniform was still spattered with Zach Whitley's blood. "It's like... none of them realize they've done anything wrong."

Buck said, "You should go home. You and Miller both. You've done your job for today."

Baker shook his head absently. "Nah, we're short-handed. I'll stay."

"A few good men," Buck murmured absently.

Baker looked at him quizzically, and Buck shook his head, smiling. "It was mighty good to see you," he said, "back at the shop. What the hell were you doing out this way, anyhow?"

"Oh," Baker said, and seemed on the verge of embarrassment. "Lunch break. There's this great barbecue joint about two miles away. Hog Heaven."

Buck said, "Family place?"

Baker replied cautiously, "Yeah."

Buck said, "We'll have to take the wives and kids there some night for dinner. After all this holiday craziness, of course."

Baker replied uncertainly, "Yeah. Sounds good."

Buck glanced around and said in a moment, "Well. Carry on." He started to walk away.

Baker said, "Chief."

Buck looked back.

"See you in church."

Buck smiled and turned to walk back to his car. He still had a twenty-year-old kid sitting in jail, waiting for Buck to tell him that his father had just committed suicide.

When Buck returned home that evening, he

was greeted by the smell of charcoal smoke on the warm summer air. A flock of starlings exploded in the sky overhead as he came through the hedge, and the grass that stretched toward the river was a particularly brilliant shade of emerald. Home had never looked so good.

Eloise was putting a bright yellow tablecloth on the picnic table on the screen porch, and she called, "Evening, Buck! We found the grill."

"Good deal," he returned. "I'll bring the steaks out in a minute."

He entered through the side door and was tackled by an excited Willis and an even more excited Thor the minute he set foot in the kitchen. He put the groceries on the counter and let them knock him to the floor, Willis hugging his neck and Thor licking his face.

"Guess what, Buck?" Willis cried. "I hardly got in trouble at all! I just have to take out the garbage and set the table for two weeks and plant three rows of cucumbers in Mama Eloise's garden. I can do that easy! And, hey, we found the grill in the garage and put it together all by ourselves! Can I have potato chips with my steak?"

"Whatever your mama says, big guy," Buck replied. He held on to the boy a little tighter than was perhaps strictly necessary, and his voice was muffled in Willis's shirt. He had to force himself to let go. "Now, let me get these groceries unpacked so we can get this show on the road, huh?"

He pushed the exuberant Thor away and

grasped the countertop to help himself to his feet. His bad leg ached from having been on it most of the day.

Jo was standing by the sink, smiling as she watched them. He went over and kissed her lightly on the lips. She studied his face for a moment when they stepped apart, and then took a handful of silverware from a drawer and handed it to Willis.

"Go help Mama Eloise set the table," she told him. "And stay away from the grill," she warned as he scampered out the back door, Thor at his heels.

She turned back to Buck. "So," she invited, "how did your day go?"

"Okay." He took the steaks out of the bag, followed by four fat baking potatoes and a loaf of garlic bread. "I broke up a baby-selling operation, initiated an ICE investigation, got shot at, rescued Junior Aikens from the trunk of a car—he's going to be fine, don't worry, even with the GSW to his shoulder..." He turned to wash his hands, drying them on a paper towel. "Let's see... oh, yeah, solved the Marianne Martindale murder, arrested Jarrod Whitley, and..." He tossed the paper towel in the trash, turning again to face his wife. "Watched a man blow his brains out right in front of my eyes. Pretty much an ordinary day in Mercy."

Jolene stepped forward and took him in her arms. Buck held her tightly, dropping his face to her hair. After a long time he was able to speak again, and what he said was, softly, "It's good to be home."

CHAPTER FORTY-ONE

The dining room of the Magnolia Inn B&B held ten round tables, each decorated with red, white, and blue striped tablecloths and centerpieces of red and white carnations with silver streamers fashioned to look like firecrackers. Every table held four to six people, mostly women. The League of Women Voters had gone all out for their July meeting.

Buck was escorted to his table by Iris Pearlman, president of the chapter, who held on to his arm as though he was a prize she was afraid of losing and who stopped at every table they passed to introduce him to someone. Buck put on his most charming smile and tried not to look at his watch.

The mayor was already seated at the table nearest the lectern, and when they reached it, Iris said, "Now, you must excuse me for a minute,

Chief. I have a few things to take care of—you know how it is when you're in charge! But you're in good company with the mayor until I get back."

Buck sat down as she hurried off. He unfolded a white linen napkin across his knee and said, "Really, Miss Corinne, we have to stop meeting like this. Seems like I just had lunch with you a couple of days ago."

She dimpled and lifted her almost-empty mimosa glass. "Next time you'll have to take me dancing."

A luncheon plate with a scoop of chicken salad atop a lettuce leaf was already in front of him, and a waitress appeared with two mimosas in hand. She set one before the mayor and the other in front of Buck. Miss Corinne lifted a finger and said, "Oh, honey, the chief doesn't drink at lunch. Just bring him an orange juice, won't you?"

Buck closed his fingers around the glass. "It's fine," he told the waitress. He turned and lifted his glass to the mayor. "Happy Independence Day, Mayor."

She returned the toast with an amused quirk of her eyebrow. "The same to you, sugar."

The drink was heavy on the champagne, and he put it down after one sip. "By the way," he added, "thanks for the bourbon."

She picked up her fork. "Just my way of thanking you for the fine job you've been doing."

He couldn't tell whether or not she was being sarcastic, so he did not reply.

She cut off a piece of lettuce with her fork and popped it into her mouth. "I hear you had a bit of excitement at Hollowgrove yesterday."

"A bit." Buck took a bite of the chicken salad. Too much celery, too much mayonnaise.

"I mean," she went on easily, pretending to focus on her own salad, "practically every member of the Whitley family in jail, and poor Zach Whitley dead. Whoever would've thought?"

She allowed a moment of respectful silence before adding, "Junior was sent home after they fixed him up at the emergency room last night, though. That's the good news. His wife is driving in."

"I'm glad to hear that," replied Buck, although he had of course checked on Junior before going to bed last night. None of this was news to him.

She looked at him intently. "What do you suppose came over Zach, Buck? You were there."

He told her what was already a part of the record, and that was all he knew. "Junior overheard Jarrod talking to Zach about the shipment of illegals that was due and apparently told Zach he was going to the police. That's when Zach shot him. I guess he didn't think he could live with the consequences of attempted homicide against his oldest friend."

Corinne Watts shook her head sadly, again allowing a moment of silence. Then she said, "And did I hear something about a raid of some kind out there this morning?"

"I'm afraid I couldn't speak to that," Buck replied, picking up his glass again.

Thirteen illegal immigrants had been unloaded from a Whitley Heating and Air truck at approximately 6:30 that morning and taken into ICE custody. Many of them were sick, all of them were dehydrated, and some had to be transported to the hospital. But they were alive. And that evidence was, metaphorically speaking, the final nail in Jarrod Whitley's coffin.

"Oh, please, Buck, don't be difficult." Her tone was impatient. "I know you were there."

"Only as an observer," he assured her. He added, "But I did hear that investigators had uncovered the partially decomposed remains of two more victims in the old slave graveyard. One was riddled with bullet wounds from what appeared to be an assault rifle. The other's cause of death is undetermined."

She made a face. "Gracious. What a topic for the luncheon table."

"Also, one of the agents told me they had been trying to tie Jarrod Whitley to a South American arms deal for years, but every time they got close to making a case it would blow up in their faces. It looks like what started out as a local investigation could end up being a whole lot bigger."

"Thanks to you," she said generously, but something in her expression made Buck think none of this was a surprise to her.

He took the compliment with a shrug. "Of

course, the whole thing is in the hands of county and state authorities now. Just like…" he added meaningfully, "it should have been in the first place."

She speared a tiny piece of chicken with her fork. "Well, now," she returned mildly, "if we'd left it up to them, nothing ever would have been done, would it?"

Buck ate in silence for a while. His dining companion finished her mimosa and signaled for another. Buck touched his mouth with his napkin and said, "You know, there were actually four ICE complaints against Hollowgrove in the past eight years. All were closed without action."

"Is that a fact?" She smiled at the waitress who brought her third—or perhaps it was her fourth— mimosa.

"At first I thought it had to be somebody pretty powerful to close down that many investigations in a row," Buck went on. "And then I thought that it actually had to be somebody pretty powerful to even go up against Whitley and report him in the first place. Somebody like you."

She just sipped her mimosa.

"So last night, while I couldn't sleep, I did a little research," Buck said. "You went to high school with Don Estes, didn't you?"

"Such a sweetheart," she replied. "We dated for a little while. Then I went off to college and he took the job at Hollowgrove. We still talk now and then."

"Like," suggested Buck, "whenever there's a chance to bring down Jarrod Whitley."

She said, "Buck, honey, let me get you another drink."

She started to lift her hand to the waitress, but Buck held up his glass, still half-full. "I'm fine." He went on, "You know, I kept wondering why the Whitleys would call the police out there to investigate a couple of thirty-year-old skeletons that they could have so easily covered up like they do everything else... especially when they were smack in the middle of committing a much more serious crime. But they *didn't* call the police. The mayor did. And Don Estes called the mayor, just like he did those other times with the customs and labor law violations. And every single time, Jarrod Whitley managed to shut down the investigations. He would've done it this time too if I hadn't kept him and his grandson in jail until law enforcement unloaded that truck full of human cargo."

Miss Corinne smiled at someone across the room, pretending only the vaguest interest in what he was saying, and took another sip of her drink.

"What's interesting," Buck continued, "is that Estes—and therefore you— had to know about the missing woman and newborn, just like he knew about the upcoming shipment of laborers. But he couldn't report that to the police without risking his job—and maybe his life. But uncovering those skeletons gave you both the perfect excuse—legal and relatively harmless—to have a police presence out there. You were counting on one investigation leading to another."

"Well, honestly, darling, what did you expect us to do?" She gave a faint, dry smile as she glanced around the room. "It was a perfect storm. The Whitleys are a blight on the face of the earth, and this was a chance to get rid of them once and for all. After all those failed investigations, they thought they were bulletproof. Somebody had to stop them." She smiled at him, tilting her glass in his direction. "I figured if anybody could bring them down, it would be you. And I was right."

Buck was unsurprised. "You didn't want to get your hands dirty or make an enemy of one of the most powerful men in the state. But if I screwed up and got on Jarrod Whitley's bad side, I was expendable." Before she could object, he went on, "The only thing I can't figure out is what's in it for you. You own stock in Hollowgrove—or, I should say, in its parent company, Aegis. Not a majority share, but a lot. So why would you want to see it fail?"

She relaxed and leaned back, crossing her legs under the table. "The Whitleys own the controlling share of Aegis, naturally, but they do report to a board of directors. Jarrod has been in the chairman's seat for sixty years, a position which he will be unable to continue to fill after all this, I can assure you. Neither will his children.

All their shares will be returned to the company in a drastically devalued state, I'm afraid. In other words, Aegis—and Hollowgrove itself, of course—will be ripe for a takeover. My dear friend Hiroko Takahashi has been wanting to do just that for years. He's a brilliant businessman. It will be a perfect outcome for everyone. Except, of course..." She paused to take a demure sip of her drink. "Poor Jarrod."

Buck said, "And you? What do you get out of it?"

She smiled. "As it happens, Hiroko has offered me an additional five percent of the company and a seat on the board."

Buck took another sip of his mimosa and set the glass down. "So," he said, "you've been pretending to be Jarrod Whitley's ally, taking his money in exchange for police protection for years, and all this time you've been plotting to bring him down." He looked at her somberly. "Miss Corinne, I hope you'll take this in the spirit it's meant, but you are a snake."

She smiled sweetly and lifted her glass. "This part of the country is crawling with them, sugar."

Iris Pearlman took the podium and tapped lightly on the microphone. "Welcome," she said, "to the July meeting of the Mercy chapter of the League of Women Voters. In consideration of our guest speaker's very busy schedule—it *is* the holiday weekend, after all!" Here she was interrupted by a few chuckles and murmurs of agreement, then she went on, "We are altering our customary agenda and placing our business meeting after the remarks of our guest speaker. We also have eliminated the question-and-answer portion of the program in order to return the very valuable keeper-of-the-peace in our fair town of Mercy, Georgia to his duties." She beamed at Buck. "So, without further ado, please welcome our new chief of police, Buck Lawson!"

The mayor squeezed his hand. "You're on, sweetie."

Buck walked to the lectern, smiling as he waited for the applause and the flash of lights from cellphone cameras to stop. Then he began, "Thank you, Mrs. Pearlman. And thank you all for having me. You know, when I first took this job, I knew I had some mighty big shoes to fill. On top of that, I wondered whether I'd like it here, and whether you all even wanted me here. It was hard to leave my hometown for a strange place and a new job with a lot of responsibility I wasn't sure if I was ready for. But in a place as sweet as Mercy, I should have known I didn't have anything to worry about. You all have made it easy to call this my new hometown."

Buck's speech lasted twenty-two minutes and was well received, judging by the rousing applause that followed his final "Thank you." Since his remarks had focused mostly on the low crime rate and high clearance rate figures provided by Lydia, as well as the community outreach programs Billy had started long before Buck took office, this was not particularly surprising.

He made his way to the door, pausing to shake hands and whisper goodbyes, as dessert was served—strawberry cheesecake, he saw with regret. A reporter from the newspaper asked for an interview, and Buck told him to call the office. A podcaster thrust a cell phone in his face, asking him to comment on events that were over two months old, and he told her the same thing. He was glad to close the dining room door on the babble of voices and start back toward the relative order of the police station.

Junior Aikens was sitting in one of the pink velvet wing chairs in the front entrance hall, apparently waiting for him. He got to his feet as Buck rounded the corner.

"Junior," Buck said, coming over to him. "It's good to see you up and around. You look a lot better than the last time I saw you."

In fact, he looked rumpled and pale, his left arm in a sling, his face lined. There were faint abrasions on either side of his mouth from the duct tape the Whitleys had used to keep him silent while he was in the trunk of the car. Nonetheless, he managed a weary smile and extended his hand. "Thanks to you," he said.

"It was a close call for both of us," Buck admitted, shaking his hand. He added quietly, "I want to tell you again how sorry I am about Zach Whitley. I would've stopped him if I could."

Junior shook his head, his voice heavy. "You couldn't have stopped him."

Buck let a moment pass. "I hear your wife is on her way."

"Not until the morning. She had to get the kids settled. They're good kids, but there's no way we'd leave a couple of teenagers by themselves at a beach house. Her sister is driving down."

"That's good," Buck said. "Do me a favor and let Frankie know before you leave town, okay? Just in case anyone has any more questions for you."

"No problem."

Buck started to take his leave. "Well, like I said, it's good to see you."

"Chief," Junior said quickly. "I wonder if I could talk to you for a minute."

Buck glanced at his watch. "To tell the truth, another time would be better. Why don't you call the office and..."

"You know those skeletons you found at Hollowgrove?" Junior said abruptly. "I know who they were. And I know who killed them."

CHAPTER FORTY-TWO

There was a small library off the foyer of the B&B with a door that closed. It was furnished in a style typical of such places: shelves lined with books, both contemporary and classic, a baize-covered table with a porcelain chess set, club chairs drawn up before a French-mantled fireplace. Buck and Junior sat in the club chairs, facing each other. Buck waited, not saying anything, for Junior to speak.

At last, Junior began. His voice was low and flat, and he didn't meet Buck's eyes. "When we were growing up, Zach and me, there were kids at Hollowgrove. Not a lot, and most of them didn't speak English, but a couple of them were close to our age. Xavier and Lorenzo liked to follow us around and we'd tease the hell out of them, you know, like kids do. They knew a little English, and they learned more hanging out with us. After a few years, we got to be, I don't know, buds, I guess. There wasn't a lot to do at Hollowgrove and the court said Zach had to spend every other weekend plus Thanksgiving there with his dad, so yeah, we were glad to have somebody to pick on and get into mischief with.

"Of course, even the kids worked on the farms, but Trey—that was Zach's older brother—he'd give Xavier and Lorenzo time off to play with us, which I guess is one reason they liked hanging with us. The other adults—I'm talking about the Spanish-speaking adults, the kids' family, I guess—didn't approve of them running with us and tried to keep them back at the camp. They must've known what was going on. Trey was teaching the kids to trust white people and to keep secrets. Of course, our secrets were about playing on the railroad tracks and stealing cigarettes. Trey's were a lot bigger.

"I guess Zach and I always knew there was something off about Trey," Junior went on. His eyes were loosely fixed on a point on the carpet some distance away. "You just kind of got a creepy vibe from him, even though he didn't exactly do or say anything to make you feel that way. Besides, we were just kids. Eight, nine, ten. But by the time we were twelve, we should have known. Maybe we did."

Junior paused, taking a long deep breath. Buck waited. He knew where this was going. Or at least he thought he did.

"One summer, the last summer I went out there, there was something different about Xavier and Lorenzo. They were quieter, angrier. They didn't want to hang out, said they had to work. Seemed to want to work. I guess I didn't think much about it, figured it was what they did, the kids of the farm workers—when they got to be a certain age, they went to work. I remember Trey hanging around the camp a lot, bringing Lorenzo and Xavier little presents—candy and new sneakers and tee shirts with stupid sayings on them. Sometimes he'd take the kids off in his truck, and I got the feeling they didn't want to go. They never wore the tee shirts or the sneakers, and I saw them throwing away the candy once.

"Anyway, it was a boring summer, and I didn't want to go back for Thanksgiving, but Zach talked me into it." He talked more quickly now, his voice tight, anxious to get the story over with. "It was a hunt weekend, quail I think, and all the adults were busy with the guests, nobody to supervise us. There was this shed on the edge of the old cotton field where Zach and I used to go to smoke weed when we could find it." He glanced quickly at Buck and away again. "The field was fallow, and the shed was just a falling-down shack where they used to store old tools—hoes and rakes and shovels and such. Nobody ever came there. Except this day, somebody did.

"Before we even got there, we heard shouting, screaming. We started running and when we got there, we could tell it was Xavier's voice, screaming something in Spanish. The door was half falling off its hinges anyway, and it was easy to see…" He paused for another breath. "Lorenzo lying on the floor, half-naked, not moving, not breathing. Xavier had a shovel and he was screaming at Trey, who was…who was buckling up his pants."

There was a long moment in which Buck thought Junior would not continue, but then he went on, each word wrenched out of him as though it were a physical thing. "Xavier swung the shovel at Trey but he wasn't very big, all he could do was hit him in the back hard enough to piss him off. He was screaming, 'You killed him, you killed my brother'—and that part was in English, or at least I think it was. So many years ago, it's hard to remember.

"But I do remember when Lorenzo dropped the shovel after hitting Trey, Trey picked it up and swung it back again, hitting Lorenzo in the head. I heard the skull crack, I swear to God, and there was a dent in the back, filling with blood. Lorenzo was on the ground and Trey threw the shovel down. It landed near the door, where we were.

"I swear I don't know what came over me. I heard this—this kind of roar coming out of my throat, and I ran inside the shack and grabbed the shovel and swung it at Trey like I was going for a home run. It hit him right in the throat and dropped him like a sack of potatoes. I couldn't believe what I'd done. The force of it had knocked the shovel right out of my hand, and my fingers were numb."

Junior was back there now, his eyes unfocused, reliving the moment. "I started to back away, just as Trey was getting to his feet. The look in his eyes... I'll never forget it. He was going to kill me. And then I saw, out of the corner of my eye, Zach standing there just inside the door. He had Trey's shotgun on his shoulder. Trey didn't even notice, he was so focused on coming for me. And then Zach shot him."

The silence this time was much longer. Buck could hear the muffled sounds of voices from the dining room as the League of Women Voters broke up. Junior didn't move, didn't breathe, hardly seemed to blink.

When he finally spoke, his tone was as dispassionate as though he was reading from a newspaper. "Trey's truck was parked not too far away. We carried him to it and drove him down to the river. Left his gun beside the body, hoping people would think it was—I don't know —an accident or something. We buried the kids beneath the floor of the shed. We didn't know what else to do. If we told the truth, Zach would be charged with murder, and his daddy...that was the worst part. His daddy couldn't find out. We made a pact on that. Trey was his favorite, and we both knew Jarrod Whitley had killed for less.

"After it was..." He swallowed hard. "After it

was done, I called my mom to come get me. I told her I had the flu, which wasn't hard to sell since I spent the rest of Thanksgiving break throwing up and shivering in my bed. I can't tell you how many times I wanted to go to my dad, tell the truth... but I never could."

Finally Junior lifted his gaze to Buck. "I know I told you Junior shot me because I threatened to go to the police about the shipment of illegal workers he had coming in. Maybe that was part of it, I don't know. But the thing was, after I got here, started going through Daddy's things and all... and honestly, seeing you with your boy and thinking about how it all could have been different... I couldn't do it anymore. I couldn't stay quiet, and I told Zach I was going to tell the truth about what happened that day. That's what he couldn't face. That's what he couldn't let happen."

"And that's why he killed himself," Buck said quietly, finally understanding.

Junior's face was haggard, his eyes bleak. Suddenly he did not look anything like his father. "Trey had this red baseball cap he wore," he said, "with his initials embroidered on the front. I guess neither of us saw it there on the day... the day it happened. But that was one of the first things the construction crew dug up, and Zach freaked. I came here to calm him down. That's the irony. I came here to calm him down and I'm the one who broke. I'm the one who couldn't take it anymore."

He sat back and squared his shoulders. "If there are charges, I'm ready. Like I said, my wife will be here in the morning, and I wanted to get this done before she arrived. She can call my lawyer. We can put our house up for bond. I'm ready."

Buck was thoughtful in his answer. "I have a meeting with the D.A. in about half an hour," he said. "I'll run this by him. But from what I know now, with a thirty-year-old closed case and no witnesses other than yourself as to what really happened...the only charge I can see forthcoming against you is assault, which could be argued to be in self-defense. I doubt the state will pursue it." He added, "It must have been hard to carry this around all these years."

Junior let out a great long breath, his shoulders, his torso, his entire being deflating. "Yeah," he admitted, in a tone that suggested an understatement. "It was."

They rested easy for a while, each processing the events of the last few moments through their own lenses. The crowd from the luncheon spilled out into the hallway, their voices growing louder. Buck said, "So, seeing as how your wife won't be here until tomorrow, this might be a good time to get that dinner we've been promising each other. If you're up to it, of course."

Junior smiled slowly. "Sounds good."

Buck stood. "Seven o'clock? My house. I'll text my wife."

Junior stood too, still smiling. "Thanks, Buck,"

he said, and it was easy to read the depth behind the words. "I mean it."

To which Buck replied simply, "No problem."

CHAPTER FORTY-THREE

O n the evening before the Mercy Police Department's annual barbecue, Buck sat on the back steps, looking over the twilight lawn. A breeze wafted in from the river, and every now and then he could hear the splash of a fish jumping. In the distance, a trolling motor droned. The muted sound of voices and occasional laughter came from the kitchen, where Jolene and Eloise were busy making an enormous batch of potato salad. Willis was having his bath. Thor was asleep on the grass at Buck's feet. It was his favorite time of day.

A couple of dozen tables had been arranged across the lawn, and a contingent of off-duty officers had brought two pick-up loads of folding chairs that afternoon. The tables were covered with red-and-white checked tablecloths, each anchored against the fluttering breeze by mason jars filled with daisies. The screen porch was draped with red, white, and blue bunting, as was the long buffet table inside. Buck went down to check the two grills that were set up on the stone patio beside the screen porch. The gas one was a super-deluxe grilling station that had been delivered by Aiken's Department Store only that morning, and he had spent the afternoon studying the user's manual, trying to learn all the bells and whistles.

"Now, that is one sweet set-up," remarked Billy as Buck opened the chrome hood of the grill. "Bet you can flip a few burgers on that thing."

"Two dozen at a time," replied Buck proudly. "Plus beans and cornbread if you've got 'em. This baby does everything except the dishes. I figured I'd cook the burgers on this one, and hot dogs on the charcoal grill."

"The one I had wasn't nearly as fancy," Billy said, opening one of the doors beneath the grill. "What is this, a smoker?"

"Yep," said Buck, "I'm not planning to use it for tomorrow but figured it would come in handy one of these times. From what I hear, the Mercy PD is big on parties."

Billy chuckled. "That we are." He looked around, smiling. "Everything looks real nice. A house like this, it was meant for people to enjoy. Now, don't forget, I've got a couple of pop-ups in the shed in case of rain. Put one over the grills and you won't miss a step."

"I saw them."

Billy said, "It's nice of you to keep up the tradition, Buck."

Buck said, "It was a rough Fourth. We all deserve a little break."

"You came through it fine, though," Billy pointed out. "Just fine."

Buck had not led the Independence Day Parade as Billy once had done. Instead, he had sat in the reviewing stand with the mayor and other city officials. He wore a discreet black armband, as did the other members of his department, in honor of Billy, and he called for a moment of silence to remember their fallen leader before the parade began.

The holiday itself had passed with remarkably few incidents, and that evening Buck had taken the family to Sulfur Springs Park, holding Willis on his shoulders to watch the fireworks on the river. Willis had not had his picture taken with Hobo, although he had managed to persuade his mother to reopen negotiations this time next year. Given the animal's age, Buck had reason to hope the point would be moot by then.

He moved with Billy through the tables and chairs, walking toward the river and the sunset-streaked sky. "My favorite time of day," Billy observed contentedly.

Then he looked at Buck, his tone sobering. "I want to thank you for what you did for my boy, Buck," he said. "When I think of all those years he suffered, and I didn't have any idea. Even in the end, it was never resolved between us." His face was creased with pain. "Why couldn't he come to me? Why didn't he ever say anything?"

"You were police chief," Buck pointed out. "He'd promised his best friend he wouldn't tell. And they both were terrified of Jarrod Whitley, maybe with good reason. Even after all these years, Zach Whitley decided to kill himself rather than face his father with the truth."

Billy shook his head sadly. "That poor boy was as messed up as everybody else in that family. He hid it well, but he was."

"Something like that—seeing two boys murdered, then killing your own brother—that would mess anybody up."

The silence fell heavy between them. Then Billy said, "You guard that boy of yours. Make sure he knows he can tell you anything. Make sure he knows that no matter what happens, there's one person in this world that'll always be on his side."

Buck said firmly, "I plan to."

Billy shot Buck a grin. "Say, I meant to tell you, I like your new recruiting poster. 'Mercy is looking for a few good cops.' Now, if you'd put that pretty young rookie on there, you're likely to get them."

Buck chuckled. "I'll run it by P.R." He added, "It was Gideon, by the way. The guy with the 300 soldiers. I looked it up."

They reached the mulched path that led between the hydrangeas to the river. Billy remarked, "You ought to fence off the river, with that little one running around."

"Construction starts next week," Buck replied. "Miss Corinne said it was against the historic district's covenants, and I told her I was overriding those covenants as police chief in the interest of public safety."

Billy chuckled. "I'll bet she loved that."

"She gave me the name of the fencing company."

"You're getting the hang of this, Buck," Billy said. Then, "What will happen with the Whitleys, do you think?"

"The old man is out on bond," Buck said. "He'll never live to serve his time, though God knows there are enough charges to keep him in prison for three lifetimes. Ballistics matched the bullets that killed Marianne Martindale to Carter's gun, and his fingerprints were all over her vehicle, so he'll spend the next few months in jail, awaiting trial. Geraldine has agreed to turn state's evidence against the rest of her family in exchange for reduced charges. And I understand Hollowgrove is being taken over by a company that has a slightly more progressive view of human rights."

"What about that poor young couple with the baby? What was their name?"

"The Gilfords." Buck pushed his way past a strand of low-hanging Spanish moss. He hated the stuff. "That's in the hands of Family and Children's Services, although it looks pretty clear cut to me. They took their baby home, and it was a legal adoption. Hope House has been closed down, of course. Eliza Summerfield is still denying all wrongdoing, but to say she's got a long legal battle ahead of her is an understatement."

They came out onto the pier that stretched twenty feet across the Blood River. Their footsteps echoed hollowly on the boards as they made their way down the pier. Beneath them, the water was like painted glass, streaked with slashes of black, gold, and red.

They reached the end of the pier and stood there for a moment, admiring the sunset. Billy said, "So what's your thinking now? About staying here." He slanted him a look. "Don't think I don't know you've been turning it over in your mind."

Buck was silent for a moment. "You know, Billy, when I came here, I didn't expect to see this much action. The other day at Whitley's place...I let Carter get the drop on me. That never should've happened. I should've returned fire immediately."

"Ah, come on, Buck. You and I both know the only cops who shoot first and think later are the ones on TV—or at the center of an I.A. investigation."

Buck shook his head. "I waited too long to enter the building. I gave Zach the chance to get his gun. And the truth is I'm not sure I would've gotten out of there alive if Baker and Miller hadn't shown up when they did."

Billy said, "Wondering if you're fit for the job,

are you?"

"More than wondering."

Billy was thoughtful for a while. "You probably think you took this job because it sounded like easy duty with good pay, and because, after the shooting, you were worried about how much longer you'd be able to stay in law enforcement."

Buck didn't argue that.

"But I hired you," Billy said, "because I could tell you wanted to make a difference. And because you were the kind of man who wouldn't stop until he did."

Buck smiled wryly. "How am I doing so far?"

"Not bad," replied Billy easily. "Not bad at all."

Buck said after a moment, "This place can take it out of a man, I'll tell you that. But Jo likes it here, and Willis hasn't even started school yet. I'd hate to uproot them. And that college scholarship for Willis would be a big help. So, I guess you've got me for another five years...or at least as long as it takes me to pay for that new grill."

Billy grinned. "You're making the right decision Buck. You'll find this place grows on you. And believe me when I tell you you're exactly what the town needs."

"Maybe." Buck was quiet for a time, watching the shadows on the water. Then he said, "Everybody misses you, Billy, even me. Especially me. I wish you could be here for the party tomorrow."

Billy just smiled, clasping his hands behind his

back, fixing his eyes on the bank across the river. "Oh, don't you worry," he said, "I will be."

The two men stood together in quiet companionship, watching the sun drop below the horizon and paint the water beneath their feet blood red. Then Buck, smiling goodbye to Billy, turned and walked back to the house alone.

ABOUT THE AUTHOR

Donna Ball

Donna Ball is the author of over 100 books under a variety of pseudonyms. Though she has been published in virtually every genre, she is best known for her work in women's fiction, mystery and suspense. Her novels have  been translated into multiple languages and published around the world. Her most popular series are the award-winning Raine Stockton Dog Mystery series, the Dogleg Island Mystery series, The Blood River Mystery series, and the Ladybug Farm series. All are available now in paperback in bookstores everywhere, as audiobook downloads, and in digital format for your e-reader.

Donna lives in the heart of the Blue Ridge Divide in a remodeled Victorian-era barn. She spends her spare time hiking, painting, and enjoying canine sports with her three dogs.

MORE BY DONNA BALL

The Blood River Mystery Series

Don't miss this exciting first installment

Unfixable: A Buck Lawson Mystery

Former sheriff Buck Lawson leaves the mountains of North Carolina to take a job as police chief of the small South Georgia town of Mercy, and soon finds himself in over his head. For one thing, his predecessor has been murdered...

Welcome To Bethlehem: A Buck Lawson Short Novella

Police chief Buck Lawson wants his first Christmas in his new hometown of Mercy, Georgia, to be a memorable one, both for his family and the police officers under his command. But while preparing to host the traditional police department Christmas party, Buck's home is burglarized by a Middle Eastern man who may be connected to far more violent crimes. As the investigation unfolds and unsettling connections to the past come to light, Buck fears this Christmas will be memorable for all the wrong reasons.

Also Available In The Holiday Anthology Deck The Halls

* * *

The Raine Stockton Dog Mystery Series

Books in Order

Smoky Mountain Tracks

A child has been kidnapped and abandoned in

the mountain wilderness. Her only hope is Raine Stockton and her young, untried tracking dog Cisco...

Rapid Fire

Raine and Cisco are brought in by the FBI to track a terrorist ...a terrorist who just happens to be Raine's old boyfriend.

Gun Shy

Raine rescues a traumatized service dog, and soon begins to suspect he is the only witness to a murder.

Bone Yard

Cisco digs up human remains in Raine's back yard, and mayhem ensues. Could this be evidence of a serial killer, a long-unsolved mass murder, or something even more sinister... and closer to home?

Silent Night

It's Christmastime in Hansonville, N.C., and Raine and Cisco are on the trail of a missing teenager. But when a newborn is abandoned in the manger of the town's living nativity and Raine walks in on what appears to be the scene of a murder, the holidays take a very dark turn for everyone concerned.

The Dead Season

Raine and Cisco take a job leading a wilderness hike for troubled teenagers, and soon find themselves trapped on a mountainside in a blizzard... with a killer.

All That Glitters: A Holiday Short Story E Book

Raine looks back on how she and Cisco met and solved their first crime in this Christmas Cozy short story. Sold separately as an e-book or bundled with the print edition of HIGH IN TRIAL.

High In Trial

A carefree weekend turns deadly when Raine and Cisco travel to the South Carolina low country for an agility competition

Double Dog Dare

A luxury Caribbean vacation sounds like just the ticket for over-worked, over-stressed Raine Stockton and her happy go lucky canine companion Cisco. But even in paradise trouble finds them, and when someone she loves is threatened Raine must use every resource at her command to track down a killer before it's too late.

Home Of The Brave

There's a new dog in town, and Raine and Cisco find themselves unexpectedly upstaged by a flashy K-9 addition to the sheriff's department. But when things go terribly wrong at a mountain camp for kids and dogs over the Fourth of July weekend, Raine and Cisco need all the help they can get to save themselves, and those they love.

Dog Days

Raine takes in a lost English Cream Golden Retriever, and the search for her owner leads Raine and Cisco into the hands of a killer. Readers will enjoy a treasure hunt for the titles of all ten of the Raine Stockton Dog Mysteries hidden in this special tenth anniversary release!

Land Of The Free

On a routine search and rescue mission Raine Stockton and her golden retriever Cisco stumble onto something they were never meant to find, and are plunged into a nightmare of murder, corruption and intrigue as figures from her past re-emerge to threaten everything Raine holds dear.

Deadfall

Hollywood comes to Hanover County, and Raine and Cisco get caught up in the drama when a series of mishaps on the set lead to murder.

The Devil's Deal

Raine takes temporary custody of what may well be the most valuable dog in the world, but when lives are at stake she is forced to make an unthinkable choice.

Murder Creek

Raine and Cisco rescue a dog who is locked in a hot car in a remote Smoky Mountain park... and subsequently discover the owner of that car drowned in the creek only a few dozen yards away. Was it an accident, or was it murder?

Angels In The Snow: A Raine Stockton Short Novella

While preparing for the annual Dog Daze Christmas party, Raine leaves on a secret Christmas errand and becomes trapped in a blizzard. Injured and alone, with a desperate criminal on the loose, a surprising canine hero comes to her rescue. But is it all a product of her imagination, or a genuine Christmas miracle?

Also Available In In Deck The Halls: A Holiday Mystery Anthology

The Judges Daughter

In this pivotal fifteenth book in the ground-breaking Raine Stockton Dog Mystery Series, the death of an old friend leaves Raine Stockton with an unwanted inheritance, an old wound reopened, and the most challenging mystery of her life.

* * *

The Dogleg Island Mystery Series

Flash

Dogleg Island Mystery #1

Almost two years ago the sleepy little community of Dogleg Island was the scene of one of the most brutal crimes in Florida history. The only eye witnesses were Flash, a border collie puppy, and a police officer. Now the trial of the century is about to begin. The defendant, accused of slaughtering his parents in their beach home, maintains his innocence. The top witnesses for the prosecution are convinced he is lying. But only Flash knows the truth. And with another murder to solve and a monster storm on the way, the truth may come to late... for all of them.

The Sound Of Running Horses

Dogleg Island Mystery #2

A family outing takes a dark turn when Flash, Aggie and Grady discover a body on deserted Wild Horse Island, and the evidence appears to point to someone they know—and trust.

Flash Of Brilliance

Dogleg Island Mystery #3

Aggie, Flash and Grady look forward to their first Christmas as a family until a homicide hit-and-run exposes a crime syndicate, and dark shadows from the past return to haunt their future.

Pieces Of Eight

Dogleg Island Mystery #4

A deadly explosion at an archeological dig on Dogleg Island plunges police chief Aggie Malone and her canine partner Flash into a dark mystery from the past, while on the other side of the bridge, Deputy Sheriff Ryan Grady stumbles onto the site of a mass murder. As the investigation unfolds, Aggie and Grady see that the two cases are related, but only Flash knows how...and by whom.

Flash In The Dark

Dogleg Island Mystery #5
Flash discovers an abandoned child on the beach, and the subsequent attempt to identify her leads to a secret organization with a plan for revenge that has been decades in the making. Unless Aggie, Grady and Flash can stop it they risk losing everything the love... even Dogleg Island itself.

The Good Shepherd: A Dogleg Island Short Novella

A missing infant, a holiday pageant, and a priest determined to do the right thing no matter what the cost all come together to present Dogleg Island police chief Aggie Malone and her canine assistant Flash with one of their most unusual cases yet. When a routine call escalates into a kidnapping on the eve of the annual Dogleg Island Police Department holiday open house, Flash and Aggie are held hostage by a desperate man whose only chance for redemption may be the grace of the holiday season.

Also Available In Deck The Halls: A Holiday Mystery Anthology

* * *

Spine-chilling suspense by Donna Ball

SHATTERED

A missing child, a desperate call for help in the middle of the night... is this a cruel hoax, or the work of a maniacal serial killer who is poised to strike again?

NIGHT FLIGHT

She's an innocent woman who knows too much. Now she's fleeing through the night without a weapon and without a phone, and her only hope for survival is a cop who's willing to risk his badge—and his life—to save her.

SANCTUARY
They came to the peaceful, untouched mountain wilderness of Eastern Tennessee seeking an escape from the madness of modern life. But when they built their luxury homes in the heart of virgin forest they did not realize that something was there before them… something ancient and horrible; something that will make them believe that monsters are real.

EXPOSURE
Everyone has secrets, but when talk show host Jessamine Cray's stalker begins to use her past to terrorize her, no one is safe … not her family, her friends, her coworkers, and especially not Jess herself.

RENEGADE by Donna Boyd
Enter a world of dark mystery and intense passion, where human destiny is controlled by a species of powerful, exotic creatures. Once they ruled the Tundra, now they rule Wall Street. Once they fought with teeth and claws, now they fight with wealth and power. And only one man can stop them… if he dares.

Also by Donna Ball

The Ladybug Farm series

> *For every woman who ever had a dream... or a friend*

A Year on Ladybug Farm
At Home on Ladybug Farm
Love Letters from Ladybug Farm
Christmas on Ladybug Farm
Recipes from Ladybug Farm
Vintage Ladybug Farm

A Wedding on Ladybug Farm

The Hummingbird House
Christmas at the Hummingbird House
The Hummingbird House Presents

20766041R00239